The Rajani War I
Outsiders

Brian S. Converse

Copyright 2026 by Brian S. Converse

This is a work of fiction. All characters in this publication are fictitious and any resemblance to real persons, living or dead, is purely coincidental.

ISBN: 978-1-7339334-4-5

For LAZDE
Always

Other Works by Brian S. Converse

Rajani Chronicles I: Stone Soldiers

Rajani Chronicles II: Resistance

Rajani Chronicles III: War

The Island of Despair *(poetry collection)*

Shattered Jewels: Tales of Wonder and Terror
(short story collection)

Recap

James Dempsey was a Detroit Police Lieutenant until he inexplicably awoke aboard an alien spacecraft. He and four other Humans, Yvette, Gianni, David, and Kieren, learned they had been kidnapped by a group of Rajani who were fleeing their home planet. Rajan had been invaded by intergalactic pirates known as the Krahn Horde.

The Rajani pleaded for assistance in ridding their world of the Krahn invaders, offering in return a gift beyond measure: objects that, when implanted into their hosts, gave them incredible powers. These Johar Stones were once the key to the Rajani's empire, built on conquest and the subjugation of other races, most notably the Sekani and Jirina.

With the Humans in dire need of training in the use of these powers, the Rajani ship Tukuli, stopped at a space station in search of someone who could build a training area aboard the ship. The station offered its own dangers, though, in the form of the Alliance Society for Peace, the police force of the Galactic Alliance. Led on the station by Ries an na Van, the ASPs would immediately jail the Rajani if they were discovered.

Amidst the new experiences and dangers, James and Yvette allowed their attraction for each other to become a fierce romance. Loners by both choice and chance, the two Humans were surprised and happy to find someone while so far from home.

With a daring escape from the station and the ASPs, the Tukuli made its way toward Rajan, only to be shot down over the planet's surface by the Krahn Horde's enormous mothership. The Humans abandoned ship, separated into escape pods, while the Rajani crew stayed aboard in hopes of steering the ship away from the capital city of Melaanse.

The Humans and Rajani crew of the Tukuli found themselves separated on the surface of Rajan, with no way of communicating with each other. They found their own way to Melaanse, though, each facing their own perils before reuniting.

James met up with the Jirina; Gianni and Kieren with the Sekani; and Yvette was reunited with Rauph and Bhakat, and later, David, who had been with Jonan, until they were captured by the Krahn. David managed to escape with the help of his comrades, but Jonan remained a prisoner.

The five Humans were able to help the scattered remnants of the Rajani society come together to form a Resistance movement, which began to make inroads in their fight to reclaim their planet from the Krahn Horde invaders. While the resistance against the Krahn intensified, a notable split begins to occur within the Rajani. Two factions formed, the Elders, who are traditionalists led by Rauphangelaa (as Keeper of the Stones) and Tumaani (as Keeper of the Past), and the more militant Valderren, led by Kedar and Welemaan.

Along with the newly elected leader of the Jirina, Mazal, and Sekani leader, Zanth, the Rajani coordinated assaults against the Krahn bases, which resulted in heavy casualties despite their successes.

Meanwhile, Ries an na Van, now a rogue Galactic Intelligence agent, began his own investigation into the Rajani, only to discover that the current planet called Rajan was not the first. His search for more information led to him ultimately kidnapping the Talondarian crown prince named Creon, which resulted in his imprisonment on Talondaria for the crime.

While the ultimate result was victory for the Rajani in defeating the Krahn Horde and capturing their leader, Ronak, victory came with a steep price, with the deaths of Rauphangelaa, Kedar, and Kieren during the fighting. They also discovered a horrifying war crime: the Krahn Horde had rounded up all of the Rajani women and children and slaughtered them. The genocidal act becomes known as the "Death of a Dream".

This news came as they also find that Yvette is pregnant with James' child. Yvette also learned from Bhakat that the Johar Stones held another dark secret: they were actually symbiotic organisms that paired with their hosts to grant them extraordinary powers.

David, who had rescued his friend Janan from prison, finally revealed to his fellow Humans that he was a serial killer who on Earth was known as the Infinity Killer. James and Yvette attempt to capture him, but he escapes and stays on the planet, while Tumaani gifts the Humans a ship, the *Bright Journey*, as a gesture of thanks.

Post-war activities included a trial for Bhakat, who broke the Rajani's most sacred law by implanting himself with a Johar Stone. Although the traditional sentence was death, he was merely banished due to his service during the fighting. Janan agreed to accompany him in his exile. The Sekani traitor known as Belani was also sentenced to death, but James intervened on his behalf, arguing that the Humans needed a pilot to get them back to Earth.

The three remaining Humans, along with Belani, left Rajan to return to Earth having been changed forever from their time apart from their home planet.

Prologue

From the private diary of James Dempsey

Kieren once asked me why I fought for the Rajani. It's a question that I have asked myself many times on the way to and from Rajan. Did we have the right to interfere, even with a personnel invitation from the Rajani themselves? Did we have the right to involve the Earth in galactic politics when we have barely begun our emergence as a space-faring species? The only answer I could give her at the time was "it's the right thing to do."

Now, I've had five years to think about it and I'm not so sure it was. The cost...was immense. Kieren is gone and David, well, David is another problem that needs to be cleaned up at some point. He was a dangerous person to begin with, but now that he has a Stone. I hate to think about what he could do if he ever returned to Earth. Yvette injured him just before we left Rajan, but I have no doubt he survived due to the Stones' healing abilities.

The case of the Infinity Killer remains open as of this writing, though I'm sure soon it will turn into a cold case, since the killer hasn't been heard from in over half a decade. I thought of visiting my old partner on the force but feel like there would be too many questions and not enough answers to satisfy him. I doubt he would believe me if I told him that both me and the killer just happened to be kidnapped by aliens. And I feel like a fool saying that the object of my investigation had lived in the same apartment as me and I never knew about it until we were on another planet.

Gianni went his own way when we got back, and I haven't seen him since then. I know he and Kieren were close on the planet, and that her death was devastating for him. I should have kept in contact with him, but both Yvette and I had our own problems to deal with once we returned, including raising a newborn. I don't think Gianni knows that we named our daughter after Kieren. She was a special person, and we tried to honor her for that, in our own way.

When we left Rajan, all I could think was that we had awakened a sleeping beast. I've seen the Rajani in battle, and even without the presence of Johar Stones, they are formidable fighters, even with as little training as they had. Rauph and Bhakat tried to sell us on the fact that the Krahn were the most dangerous fighters in the galaxy, but he neglected to tell us who had held that title for thousands of years before the Krahn had crawled out of their primitive jungles. I don't blame him for trying to save his species. It was plain wrong for the Krahn Hoard to attack a peaceful civilization, no matter what their crimes were in the past. Only now, we must all live (or die), with the consequences of that act.

When we returned to Earth, I thought I would never want to leave the planet again, but as time went past and I started spending more time on *Bright Journey* than I did on Earth's surface. It has become a bit of a sanctuary, and it allows me to be alone with my thoughts—something that I haven't had since this whole saga began.

Don't get me wrong, I love spending time with Yvette

and little Kieren on Earth and when they come to visit me on the ship, but I also like spending time alone on the ship reading my long-lost poetry collection, or speaking at length with Belani, our Sekani pilot, about several issues, both "foreign" and domestic, as it were.

Belani's English is improving every day. He has a unique (you might even say alien) perspective on things. Besides, I still don't think Yvette's father likes me very much, and since I don't have a place to stay on Earth, it's either his place or my ship. I guess you could say that the ship is my equivalent of a study or den, except that this den is orbiting the Earth instead of being off the hallway to the right.

Speaking of the *Bright Journey*, I also enjoy teaching the ship's computer, Bob, everything I can, which could be a full-time job if Belani wasn't helping. It still amazes me that the Rajani had such complex AI available to them on their ships, but they turned off the learning capability for them. Of course, this is just an assumption of mine based on Rauph's ship. He may have been the only luddite among the masters of Rajan, but Belani seems to think the same. He was as surprised as I was to discover the vast capabilities inherent in the ship's computer once we turned it on fully.

I can't help but think that our part in this story has not yet finished being written. We're too near the action, relatively speaking, and the Johar Stones are too valuable a commodity for no one to come searching for three beings implanted with them, even if they're located on a little backwater world like Earth.

We'll see what the future brings, but I highly doubt it's going to be peaceful.

Chapter 1

A large space port spun slowly in the blackness of space. Spaceships, both large and small, entered and left the station. There was no night and day aboard the station, only the passing of Talondarian Standard hours. If you wanted natural daylight, you had to travel to the blue and green planet below, known as Mandaka.

The Mandakan Space Port was a place offering rest for the weary crews of the ships that docked there, entertainment for those who enjoyed gambling, and a variety of black-market items available due to a thriving clandestine smuggling industry. The pleasure district also served those with a need for physical gratification. Nothing was out of the question, and the pleasure district was booming.

The station was owned by the royal family of Mandaka. The planet had no other notable exports, so they took advantage of a favorable location in Galactic Alliance space. There were few rules—but breaking them could get you banned for life or even ejected from the station—with or without your ship.

The Galactic Alliance (known mostly as the GA) also had a heavy presence there, with the Alliance Society for Peace officers (commonly referred to as ASPs) routinely patrolling near it, and a permanent outpost within its walls. There was also a level of the station dedicated to diplomatic purposes within the GA. There were both offices and lodgings for important individuals from a variety of GA member planets. Many of the diplomats and their staff appreciated having notable vices close to their official dealings.

The game of Ships was being played at several of the tables in the casino area of the port. The game featured cards illustrated with a variety of spaceships and notable people from different worlds and with different points assigned to them. It was a popular game among the pilots who frequented the station and was basic enough that inhabitants from most planets in the GA could understand its rules.

One of the players, a Kkathrewn—a purple humanoid with three eye stalks and three tentacled fingers on each hand, placed his bet, and the turn went to the next at the table, a large cat-like alien with a patch over one of his eyes—a Sh'Kallian. Next at the table was an alien with a robotic body with a clear abdomen where the amphibious alien floated in a mixture of methane, carbon dioxide, and nitrogen. Small cords ran from its body to its mechanical shell, powering the mechanisms that allowed it to move its artificial suit.

Next at the table was a young Talondarian woman who had introduced herself simply as Amera. She was tall, with bright red hair flowing past her shoulders and dark blue eyes that seemed purple in the right light. The last occupant of the table was a large Rajani with a shaved head and a flowing white beard and enough grumpiness to spare. It was rare to see a Rajani outside of their home world, and even more rare to see a bald one. The lack of hair accentuated his large, pointy ears and gave him an even more sinister look than usual for one of his species.

The expansive room around them was loud with the

sounds of bets being called and money being lost or won and general socializing and conversation. There were calls for drinks and beeps and clangs from gambling machines as well. Most of the players spoke Talondarian Standard, the official language of the GA, but there were also mutterings in a variety of languages when things didn't go their way.

Their table was close to a winding stairway that rose up to a more exclusive area of the port, where only high rollers were allowed, and the minimums were much higher than those below. The Rajani's companion had gone that way only a Talondarian standard hour before.

The Kkathrewn played a card after all the bets were made. "Ah, D'pac!" he shouted excitedly, his eye stalks turning an amusing shade of green for a moment. The Sh'Kallian hissed his disappointment as he laid out a Domdari trawler. He sat and crossed his arms, glaring at everyone around him. The amphibious alien played, its mechanical body rumbling and wheezing as it laid down its card, a Talondarian Starship. A sound like air escaping came from it, and everyone realized it was laughing.

The Talondarian woman reached for the table and rested her hand lightly on the card lying face down on the surface. "Would anyone care to raise the bet? Double or nothing?"

The robotic amphibian pointed at her. "Just get on with it," its mechanical voice said.

She turned to the large Rajani next to her and smiled.

"Just play your card, human," he said, and took a gulp from the mug sitting at his place.

"I don't' know the word you just called me, but it sounded almost as ugly as you are," she said, her smile staying in place. She turned the card over.

No one saw what card she played as suddenly there was a loud commotion above them in one of the balconies. The sound of weapons fire was followed by shouting as a small figure flew over the balcony and landed on the table eight standard feet below, just as the Talondarian was reaching for the pot. Credit chips flew everywhere as the diminutive figure tumbled off the table.

"Janan!" the Rajani yelled, standing up. "You said you wouldn't get into trouble."

"It's not my fault, Bhakat," the little blue alien said, himself standing and placing a steadying hand on the table. "He's a sore loser. Can I help it if he's also the royal heir of Mandaka?" He began laughing at the absurdity of it all. Bhakat did not join him in his mirth.

He looked up just as a well-dressed Mandakan leaned over the balcony above them. "There you are you Sekani cheat!"

"Uh, oh, time to go," Janan said, looking around for the best exit route.

As the prince began to shoot at them, Bhakat suited up—completely surrounding himself in a suit of energy, which sent the rest of the players scrambling except for the Talondarian. Her eyes went wide, but she seemed otherwise unaffected by the appearance of a full-grown male Rajani in a Johar Stone power suit. She ducked down and then pulled out her own gun and began firing back at the prince.

"Bloodfire," she yelled as a hole was blown through the table next to her. "Do something, you idiots. You're the ones who started this."

Bhakat looked at her briefly before leaping up to the balcony. He quickly took the gun away from the faltering prince and broke it in half. "That's enough of that. The Sekani is under my protection. Whatever slight you think he may have caused should be forgotten. Understood?"

The prince stood there, his mouth agape and fear in his

eyes. He nodded once, and Bhakat sighed before turning and jumping back down to the floor below. His impact demolished the table, with Janan jumping out of the way to avoid being demolished himself. He settled down next to the Talondarian woman, who was squatting down on the floor.

"Is he gone yet?" Janan asked, his eyes now squeezed shut.

"Which one, the big ugly one or the short ugly one?" she asked.

Janan opened his eyes. "Well, I guess it's a matter of perspective. They're both big to me." He saw Bhakat standing nearby and then stood as well, followed by the Talondarian, who was looking up at the crown prince of Mandaka, who still seemed to be in shock.

"As you said, Janan, it is indeed time to go," Bhakat said, beginning to walk away.

The two friends hurriedly left the gaming area, not caring that the Talondarian female was following them.

"Hey, wait for me," she said. When she caught up to them, they were almost to the elevator for that floor. "My name's Amera."

"Hi Amera," Janan said, smiling up at her. "I'm Janan. The big guy is Bhakat."

"I'd say it was nice to meet you, but I'd probably be lying," she said, though she smiled back at him.

Janan was again surprised at how human she looked, though there were enough differences that telling a human and a Talondarian apart was easy enough if you looked closely.

"Listen," she said as they reached the elevator. "I know of a safe place we can go if you two need to lie low."

"No," Bhakat said without looking at her. He was still suited up, ready for another attack from the prince or his men. "I'm sorry that you were involved in that...disruption back there, but you can't be seen with us."

"We may need her help, Bhakat," Janan said. I didn't exactly have time to collect my winnings up there, and we don't have money to refuel at the moment."

Just then the elevator doors opened, and they found themselves face to face with a large, black, hairy beast of a creature. It smiled at them all, flashing its sharp white teeth in the process.

"Punjor!" Amera said, surprised.

"Shit," Bhakat said in English.

All Janan could do was laugh.

◊

"What do you mean the ASPs aren't available?" Artral, the Mandakan crown prince, asked through his comm unit. "I was attacked in my own casino today, and I want someone punished!"

"We will get someone to your location as soon as they become available, your highness," said the voice on the other end. "All of our personnel are handling other matters right now."

"You had better get someone here soon, or my father will hear of it." He angrily cut off the communication by smacking the communicator device located behind his ear, then winced at the loud feedback sound he got from it. The ASP unit on the station hadn't been the same since the old ASP unit chief had left under mysterious circumstances a few years before. Ries an na Van had been a competent, if eccentric ASP commander, and had kept his unit on top of these types of things, from what Artrell could remember.

Perhaps it was time to get some of his own security people involved in the investigation of just who the Rajani and Sekani were who had so blatantly tried to rip him off on his own space station.

◊

The ride in the elevator was silent until Bhakat finally spoke. "I assume your boss wants to speak to us for some reason?"

"Unfortunately, Zazzil is no longer with us," Punjor said, quietly.

"Did you kill him?" Janan asked. His eyes grew wide when Amera's knife blade kissed his cheek. He hadn't even seen her pull it out.

"That was my guardian you are speaking of," she said. "Zazzil was very old for his species. His death, though inevitable, was also tragic for all of us."

"My apologies," Janan said. Once Amera withdrew and sheathed her dagger, he turned to Punjor. "I'm sorry I was flippant. I know that my former boss, Rauphangelaa, held Zazzil in the highest regard."

"Thank you," Punjor said. "Zazzil felt the same. And Rauphangelaa is...?"

"Dead," Bhakat said. "He died on Rajan during the conflict with the Krahn Hoard."

"Seems that bad news is everywhere these days," Amera said.

"Indeed, it is," Bhakat said.

"So where are you taking us," Janan asked. "I hope you won't be turning us in to the Prince of Mandaka or the ASPs?"

"Not unless I'm forced to," Punjor replied. "I can shelter you for a short time, but then we'll have to get you off the space station. If we're caught with you, I'll have to claim we captured you and hand you over."

"And what will we owe you for this assistance?" Bhakat asked.

Punjor smiled widely, displaying his impressively sharp

teeth.

"I don't like that," Janan said quietly.

"No, I don't either," Amera said, matching his volume. She bent over and rubbed his face where she had placed her blade. He noticed that his face had been bleeding as she pulled her hand away. "Sorry about that," she said. "Sometimes my blade thinks faster than I do."

Janan shrugged it away. He smiled up at her to show her that her apology was accepted. Her consideration for him was surprising. She returned his smile.

◊

Artral walked into his command center aboard the space station. Being the crown prince of Mandaka did have its privileges, especially when your father owned a large space station and put you in charge of running it.

"Where are they?" he asked the closest person, a young aid named Trelfer.

"We lost them when they entered the elevator, your highness," the aid replied, keeping his eyes downcast.

"What? How can you have lost someone on this station? Especially when both are so conspicuous?"

"There was a problem with the surveillance camera in the elevator as soon as they entered. And we couldn't track where it stopped."

"Unbelievable," Artral said. Then louder, "Unbelievable! Why the hell are we paying you incompetent fools?" He walked swiftly to the door of his private chambers. "Someone better get me a drink right now, or you're all fired!" He slammed the door of his suite to show he meant business. All of the aids looked around at each other, then quietly went back to whatever they were currently working on. It wasn't the first time they'd been threatened by the crown prince.

◊

The door to the elevator opened, and they all followed Punjor out and to the right down the hallway. They were in a secluded part of the station now. This was where many rooms were available to those who weren't interested in games. It was quiet and sparsely inhabited.

Punjor came to a door and passed a card over a sensor. The door opened, and Punjor stepped back, motioning that they should all enter. As Janan entered, he could see the large, now empty, aquarium-like section of the room. It was true: Zazzil was no longer there.

"So, who is in charge now?" he asked no one in particular.

"I am," Punjor said.

"It wasn't what you'd call a peaceful transition of power," Amera said from behind him.

"No airing the inner workings of the organization, thank you," Punjor said. "Zazzil may have given you leeway in your actions, but I will not."

Amera just smiled and rolled her eyes.

Punjor walked to a large table set up near the corner and sat down. He motioned for them all to join him. Once they were seated, Punjor pushed a button on a device located on his wrist. Almost immediately, a door opened opposite the door they had come in, and a short, three-legged creature covered in long red hair entered with a tray of glasses full of a dark liquid. The alien placed a glass in front of each of them, bowed to Punjor, then left without saying a word.

Janan sniffed at the liquid in the glass, then smiled when he recognized the odor. It was a drink called fernta that came from Rajan. He took a sip, then a larger gulp. He set down the cup and smiled again at Amera as she drank. He nodded appreciatively when she downed half the glass, then burped and smiled back at him.

"I never thought about an inter-species relationship

before," he said. "But I think I love you."

Amera laughed and he joined her, though he was only half-joking.

"Now, what is your price?" Bhakat asked. He hadn't touched his drink.

"We will get you off this space station, but you have to take the girl with you," Punjor said, motioning towards Amera. "We've already filled your ship with fuel and supplies in anticipation of your journey away from here," Punjor said.

"What?" both Amera and Bhakat said at the same time.

"She's too exposed here," Punjor said. "It was fine when she was younger and content to stay in her room or roam the halls when they were deserted, but you just saw—she's old enough now to venture out on her own...and find her own trouble." He looked down at Janan as he said the last part.

"Too exposed to what?" Janan asked.

"Everything," Punjor said. "As we've said, my rise to this position wasn't uncontested. There are new factions on the station who would gladly sell her out for a few Galactic credits."

"Who is she?" Bhakat asked, looking at the girl.

Punjor sighed. "I am not at liberty to say at the moment," he said. "At least not until you promise to take her with you. I can think of no safer place at the moment. As I said, Zazzil thought very highly of Rauphangelaa. I was hoping to give her into his care, but now, you'll have to do."

"So, I'm just to go with these strangers that I've only just met and never return?" Amera asked.

"That is the best I can do for you at the moment," Punjor said, standing up and beginning to pace. "I'm sorry, Amera, but it's become too dangerous here." He turned to Bhakat. "It's also become dangerous for your human friends. I'm told there is a price on their heads."

"What?" Janan said, standing up. "From whom?"

"The Kran home world, for one," Punjor said. "Possibly Rajan as well."

"Welemaan," Bhakat growled.

"Must be," Janan said. "Tumaani would never..."

"It doesn't matter," Punjor said, stretching impossibly long arms. His muscles were thick ropes along his arms and legs under his dense hair.

"I have a few things I need to pack," Amera said.

"It's been taken care of," Punjor said. When I saw that you had met up with these two, I made the decision and ordered your belongings made ready to leave."

"Just couldn't wait to get rid of me, huh?"

"You know it's not like that, Amera," Punjor said, placing a hand on her shoulder. "Zazzil swore to protect you, and he did until he could no longer. I honor his wishes even now. It would be all too easy to turn you over to interested parties, but instead I am placed in danger myself to see you escape this station safely."

"Don't hurt yourself," Janan said. "Patting yourself on the back that hard, you could pull a muscle or something."

Punjor looked down at the small blue alien, then began to laugh. "Guard her well, little Sekani." He walked over to a metal shelf and pulled a small gun from it. He brought it over and handed it to Janan. "A gift to help guard Amera."

"Thank you," Janan said, surprised by the offering. It was a beautiful weapon. The power jewel glowed dully in the handle, letting Janan know that it was charged and ready to fire.

"Bhakat, I won't insult you by trying to give you a weapon as well. From what I've seen, you are a weapon."

"Indeed," Bhakat said. He drank the last of his fernta and stood. "Your offer is accepted. We will take the girl and protect her as best we can."

"Thank you," Punjor said. "I don't want to know where you are heading from here. It's best if no one knows.

"I agree," Bhakat said, looking at the Talondarian female. "Now, who is she?"

"She is Amerina Tordor. Her parents were the rightful king and queen of Talondaria, until their untimely deaths. She is the true heir to the Talondarian throne."

"Shit," Bhakat and Janan both replied in English at this pronouncement.

Interlude

Maliq, High Vasin of the planet Kran and Vasin of the Qadira Clan, sat on his throne and pondered the news he had just received. It wasn't good. "You're sure that he's betrayed us?"

"Yes, Vasin," his chief councilor, Xenic, replied. "He now works for the Rajani. We lost contact with him some time ago. Until today."

"And?"

"His message was short. He apologized, but said that he needed to make a living, and the Rajani offered more. For a bounty hunter, I must admit that he is exceedingly polite."

"Blasted Rajani," Maliq said quietly. Again, he cursed his brother for a fool for having the audacity to attack the planet known as Rajan. The three aid ships that he had sent to their planet had never returned. "Contact the Outsiders."

"Vasin, they've worked for the Rajani in the past."

"They're mercenaries. They will work for whoever pays them. Let us hope that this time we offer the higher amount."

"Yes, Vasin."

"You may go. Keep me apprised of any negotiations," Maliq said. Xenic bowed and then turned and left the throne room without another word.

Maliq sat for a moment after his councilor had left. He'd had a simple plan: bring the Humans to the Krahn home world and tell them what had happened since his brother's failed attack on Rajan. Explain their current position, which was precarious. Implore them to help him stave off an attack from the Rajani. He was willing to negotiate reparations for the attack, though he wasn't sure what Krahn could offer them that would be enough.

He should have foreseen that the Rajani might block that plan. On top of that, his correspondence with the Galactic

Alliance was bearing no fruit. It was almost as if he was being ignored. It was maddening, to say the least.

News of his brother's failed invasion of the Rajan home world had reached him a few Standard months after he'd sent the supply ships in a gesture of peace. There were conflicting accounts of whether his brother was still alive or only captured. Speculation had ridden wild as to what would happen, and he'd ordered the planet to be on alert for the rest of the Standard year. Yet nothing had happened.

Word was that the Rajani were busy rebuilding their city and Maliq had lowered the alert level once more, hoping that it was the end of hostilities. Then he'd been informed that along with building their city, the Rajani were also seen building ships from what they could scavenge from the war. The Rajani were on everyone's radar now, not just his. Many ships now passed by the planet, using long-range scanning and photography equipment—interested in seeing what was happening on the surface.

He hadn't dared to send any of his own ships near the planet again and was forced to pay for information from others. Finally, he heard what he feared the most—that the Rajani were preparing a large fleet of ships to leave Rajan. He hoped he was wrong, but his assumption now was that they were going to attack Krahn in retaliation. He'd heard that his brother's forces had rounded up their women and children and slaughtered them all, and he knew they would seek the blood of all the inhabitants of Krahn as retribution.

His only hope now was to prepare his people for war and do all he could to avoid it. Hopefully the Humans would help negotiate with the Rajani without the need for bloodshed, but he wasn't counting on it.

Chapter 2

The small ship floated in orbit around the single moon of the planet known as Earth. The bounty hunter was sitting in the only seat in the cockpit of the ship, which had a undersized, though adequate, cargo hold, as well as a place to expel bodily waste, and not much else. He was relaxed and sipping water from a straw that was built into the cockpit next to him, which provided filtered water from the ship's hydraulic system.

The ship was not large enough to have a gravity well of its own, but he was strapped in properly and unconcerned about the lack of gravity. He had hunted before with the ship, and with the money he'd make from his current hunt, he'd be able to trade in this ship for a larger one with its own gravity and more comfortable amenities.

Starspanner mission journal. Captain Atalik Nar recording.

Far be it from me to question the motives of an employer, but I have been watching the inhabitants of Earth, these Humans, for some time now, and the impending Krahn/Rajani war is the farthest thing from their minds. It's my opinion that if they were left alone, they wouldn't get involved and may not even find out about it at all, unless it became messy and spilled over into their limited sphere of detected space.

But I'm paid for a service. It's my job to drag these three individuals back into the maelstrom—to make sure they don't fall into the wrong hands—or fight for the wrong side. So, I'll take the Rajani leader's money and do my job, as always. I have a reputation for completing paying hunts, and I won't do anything to jeopardize it, no matter what my personal feelings may be.

Once again, the Galactic Alliance is abuzz with talk of the Rajani. The warriors of Rajan have a reputation that spans the galaxy. Their fighting prowess and utter ruthlessness in battle are still feared thousands of years after their last conquest. Someone was foolish enough to poke the monster. These Humans may not know it, but they have been thrust into intergalactic politics and there is no way to escape. Now that their 'Earth' has been discovered, there can be no return to their protective obscurity.

None but these three have any inkling that there is anything beyond the pale blue of their sky. Their species has only traveled to their moon and back. They're about as primitive as can be—I doubt they would even gain admittance into the Galactic Alliance at this point in their evolution. Yet the three Humans and their actions have sent a wave of unease throughout the galaxy, and the Galactic Alliance itself.

I've been on the trail of the three Humans that returned to Earth from Rajan for a short time, and so far, I've haven't been able to track down any of them. I assume that the human male named "James the Human" is on his ship somewhere near the planet. The ship is in orbit, so it shouldn't be difficult to find when the time comes, unless he's discovered a way to completely camouflage it from detection. I paid a large sum for the cloaking device on this ship, small as it is, and from what I've been told, the Bright Journey was not equipped with one when the leaders of the Rajani gifted it to the Humans for their service.

The other male has seemingly dropped off the map. He may have been terminated on Earth or disappeared completely from what I can tell. He may turn out to be the most difficult to find, but I have his last known location from my employers, so I'll try there first.

The Human female named Yvette has been tricky as well. Her last known address is coming up empty. No signs that she still occupies that location. I've fed everything I know about her into the somewhat archaic computer on my ship, so I should have answers soon. Until then, I've been studying this Earth and its civilization. As I said, they're a primitive species, for sure, but an interesting one. Their resemblance to the Talondarians is striking, of course, and I have to wonder if there is a connection there...

Suddenly the ship's AI began to speak over the intercom.

<Computer extrapolation complete.>

"Go."

Atalik looked at the readout on another screen as the AI spoke. The screen showed a map of the Earth with a black spot located relatively near the spot where the Human female was supposed to be found.

<Human city known as 'Port Hope.' probability rating is at 97.564%>

"The Human female?"

<Affirmative. Human female. Designation: Yvette Manidoo. Strong probability she is residing there with her biological sire, Human male: Designation Josiah Manidoo.>

"Good. Set course for those coordinates. Engage cloaking shield."

◊

Yvette Manidoo struggled as she fought her adversary, knowing that to let it win would only bring more trouble than she wanted to deal with at the moment. She gave one last tug on the belt that held the car seat in place and was finally rewarded with enough slack in it to click the button and free the car seat from its normal place in the back seat of the Cadillac Escalade. She needed to put down the back seat so she could fit all of her groceries in the rear compartment of the large SUV.

She was grateful that her father had retired to his ranch well away from town, except for times like now when she had to go grocery shopping. She had to buy food for the entire month, and that meant lots of boxes and cans. Kieren's favorite cereal alone seemingly took up half the available space. James constantly warned her that they needed to stay obscure, so she hardly ventured from the ranch, except for the occasional trip to the grocery store.

When Yvette had returned to Earth, her first thought was to find an OBGYN doctor. The trip home had been relatively uneventful, but she knew she would eventually have to receive prenatal care. The thought of giving up the baby or having an abortion never entered her mind, and she knew that James had felt the same way. This child was wanted. This meant that she had to make the decision of whether to return to normal society after presumably being listed as missing for over a year. She decided that she didn't want the hassle of being a shiny new object for the press and other curious parties, and she certainly didn't think her father would, either.

She had travelled by bus to her old apartment after James dropped her off with the ship's lander a few miles outside of Detroit. She had not been to the point where her pregnancy weight was a hindrance to moving about comfortably, but it was fast approaching. She'd found that her apartment had been rented out to someone else. More than likely her possessions had been donated or sold.

She had known then that the only course of action would be to contact her father. She'd had enough cash in her wallet from when she was initially taken to pay for the bus fare into the city, but that was all. She had been pleasantly surprised to find that one of her credit cards was still active, though she hadn't used it for at least a year. She went to the store and bought herself the first real Earth food that she'd had in a long time, as well as a pre-paid cell phone. She ate her baked chicken sandwich and potato chips while she found a secluded place to make a call.

Her father had picked up the phone after a few rings—she had feared that it would go to voicemail.

"Hello?"

"Dad?" She wasn't sure what else to say.

"I'm sorry, who is this?"

"Dad, take a deep breath. It's me, Yvette."

"Yvette. Where in the hell have you been?" She could tell that he was crying, and then she started crying.

"I'm sorry, daddy," she said. "I didn't mean for this to happen. Where are you, DC?"

"No, no, I'm done with that place. I'm at the ranch. Where are you?"

"I'm near my old apartment. Daddy, can you come pick me up?"

"Of course, honey. I'll be there in about three hours. Don't move."

"Thanks, daddy. I'll wait out in front of the apartment. Do you remember the address?"

"Wouldn't be able to forget it," he said, then hung up.

She smiled as she loaded the last of the groceries into the SUV. He'd made it in two and half hours, which meant he must have been flying down those country roads in the thumb. He'd pulled up to the curb and had hopped out of the same SUV she was driving now, which was surprising given how bad his hip was—he'd told her later he'd had hip replacement surgery. She had been showing considerably by then, so he had stopped short for a moment to study her protruding baby belly before embracing her as they both began to cry again.

That was five years ago. Her father had been able to get her in to see a private doctor for the birth of her daughter. He'd also been able to procure fake identities for her, James, and Kieren. She hadn't asked how, and he didn't tell. She was sure that he still had a few clandestine contacts in the political world that could have helped him. All she cared about was that they were safe, and if she ever got pulled over by the police, they would run the license of Tricia Palagos, who grew up in Texas and moved to Michigan for her job at the local school, where her daughter Kieren would be attending the following year.

Yvette shook her head, wondering how the time had passed so quickly. How was it almost time to send her baby to kindergarten? She packed the rest of the groceries into the SUV and closed the back door. She had a half hour drive ahead of her back to the ranch, and then she had a date.

She smiled at the thought of her date. James was planning on sending down the lander to pick her up and bring her to the *Bright Journey*. It would be good to talk to Belani again, and then she could scold James about not being around much lately as he seemingly spent more time aboard the ship than at home. She knew part of it was that he didn't think her dad liked him, and he was correct in that regard, but Kieren missed her daddy.

James had been with her throughout the end of her pregnancy and for the first few years of Kieren's life, but lately he had been spending more time away, and she wasn't sure why. He'd vaguely mentioned wanting to be ready if the Rajani—or anyone else—made another appearance, but she also knew that he was a solitary person, still not ready to be in a family. On one hand, she couldn't blame him, but on the other, she was almost ready to give him an ultimatum.

Kieren needed a father around. She needed...well, she needed him too. They hadn't had the conversation about marriage. Both had been through a life-changing experience and when they returned, they were changed forever. She knew that he still loved her, and she loved him, but neither was sure that marriage would change anything, since neither of them were on the grid and any legal marriage would be null and void before the license was even signed.

She was on a main road leading to the turnoff to her father's land when an energy beam pierced the SUV's engine and suddenly Yvette was coming to a stop with a large, smoking hole in the hood of her father's car. She quickly unbuckled, got out of the car and suited up, her energy suit a dark yellow that glowed in the last light of the sun.

She looked around her, trying to pinpoint where the blast had come from. Finally, a tall, humanoid figure stepped out from behind a copse of trees about a hundred yards from the road. She turned towards it, wondering what she was dealing with. The figure didn't fire again at her and was walking unhurriedly towards her position next to the car.

"You've made a big mistake," she said. She looked down at the hole in her dad's car. "A very big mistake." She knew her father was going to be pissed off, to say the least.

"Please come with me, Human," the figure said as it got closer, its voice sounding mechanically generated. "Your friend Gianni is already on my ship waiting for you."

"What?" she asked, confused. Gianni was already with him? That didn't make much sense at all.

"Please come with me, Human," the figure said again. It was now about fifty feet away.

"How about you pay for my dad's car and then fuck off?" she said. She began to run towards the figure, who she now assumed was some alien being. She could recognize a voice translator device by now. He was also in a type of protective suit that obscured his features, though the size of his body seemed too thick to be human at all. She formed twin spears out of her arms as she got closer to it.

The being raised a large rifle and hit a button on it, then aimed it at her. She didn't think anything could penetrate her suit. At least nothing had yet. She was preparing to dodge whatever the rifle shot when she saw a strange sight – a bubble of energy was released from the end of the rifle and engulfed her before she could dodge it. She stopped her momentum for a moment, looking at this new situation. Then she extended both her hands and tried to pop it, but it just extended around her, not showing any signs of breaking. She then noticed that it seemed to be getting slowly smaller.

Suddenly the figure was there next to her, and it injected something through the bubble. Oh, damn, some sort of gas, she thought as her world began to darken. Daddy's car, she thought, before falling unconscious. Her suit disappeared.

◊

Jophen Dar walked down the street in the Human city known as Detroit. He still couldn't pronounce the alien name of the city. It was dark and he had his hood up over his long brown hair, so he blended well enough into the local populace. He looked around before tapping the communication and translating implant located just behind his right ear.

"Reilla, any luck pinpointing the location of the Human ship?"

"Not yet, Dar. Making any progress on your end?"

"No. This, what did you call it, 'apartment complex' is nearby." He walked a short distance before looked up at the building and muttering, "I can't believe I'm here again on this planet."

"Yes. Apartment complex," the voice in his ear said, ignoring his last statement. "A type of low-cost, high concentration housing unit."

"I'm right outside the structure," he said. "For all of his reputation and the fear and respect our employer gives him, I'm surprised he doesn't live in some type of warrior's habitat."

"The Humans, I'm told, are an eccentric species. Besides, we know that all the Humans lived in that structure at one time. Perhaps there is more to the complex than meets the eye. Like I told you before, that's his last known location, so he may not be there at all. I remember you telling me that it was a strange place the last time you were there."

"That's an understatement. You should see all the things I have since coming down here. The last time was a quick in and out with the human cargo."

"We really don't have time, Dar."

"I know, I'll tell you later. I'm going in. Comms silent until I say otherwise."

"Copy that."

Dar opened the front door of the building and went inside. There was an unoccupied counter to the left, behind which he could see a few desks with computer monitors set up. He saw stairs to his right and moved towards them. The quarry was said to live on the fourth floor. He walked quickly upwards and checked his gun and sword to make sure they were situated in case he needed them. His employer had said that he wanted all the Humans brought to him alive and unharmed, but Dar would do what he had to do to protect himself. This Human had been upgraded since last Dar saw him.

He came to the correct floor and memories of the last time he was there flooded into his mind. He remembered this area of the building now that he was there and was feeling a bit of déjà vu when he heard a door opening at the far end of the hallway. He hurriedly ducked back into the stairwell as he saw a large creature walking down the hallway and then stopping at the doorway of one of the units. The figure pressed a finger to his ear as if listening to something, then attached something to the middle of the door.

Dar fought down the feeling of rage and frustration. Atalik the bounty hunter. He'd been told that he would have competition from other interested parties but hadn't known that they had hired the dangerous bounty hunter. Dar knew he was outgunned on this trip. It wouldn't do to needlessly put his own life in jeopardy. He'd run into Atalik before, and he was a formidable opponent.

"Blast," he whispered. He would have to make a new plan. If the Human known as Gianni was indeed in the apartment, then he was, for the moment, out of reach.

◊

A closed fist pounded on a door from the other side. The room was dark and messy. A man's voice came from the other side of the locked door. "Come on, man. Open the damn door!

More pounding. Finally, some movement. A pillow was thrown towards the door. "Go away! Asshole."

The pounding intensified. "Dammit, G, I'll break the door down."

Finally, the door opened. "Jesus..." Gianni Moretti said, squinting at the light. His long, dark hair was in messy curls around his head, some of it was sticking up on top, making him look like he had just rolled out of bed, which he had. He scratched at his goatee as he looked out from the dark room.

"Damn, bro, you look like shit."

"You're lucky you're connected, or I'd shoot you, Tommy." Gianni laughed as the man embraced him, and he hugged him back.

"Good to see you too, man," Tomas said, smiling. "Not so great smelling you."

"Shut up. You got the stuff?"

Tomas held up a large black briefcase. "Right here."

Gianni extended his arm towards the inside of his room. "Welcome to castle Moretti." The inside Gianni's room was a total mess. There were beer cans, beer cartons, beer bottles, bottles of three different types of Kentucky whiskey, and other types of empty liquor bottles. There were also fast-food buckets, burger containers, pizza boxes, and other junk food trash.

"Moretti? Or DeMilo? The hell, G?" Tomas said, looking at the sprawling mess. "How long you been holed up here?"

"Too long," Gianni responded. "And I don't go by DeMilo no more. And I won't be going by Moretti, either, I assume?"

"So, you woke up from a coma and instantly began drinking everything in sight?" his cousin asked, ignoring Gianni's question.

"Something like that. I've been dealing with some heavy shit for a few years now."

Tomas went over to the windows and opened the blackout curtains, and a bright shaft of light entered the apartment. "Much better."

Gianni moved some pizza boxes from the couch and then sat down. Tomas inspected his cushion a moment before sitting. He made sure not to touch his back to the back of the couch. It looked like there might be a large stain back there. He pushed away the glass coffee table that was also overflowing with debris. He placed the briefcase he was holding onto the floor in front of him and opened it.

"Okay," Tomas began. "Social security card. Passport. Driver's license. All in the name of Anthony Puntini."

"Puntini?"

"Hey, it was the only name I could get besides spaghetti," he chuckled at his own joke. "Your name is Anthony Puntini now. You were born in the Bronx in 1986." He looked at Gianni a moment before adding, "of course to look at you, maybe I should've made it 2006."

Gianni ignored him. "Did you have to make me Italian? That's cutting it a little close, don't you think? And Puntini? That kind of sucks."

"Like nobody is going to know you're Italian." Tomas said, leaning back, having forgotten about the stain. "Just like nobody is going to believe that supposed 'coma' story you gave me to cover all that time you've been gone. Almost six years now! All I know is that I went into your loo to take a piss, and when I came out, you were gone. What really happened man? I thought you were dead! Everyone thinks you're dead. Your uncle says you'd better be. And why haven't you gone to see your mama? She's still distraught."

Gianni held his right hand over his eyes as he leaned forward. "You don't know how close it was, Tommy. God, the things I've seen. I just haven't been ready to see momma yet."

Tomas leaned forward towards Gianni. "You can tell me. I'm still your boy."

Gianni smiled at him now. "How about you tell me what happened to my cat?"

Tomas smiled back. "Stop trying to change the subject. C'mon, you can tell me."

"Fine," Gianni said, leaning back. "But you won't believe me."

"Try me," Tomas said, leaning back and again forgetting again about the stain on the couch.

Gianni began at the beginning, when he awoke aboard the Tukuli. Meeting his fellow humans and then the aliens who had kidnapped him. The decision to help the Rajani and the implantation of the Johar Stones. He told him about Kieren and fighting on Rajan, and finally, about losing her, and coming home. Time passed, and the shadows grew larger around them.

"You are so full of shit."

"I said you wouldn't believe me," Gianni said, chuckling.

"Aliens."

"Hand to God, yeah."

"Spaceships."

"Yeah."

"Damn bro."

"You keep saying that," Gianni said, laughing.

"Yeah. I do. How am I supposed to take it when my own cousin won't level with me? Maybe you should stick with the coma story. Or better yet, that you were lying low in Europe for a while. Something plausible."

"I guess there is only one way to prove this to you." Gianni stood up. "It's been a little while since I've done this. Give me a sec." Gianni suited up, his body surrounded by an energy field. "Ah. Like riding a bike." He laughed at the expression on his cousin's face. "See, I..."

Suddenly the thin door of the apartment exploded inward as the large alien named Atalik pushed his way through. The small explosive device he'd attached to the door was designed to blow material only one way. Tomas dove away from the flying materials but was struck in the head by a large piece of the door, which knocked him unconscious.

Gianni stood there facing Atalik, who was much larger

than he was. "What the hell did you do to my apartment, asshole? Do you know how much the security deposit was on this place?"

"Come with me, Human," the alien said. "Your female friend is already on my ship."

"I have a lot of female friends, dickhead," Gianni responded. "Don't think any of them would go with you willingly."

Without another word, Atalik aimed a blocky gun at Gianni and fired. Gianni was ready for either a projectile weapon or even laser, having faced both on Rajan, but instead a bubble of energy surrounding him. Gianni was standing inside of the bubble, wondering what had just happened. He fired from his hands, and watched as the energy bounced back at him, re-absorbing back into the suit. He held his hands out to the bubble, feeling the resistance against his hands, but not as if the bubble were solid. It felt more like soft plastic.

"Son of a bitch...what the hell is this stuff?" He felt the bubble beginning to shrink against his hands. It was getting smaller.

Atalik approached the bubble with a device shaped like a syringe. He injected the contents of the syringe into the bubble. "Sleep, Human," he said in Talondarian Standard.

The liquid from the syringe started to take gaseous form inside the bubble, causing Gianni to start coughing. He fired again, instinctively, though with the same results. He was beginning to feel lightheaded and fell to one knee. He looked up at the large alien outside the bubble. "You son of a..."

Gianni fell unconscious on the bottom of the bubble, and his suit disappeared. Atalik stood over the top of him for a moment, looking down at his latest successful hunt. He looked over at the other Human, wondering if he should kill him, but decided that he wasn't paid enough to clean up loose ends. Atalik didn't like to take life needlessly. He always prided himself on taking his bounties alive to face whatever consequences they were due. He pressed a button on the side of the gun he was carrying and pointed it at the bubble. When he fired, the bubble dissolved, leaving the unconscious form of Gianni lying on the floor amongst the other debris.

◊

Atalik secured the Human male over his shoulder. The effects of the gas would last for long enough for him to transport his prisoner back to his ship, which he'd parked in an open space near the complex, making sure not to crush the play structures located there. His ship was camouflaged to the casual observer, but such destruction would bring unwanted attention from the local authorities.

He opened the hatch to the cargo section of the ship and walked in, pressing the button to close it behind him. He walked a few paces to where the body of the Human female was lying, secured for transport. He laid the Human male next to her and strapped him in as well, then opened the small case nearby that held the intravenous fluid that would keep him sedated for the trip to Rajan.

After finishing hooking the Human male up to the IV and checking that female's IV was still secure, he walked to the metal ladder that led up to the cockpit of the ship. He looked back once more at the two humans. "Sleep well," he said softly and then climbed the rungs.

It was time to find James the Human.

◊

The small transport ship circled once around the larger ship near the northern pole of the planet called Earth. Finally, it docked near the rear of the larger ship and the airlock clicked into place. Dar unbuckled and left the pilot's seat. He was feeling frustrated. Atalik had found both the male and female Humans before he could.

"Well, that could have gone better," he said after pressing the commlink button behind his ear.

"What is that, Atalik two, Dar zero?"

"Whatever, you little blue-faced..." he whispered.

"What was that? I couldn't quite hear you..."

"Oh, nothing. Just can't help but feel like we've failed. We're not going to get paid. We'll never get hired by anyone else ever again when word gets out. Which means we'll be cleaning up hydro-trash on Kordella III for the rest of our lives. Hope you can swim."

"Oh, come on now, it's not that bad. Actually, I do have some good news to report."

"And what's that? Did the Rajani change their minds about this asinine war of theirs?"

"Not quite that good, sir."

Dar pushed open the door of the airlock and entered the main portion of the ship. Standing in the hallway was a small blue alien, her white hair cut so that it was short on the sides of her head and longer on top. "Well, what is it, Reilla?"

"I found him," she said with that twinkle in her red eyes that he knew so well.

Chapter 3

In the early morning light, Welemaan tuc Xenaani sat in his empty house and thought of everyone he had lost because of the Krahn Horde's attack on Rajan. The list was endless. He'd lost his entire family, his friends, including his best friend, Kedar, and so many others. He thought about the day ahead as well. He needed to visit the salvage site where the Krahn mothership had crashed and the shipbuilding hangars which were right next door. He needed to visit Zanth to talk about affairs of state. Lastly, he needed to check on preparations for that night's feast for the Human named David.

David was a wonder and had been an irreplaceable asset when it came to communication between the Valderren and the residents of Rajan before the infrastructure was fixed. It took almost a year for recovery efforts to clean up the results of the war and begin to rebuild. They had recycled as much of the building materials and other debris as they could. What was left was still in large piles on the outskirts of the city.

Then had come word from some scientists that their species was dying. The woman and children had been killed by the Krahn. Very few were left—those who had been hidden from the Krahn and not captured—and there were not nearly enough to continue the species. Rebuilding had turned to despair, and then to hatred. Welemaan had saw his chance to consolidate his own power and took it.

The Elders had called for peace and research into artificial methods to prolong the species, but Welemaan and his Valderren had called for vengeance. His argument had won, and he was now the leader of the Rajani as they now concentrated on the business of building starships to attack the Krahn home world. They had nothing more to lose.

Welemaan had used all his influence to begin shifting rebuilding efforts from the city of Melange to salvaging the Krahn mother ship, as well as the three Krahn supply ships that had arrived. They had been lured to a landing spot in a field outside of Melange and after landing, had been overrun by Rajani forces and all their crew members killed except for their captains, who were now prisoners alongside some remaining Krahn Horde members, including Ronak. Welemaan even had the Tukuli, Rauphangelaa's old ship, salvaged from the bottom of the ocean and used for spare parts.

Welemaan had used his newly-found power to publicly chastise the remaining Elders—even going so far as to imprison some for speaking out against the new Rajani government. Dissent was seen as sedition now by most Rajani. The hatred they all felt was enough to turn them against any voices of reason. The old fool Tumaani was amongst those imprisoned, which made Welemaan sad, but the Rajani Elder had stood in the way of their mission. It couldn't be helped, much as Welemaan hated doing it.

He sighed and stood up. He had a busy day ahead and may as well begin. There was no use contemplating the past now. There was work to be done.

◊

David felt that he was becoming better at impulse control. He was able to quash certain urges before they became obsessions and was able to maintain his status as a contributing member of Rajani society. There were times, though, when he couldn't help himself.

This night, however, was special. The Rajani were having a feast, and David was the guest of honor. It wasn't just a feast in David's honor, it was also a celebration of how far they had come at putting the Krahn Horde attack behind them and moving forward as a society, integrating both Rajani and Sekani together.

The Jirina had been invited but had politely declined. It was understandable, given how much they had lost during the fighting, and how opposed to violence they had become. Their leader, Mazal, had taken his people and moved out of the city. They were now the principal food suppliers on Rajan, having taken over farming duties from the Elders. For the most part they were left alone, and Mazal only attended important strategy meetings that affected the Jirina. He had pledged that they would not fight against the Krahn off-world.

David was in no particular hurry to get to the feast, though he could have gotten there in a fraction of a second if he really wanted to. He was enjoying the nice weather and a feeling of freedom that he'd never had back on Earth. Now, when images of his father flashed through his mind, he could shrug it off and not be thrown into rage or depression. Especially not on a beautiful day like today.

He saw Zanth and a few other Sekani warriors also heading towards what could only be called the new town square—the feast would be outside due to the fair weather. "David, how are you?" Zanth called to him, waving him over with the relatively primitive-looking mechanical left arm that replaced the one he had lost in the fighting five years before.

"Good evening," David said when he had come closer to where the group stood waiting for him. By this time, he had learned both Talondarian Standard and a fair bit of Sekani. He was practically a celebrity to the Sekani, having saved the life of Zanth by quickly taking him for medical attention after he had lost his arm.

"Good night for a party," one of the Sekani said.

"Yes it is," David replied.

"I wanted to speak with you," Zanth said. "Sit next to me at the feast."

David wondered what was on the Sekani leader's mind. He had to think for a moment to remember if he'd done something, or killed someone, who might be too important. He didn't think he had.

"David?" Zanth asked.

David realized that he had probably lost all expression, which happened sometimes when he was too far inside his own head. He smiled. "Yes, that sounds great."

"Good," Zanth said, looking at him a moment more, then turning back and speaking with one of his Sekani companions. "Jinda, please make arrangements for David and me to sit together at the feast. Explain to Welemaan my wishes." The Sekani looked a moment at David, then nodded and ran ahead to make the preparations.

◊

David felt famished, as he did so much after expending energy when he used his powers. He had piled up an enormous amount of meat and root vegetables on his plate, as well as a large glass of fernta. By now those who knew him knew about his incredible appetite, so no one gave him a second glance when he sat down with the stacked plate of food.

Soon Zanth and many others were seated as well at the tables that had been placed around a central square, which was made from a concrete-like substance. The square was empty and surrounded on all sides by a reinforced cage of metal. David was halfway finished with his plate when Welemaan stood up from his place at the head table and raised his arms in an effort to get everyone's attention. After a moment, he spoke.

"Welcome," he began, his voice amplified by the comm unit and speakers that were installed around the square. This brought on cheers and hooting from most in attendance, which from what David could see, was just about everyone. Every time the tables would fill, there were workers who set up another to accommodate latecomers.

"I'll be brief," Welemaan continued. "We are here for a celebration!" Another roar from the crowd. "Tonight, we celebrate our victory over the Krahn Horde," (hissing or booing, or at least that's what David thought it was, at this), and the peace between our great species," he said, looking over to Zanth and nodding. Zanth stood and raised his mechanical hand over his head in a fist. Everyone screamed or tapped the table in front of them, which David knew was a form of applause. "We thank all of you for your courage and your sacrifice. We also thank David of the Humans for all that he's done to help us both in the war and ever since!"

Another roar of applause as David stood up and waved to the crowd. I could get used to this, he thought. He sat back down while several Sekani chanted his name briefly.

"Yet our work is not finished," Welemaan said. The crowd quieted down. "We still have a great deal to accomplish in a short amount of time. But I think we can do it! I think we will overcome any obstacles in our path, and we will fight, and we will win once again!" The crowd was almost in a frenzy, David included. Welemaan let them all naturally quiet down again as they all released their pent-up energy.

"Enjoy tonight, because tomorrow begins a new dawn for Rajani and Sekani alike. Enjoy the show!" He sat down as another round of applause erupted.

David wasn't sure what the show would be, but from the look of the new cage barrier, he was certainly intrigued. He saw a large transport shuttle slowly pull up near the square. It was pulling a covered trailer. Others began to notice it as well, and a wave of chatter began as the anticipation grew.

Two Rajani got out of the front of the transport and then began to open the door to the rear of the transport. The crowd almost hissed when the first Krahn warrior got down from the doorway, followed by four more. They were captured prisoners from the war, and they looked in rough shape, as far as David could see. They had been imprisoned for years in the old prison, and it was evident that they had not been fed well.

The Krahn were led through the crowd along a walkway that went straight to the wide gate on the cage structure. All of them looked at the ground, their hackles lowered in submission. David thought they all looked like featherless parrots. He laughed, and the Sekani near him began to laugh as well. Soon the laughter turned to jeering and screaming, all of it directed at the Krahn. The Sekani especially hated the Krahn for what they had done when they arrived on Rajan. Many Sekani had been butchered and eaten by the Krahn warriors.

The Rajani guards opened the gate and pushed the Krahn prisoners into the cage before slamming the door behind them. One of the guards brought out five small knives from a satchel around his waist. He threw them through the bars at the feet of the Krahn.

The crowd quieted down again as the Rajani guards went back to the trailer and opened it up. One of them pressed a button on a control panel on the rear of the trailer, and a platform began to extend out from within the trailer. On the platform, strapped down securely, was a horror show. David stopped eating, seeing the creature that had been captured and was now strapped to the floating platform. He absent-mindedly rubbed his throat, remembering the last time he'd seen one. It had been choking his friend Janan to death.

The kleng beast was a small specimen, only about a dozen feet across. The mass of it was taken up by the tentacles it used to capture prey and dig through the sand of the desert. There was no sand now, and David was appalled at just how horrible the creature was when it was fully visible and not just a bunch of tentacles sticking out of the sand.

The platform was directed towards the cage and the Krahn within it. They all looked at what was coming and backed up slowly to the other side of the cage away from the gate. The platform reached the gate, and the guards opened it, allowing the platform to pass through. One of the guards stayed outside as the platform was lowered all the way to the ground. The other guard reached down and pressed a button on the platform before quickly backing away. They closed the gate and secured it just as the straps over the kleng beast automatically contracted, leaving the beast free.

There was a moment of silence as the beast noticed it was now unhindered by the straps. Its many eyes turned in its body and looked around. David had a feeling that it couldn't see very well. One of the Krahn warriors stepped forward, his knife clasped in one hand.

Zanth leaned over to David. "They have been told that if they kill the kleng beast, we will let them go." He laughed, and David smiled, knowing it would never happen, even if a miracle happened and they managed to kill the beast.

Soon, the other Krahn followed suit and began to surround the beast, their daggers held ready. The beast finally caught sight of them and let out a low roar that sounded to David like a garbage disposal back on Earth. Then the fight began.

In just a few minutes, the kleng beast was bleeding from several superficial wounds, but had four of the Krahn wrapped in tentacles. Two of them were certainly dead, their bodies mangled and bent by the strength of the tentacles. One Krahn struggled weakly as the tentacle around his neck strangled him to death. Another stabbed repeatedly at the tentacle around his right leg. The last Krahn had lost his knife and was circling around the beast looking for an opening in which to get ahold of it.

David and other members of the audience winced when the kleng beast pulled the Krahn's leg out of the socket, then completely off its body. It held the leg up above the ground as the Krahn bled to death on the concrete. There were four dead Krahn now, and the kleng beast began to feed on them, eating the leg first in a cavernous mouth that seemed full of teeth. The last Krahn took the opportunity to grab his lost knife as he backed away from the distracted beast. He circled it slowly, looking for a vulnerable spot. David smiled as the crowd around him quieted down, wondering what the Krahn would do.

Evidently the Krahn saw his chance and lunged towards the kleng beast, his dagger extended towards one of the large eyes. The dagger penetrated the eye just as a tentacle wrapped around the Krahn's head. Another tentacle wrapped around his waist as the kleng beast released a roar of pain. The tentacles tightened around the Krahn warrior and David knew what was about to happen next. He could see it in his mind clearly.

The tentacles pulled the opposite way from one another and the Krahn warrior separated in a burst of blood and tissue, his head and upper chest now in one tentacle, and the lower part of his body in another, still connected by intestines. Each part was brought to the mouth and that was the end of the match.

The Sekani and Rajani cheered loudly as the beast finished his meal. When it was clear that the festivities were over, many Rajani and Sekani rose and left, knowing that they would be working the next day. Some took their time watching the kleng beast eat as they drank fernta and reminisced about the fighting.

Zanth patted David on the shoulder. "Well-deserved recognition for you," he said.

"Thank you, Zanth," David said. He had finally run out of food and felt satiated. He sipped his fernta.

"I guess there's no better time to tell you than now," Zanth said. "We are bringing your friends back to Rajan. Hopefully they will once again decide to fight for us."

"My friends?" David asked. The meat in his stomach seemed to turn rancid and he felt nauseous. "You mean the other Humans? James?"

"Yes, James, his mate, and Sedan'ka," Zanth said.

David knew that Sedan'ka was the name they had given to Gianni when he fought with them against the Krahn Horde. No one on Rajan knew what had happened between him and the other three when it was time to leave Rajani. Most of the Rajani and Sekani had no idea that he was a wanted murderer back on Earth, and that the other Humans had learned his secret just before leaving Rajan. They had fought and David had been wounded by Yvette, or 'James' mate' as Zanth referred to her.

"You're bringing them here?" he asked. "They agreed to that?"

"Well..." Zanth said. "The Council made the decision to bring them here to get their answer in person."

David looked at him for a moment, not remembering ever seeing Zanth with a sheepish expression on his face. "You kidnapped them again?"

"Well..."

"Oh shit, James is going to be pissed," David said in English. "You're bringing them here against their will and expecting them to fight for you?"

"It worked before," Zanth answered. "We are facing long odds. The Krahn are sure to outnumber us. We can use all of the help we can get."

David nodded and stood. "Well good," he said absent-mindedly. He needed to leave—to think about the implications of what Zanth had just told him. And he needed to prepare for his revenge. Whether the others would fight or not was irrelevant. They couldn't fight if they were dead.

◊

Welemaan returned home from the feast to find David waiting for him at his front door. "David, did you enjoy the festivities?" he said as he smiled a greeting to the Human.

"I had to find out from Zanth that James and the others are coming to Rajan?"

Welemaan felt his smile falter. "It was thought best for him to tell you."

"And at the feast, where I was less likely to cause a scene and get upset."

"David..."

"No, it's fine. They're coming. I get that. But why wasn't I consulted before you made the decision?"

Welemaan sighed. He felt too tired for this conversation. "Because it was for the leaders of the Rajani and Sekani to decide. I'm sorry, I did not think you would be upset by this."

"I told you what happened when they left," David said, clenching his fists. "Do you think I've changed my mind about them since then?"

"No," Welemaan said. "I suppose you haven't, not that I blame you. But they are not to be harmed unless necessary. Do you understand? They will be our guests, not our prisoners."

David was silent as he thought it over.

"David, do I have your promise that you won't do anything rash when they arrive? We can work this out to everyone's benefit."

"You mean to yours," David said, a sour smile on his face.

"They are not to be harmed," Welemaan said more forcefully. "That is the end of it. Goodnight, David."

David looked at him a moment and then was gone in a rush of air as he took off. Welemaan wasn't sure which way he even went. He looked around once and then put in his security code at the panel next to the door. He had to think about the implications of his conversation, but at the moment, it was more important to get some sleep.

He would worry about David later.

Chapter 4

James Dempsey was aboard *Bright Journey* waiting for Yvette to call so that he could send Belani down on the smaller transport ship. The smaller ship was easier to maneuver and took far less fuel to operate within the planet's atmosphere. He placed the book of poetry he had been reading down on a nearby table. He wasn't sure if he liked Philip Larkin as much as some, but decided he was better than others he'd read recently.

"Bob, any word from Yvette?" he asked the empty room. The computer's nickname came from an old television show. Robbie the Robot had become Bob for short. He'd tinkered around with the AI's settings and now the computer was able to speak English relatively well. His inflection and syntax still needed some work, but it didn't sound like a stilted computer voice, at least. It was creating its own personality, which was fascinating to both James and Belani. By giving the computer a name, he had given it an identity.

The ship's computer also had enough storage space that the AI could store years of interactions and experiences, a virtual memory, and tap this resource as it made decisions. James could even remember the moment the AI seemed to have become self-aware, and it scared him a little at first. Bob now thought of itself, or himself now (he had extrapolated from his name that he was male), as the ship itself. He was the mind that controlled the body.

James had opened Bob's receivers as wide as possible, enabling him to access most transmissions coming from the planet below. Bob could tap into radio and television signals, as well as worldwide web broadcasts of all types.

"Nothing yet, James," the voice of Bob said over the ship's speaker in the room.

"Must have taken longer than she thought to grocery shop," James said out loud.

"What is the purpose of a date?" the voice asked.

"What kind of question is that?" James asked.

"Are you referring to the validity of the inquiry or to the intentions put forth by it?"

"Actually, that is what's known as a rhetorical question. It didn't really call for an answer on your part, Bob."

"Didn't call for...erroneous input."

"Yeah, yeah, I know. Humans don't make any sense."

"Will you answer the original question? I was wondering why you needed to date someone who you have already mated with. My records show that usually the date comes before the act of mating commences."

"Wow," James stopped from laying out his nice clothes and thought for a moment. "I don't know that we have the time now to go over this. How about this: when two people want to get to know each other better, they go on a date. They spend time together to learn about each other's beliefs, habits, and try to figure out if they're compatible personalities. Usually, they are on their best behavior. When people who have known each other a while go on a date, like Yvette and I now, it's because we want to have a somewhat special occasion where we can be together without worrying about things like childcare or how we're going to keep paying for groceries on Yvette's salary."

"Young Kieren is not coming?"

"Not tonight," James said. "Her grandfather is taking care of her."

"And a date is a part of the Human mating ritual, even after you have successfully mated?"

"Yes, Bob. Even after we've mated." James smiled and shook his head. "How much time until she is supposed to call? Has to be getting close." James had set a deadline for her to call to fit into the window of when the *Bright Journey* was over her location while it orbited the Earth. It saved on time and fuel for the lander aircraft.

"Ten minutes, eight seconds. Shall I give you a minute-by-minute countdown?" To James, the AI sounded almost excited at the prospect.

James waved away the request. "That won't be necessary. Women are always late. But I'll have to tell Belani to fire up the engines and maneuver back to the proper orbital location if she's too late."

"On Galabas IV, if a female is late, the male will cut off one of her tentacles for every minute he's had to wait."

"I don't think that will be necessary, either," James said. He finished dressing in his good clothes and looked in a nearby mirror. His hair was getting a little long. He still hadn't been able to find an acceptable cutting appliance on the ship. He would have to go to a barber down on the planet like he first had when they returned from Rajan and his hair was a mass of long dreadlocks. He'd told the barber to shave it all off. A fresh start, and a symbolic closing of his adventures with the Rajani.

He looked at himself now—a forty-eight-year-old black man who looked like he was no older than half that age. The

Johar Stone implanted in his head had brought him back to peak physical performance, which included looking like he was much younger than he was.

"Proximity alert! Proximity alert!" Bob said loudly over the intercom.

James began running towards the bridge. "What the hell?! Bob, status report!"

"Unknown vessel now two hundred earth miles away and approaching quickly."

James was running down the long hallway. "Is it Rajani?"

"Negative. By all accounts, the vessel is not registered on any known planet's list. Could be any designation."

James is now at the bridge and is almost through the door. "Damn, what's that supposed to mean?"

"Ship has been built to its own specifications, which are not in line with any known civilization. A common effect among ships of the Somani. Or Korflath. Or Krahn Horde. Or..."

James is getting into the captain's chair. "Krahn?! Shields up!"

"They were up upon detection of the ship within my operational sphere. What are your orders?"

"Standby."

Just then, the bridge door opened, and Belani entered, his eyes wide. He had been sleeping in his quarters. He nodded at James and sat down in his pilot's chair. "Bob, bring up the ship on the main screen."

The screen lit up and James could see the outline of a ship against the blackness of space. It hardly reflected the sunlight that streamed around it. "Doesn't look like a Krahn ship," he said.

"No," Belani agreed. "Bob, can you magnify in on it?"

The ship grew larger, and they both sat for a moment

observing it.

"Bob, how big is the ship in relation to *Bright Journey*?"

"Smaller in length and mass. Approximately three-quarters my size."

James thought for a moment. "Are you able to send them a message in Talondarian Standard? Ask them what they want? Also, plan an escape route in case they're hostile."

"Done." There was a pause. "Incoming transmission."

"That was quick," Belani said, turning to look at James.

James shrugged.

"Shall I play it?" Bob asked.

"Yes," James said.

There was a moment's pause, then a rough male voice came over the speakers. He spoke in Talondarian Standard. Although James had learned a bit of the language, he was thankful that he'd had a translation device implanted behind each ear, much like what the Rajani had when they first visited Earth.

"James Dempsey, this is the starship, *Freedom*. We come in peace. Please allow us to come aboard. This is an urgent matter." The message began to repeat, and James motioned for it to be cut off. There were cameras outside and inside the ship, which Bob used to his advantage. He had eyes almost everywhere.

"Originating language?" James asked.

"Talondarian Standard," Bob replied.

"Damn," James said. "Belani, what do you think?

The Sekani pilot just shrugged.

"How about you, Bob?"

"I am not programmed to make judgment decisions of this magnitude."

"Fine. Open the channel for me."

"Done."

James leaned forward in his chair, talking to the other ship. "*Freedom*, this is *Bright Journey*. What are your intentions?"

"This is Captain Jophen Dar. We are here to save your life, Human."

◊

One of the first actions James had performed when he returned to Earth was to have a translating device implanted behind each of his ears. He was competent with Talondarian standard, but there were thousands of new languages in the Galactic Alliance. The implants also enabled him to speak with Bob and Belani when off-ship, which was helpful when he was down on the planet's surface and needed to talk to one or both of them. He had tried hard to convince Yvette to also implant a device, but she was adamant in her rejection, saying that she'd already had enough machines messing around with her head.

He kept pressing, and she finally relented, agreeing to one implant behind her left ear—though she told him that if it left a scar, she would kill him. He didn't think she truly meant it but was happy when the operation was finished, and she was scar-free.

Yvette was in the back of his mind as he made his way down to *Bright Journey's* cargo hold. It hadn't left him that she still hadn't contacted them. Yvette could more than take care of herself in most situations. He wondered if this spaceship had anything to do with her continued silence. It was too coincidental not to be.

He stopped in the hallway that held the double-wide doors to the cargo bay and punched in a code. The doors opened, then a thin, shiny power grid appeared in the doorway—a shield, just in case the other ship's inhabitants proved to be hostile. He'd told Belani to stay on the bridge in case Yvette called or they needed to get out of the area in a hurry—he wasn't sure what to expect from this Dar character.

"Bob, are we ready for airlock connection?"

"Yes. My scans show that the ship is manned by four beings. A humanoid—presumably Talondarian, a Sekani, a Shif, and a Sh'Kallian."

"Sekani? Interesting." The mysteries were deepening.

"Airlock connection complete. Shall I open the outside door?"

"Yes. Let's see what they have to say." James crossed his arms and waited.

Soon the cargo airlock door opened, and a figure stepped through. James noticed that he was wearing some type of dark armor as well as a helmet that hid his features. On one leg was what looked like a sword in a scabbard, while the opposite hip had a pistol holstered on it. James assumed that this was Dar. The alien walked slowly over to the doorway where James stood.

"You don't take chances, do you?" he said in Talondarian standard.

"Better safe than dead."

"Ah, very true. Earth colloquialism, is it not?"

"Something like that," James said. "Enough small talk. What can I do for you?"

"It's what I can do for you, Dempsey," Dar said. He reached up with both hands and took off his helmet. James could see that he was a Talondarian, and that he had long brown hair and a series of scars running from his left eye down to below his chin. "I have been hired to protect you and the other Stone Soldiers in the impending Rajani/Krahn war." He smiled as he said this.

"Stone what?" James said, confused. "Hired by who?"

"Whom" he heard Bob say in his implant.

"Shut up Bob," James whispered.

"What was that? I didn't catch it," Dar said.

"Not important," James said.

"Well neither is who hired me," Dar said. "What is important is that we rescue your teammates from Atalik."

"What's an Atalik?" James asked. "Okay, look, this is going way too fast. Why don't you start from the beginning? Put your weapons on the ground and stay a while."

"Fine," Dar said. "I assure you that I mean you no harm." He unbuckled his belt and placed the sword on the floor and then placed the gun next to it.

"That's what the Rajani said, too. Step away from them."

Dar did as he was told. "You can drop your shield now."

James stood there a moment studying the alien.

Dar sighed and then dropped to one knee with his right hand over his heart. He was no longer smiling. "I pledge my honor to this truth: I mean you and your people no harm. I take this pledge of my own free will. Do you accept my pledge, James the Human?"

It was now James' turn to smile. "So, you can be serious. Know this, if you have taken a false pledge with me, you will regret it. Bob, you can drop the shield."

The energy shield in the doorway disappeared. James stepped forward and held out his hand to the alien. "Welcome to the *Bright Journey*."

Dar stepped forward and grasped James' forearm in his hand and James grasped his in return. "We have much to discuss, Dempsey." He smiled then. "Do you have anything to drink?"

James smiled back. He had just the thing.

◊

James led Dar down the hallway aboard the *Bright*

Journey. He still didn't trust him, but the Talondarian had given a pledge. That had to count for something, he guessed.

"I've never met a Talondarian," James said.

"I would like to say I've never met an Earth man," Dar said. "Technically you're the first I've talked to, I suppose."

"Oh," James said, turning to look at him.

"You wouldn't remember, of course," Dar said. "But you've been aboard my ship before."

"Really?" James said. He felt a chill go down his spine. They walked through a doorway and James sat in the nearest chair. He had refitted the room to be more comfortable for humans to gather, placing the oversized chairs in storage and replacing them with more human-sized furniture. "Please sit down."

Dar sat across from him and looked around. "By the way, I'm happy to see that you have a personal translator. I was afraid we would have to resort to the use of one of those old-fashioned translating devices that the Rajani still use.

"You seem awfully familiar with the Rajani," James said.

"I am," Dar replied, sighing. "Unfortunately. You see, it was me and my team that first took you from Earth and brought you to Rauphangelaa aboard his ship. It was a job, and we needed the work."

"So you kidnapped five Earthlings without a second thought."

"We needed the work," Dar repeated, shrugging.

"Jesus," James said.

"That word doesn't seem to have a translation accorded to it," Dar said.

"Just think of your most common expletive," James said.

"Ah, understandable. Thank you for being so calm about all of this. I do know that you've had Johar Stones implanted in you, so I appreciate the fact that you haven't become angry enough to use it on me or my ship."

"It may come to that if you don't tell me why you're here."

"First, wasn't there mention of a drink?"

James smiled, though he wasn't happy at the moment. Emotions were swirling through his mind. Memories of first waking up aboard the Rajani ship. Of first experiencing the power of the Stone within his skull. He'd always wondered how he'd been transported from his apartment in Detroit to the Tukuli. If the Talondarian was telling the truth, he'd found his answer.

"Just a moment," he said. "Bob, how are we doing on time?"

"Ms. Manidoo should have called fifteen minutes ago," Bob responded.

"What? Why didn't you tell me?"

"You told me not to give you a countdown."

"Shit," James said, standing up.

"Before you do something rash, I have something else to tell you," Dar said. "You may want to sit back down."

James sat on the edge of the chair. "Yes?"

Dar sat forward as well. "My mission was to bring all of you with us. It took some time to locate your ship, and in the meantime, I went looking for the other Humans, Yvette and Gianni, on the planet's surface. I was too late. A bounty hunter named Atalik had already captured them."

"Captured them? How?" James asked. "Both of them would have fought him."

"And they did, but he's very good at his job," Dar said. "Our orders were to keep you all safe, and I believe his were as well. But they are now on their way back to Rajan."

James stood up and began pacing. "Back to Rajan. Shit. Shit. Shit."

"I'm sorry," Dar said. "I did what I could, but Atalik had a head start. He was originally hired by the same party that hired us."

"What? What do you mean?"

"Here's where it gets a little...uh...dicey," Dar said, rubbing his beard and looking a bit peevish. "We were hired by the Krahn to bring you to their world."

"What?!" James suited up instinctively.

"Now, now," Dar said, standing up and holding his hands out towards James. "No need for that. Really, I'm not here to hurt you or take you captive again."

"The Krahn," James said. "They're the ones who started this whole mess."

"That's not entirely true," Dar said. "Ronak started the entire thing. His older brother, Maliq, is the one trying to find a peaceful resolution to the problem. That's why he wants to speak with the three of you. He wants you to come to Krahn so that he can explain his position in the hopes that you can then go to Rajani and reason with them in person. He does not want war."

James stood for a moment more before his suit disappeared. "Give me one good reason why I shouldn't throw you off my ship and head to Rajan myself."

"Because you are an honorable Human," Dar said. "Everyone has heard about the great James the Human who helped to liberate the Rajani home world from the Krahn Horde. World travels quickly in the Alliance. The Rajani are of great interest to most denizens of the GA. Especially now when it looks like they are gearing up to go to war again."

"What assurances do I have from you that this isn't some type of trap?"

"All I can say is again, I pledge that it is not," Dar replied. "And so do my crew."

"How many are in your crew?"

"Besides me?" Dar said. "Three others. My pilot is a Shif. My weapons expert is a Sh'Kallian, and my pain in the ass is a Sekani."

James nodded. It fit with Bob's scans of the ship. He was being truthful about that, at least. "Bring them over here and we can talk more about our course of action," James said. "We might as well do it over dinner, since Yvette is not coming."

"Thank you," Dar said. "I appreciate your trust."

"You don't have it yet," James said.

"Understood. And that drink?"

Chapter 5

Ries an na Van, prisoner of the Talondarian Empire and former Galactic Intelligence agent, was having a bad day. Not that any of the previous years were that great, but this day had found him actually wondering if he would survive. He had been moved from his solitary cell in the prison to one of the general holding cells. It meant that he was no longer kept in the same cell for most of the day, but it also came with risks, such as what he faced now. He had gone to the cafeteria for breakfast, and had somehow managed to anger Halone, one of the more connected denizens of the prison. It meant that not only did he now have to watch for Halone, who was a Dergen and approximately three Standard feet taller than him, but also a collection of his sycophants.

Since he had no friends of his own, this was proving to be a problem. He spent all of the breakfast hour with his shell to the wall, watching to make sure no one snuck up on him while he was eating. It was highly distracting as well as frustrating. The guards were little help, as all they did was clean up whatever carnage that occurred on a particular day.

Finally, the bell had rung that signaled an end to breakfast, and all of the prisoners began to shuffle out in single-file lines to go to whatever their prescribed job station were for the day. Ries had not received a notification yet as to what his would be. He stayed sitting at the table until almost all of the others had left before standing and dumping the remains of his food in the trash bin, then placing the tray on the stack that needed to be washed. He hoped that his new job station wouldn't be washing dishes.

He was surprised as he turned to head for the door by the figure waiting there, looking at him. It was his old pilot, Jerboxh. The Sh'kallian pilot was the last person he'd expected to see there.

"Ries, you're looking well," Jerboxh said, smiling.

"And you look like a dung heap," Ries answered. "What do you want?"

"I've been sent to speak with you," Jerboxh answered. "And possibly help you."

"Help me?" Ries said. His mind was screaming, TRAP!, but he didn't let the emotion show on his features. "How?"

"Let's go somewhere a little more private," Jerboxh said. "Follow me."

Ries thought the pilot was stupid to turn his back, but that could also be a trap. If he attacked the Sh'kallion, he would ruin any chance he had of getting out of prison. He decided to bide his time and wait for the opportune moment.

Jerboxh led him to a private meeting room, one meant for prisoner visits from important individuals. He opened the door and motioned for Ries to enter before him. Ries scowled. He didn't want to turn his back on the pilot but seemed to not have a choice. He slowly walked through the doorway and stopped in his tracks in surprise.

Seated at the lone table in the room was Creon, the Talondarian prince who had imprisoned him.

"Come in," Creon said. "Take a seat."

Ries slowly entered the room and sat down opposite the

prince.

"Close the door," Creon said, and Jerboxh nodded, stepping back into the hall and closing the door behind him.

"To what do I owe the pleasure," Ries said, hoping his sarcasm was evident.

"Pleasant as ever, I see," Creon said. The prince looked only a little older than he had the last time Ries had seen him. His hair was a little longer, and he had grown out the makings of a beard and mustache.

Ries just sat and waited to hear what Creon had to say. He wasn't in the mood to play games.

"I'm in need of certain information," Creon said. "A while after your attempted kidnapping, I began to do some investigating of my own."

Ries was curious now but wouldn't let it show.

Creon waited for a heartbeat but then continued when Ries didn't speak. "Tell me what you know about Rajan."

Ries wasn't as surprised by this question as he felt he should be. "Which one?"

The prince smiled. "Ah, that's the question, isn't it? There's the planet that everyone knows about. The one that was attacked by the Krahn Horde a few Standard years ago. Then there's the other one."

"Well, I'd like to help you," Ries said. "But being locked up in this place has somewhat fogged my memory."

"Should I get a pain inducer?" the prince asked. He smiled.

Ries should have known that this would come up. The last time they were together, the prince had been restrained and Ries had maybe gone a little over the top in his quest to find the rogue GI agent named Oderey T'van. "That won't be necessary. I'm sure we can come to some form of agreement."

"Such as?"

"You let me out of here, free to be on my way, and I'll tell you everything I know."

"Unacceptable," Creon said. "Jerboxh, come in here."

Ries watched as the door opened and the Sh'Kallian stepped in once again.

"Get me a pain inducer," Creon said.

"Wait," Ries said. "How about, you let me out under your care, and I'll tell you."

The prince thought for a moment.

"You can't seriously be thinking about taking his offer?" Jerboxh said. "We can't trust him."

"I know we can't trust him," Creon said. "Which is why you will guard him at all times."

Jerboxh scowled at this, then looked at Ries with murderous intent. Ries smiled back at him.

"You will tell us everything we want to know, and you won't try anything stupid," Creon said. "In exchange, you will be released to my custody from this prison. Depending on how helpful you are, you may well yet find your freedom. Or you may be returned here to live out the rest of your life being a Dergen's sex slave."

Ries gulped at the prospect – he wasn't exactly compatible to a Dergen's...anatomical excesses. He decided that he wasn't going to get a better offer. "Agreed."

◊

Creon knew if his father found out about his investigations into the Rajani, there would be hell to pay. His father was a powerful ruler and would see anything going against his wishes as treason, even if it was his own son. Creon had only been curious about why the ex-agent named Ries would go to all the trouble to torture him and then not kill him on the Mandakan space port. He knew that there were elements on the space port who were against his father's rule, but to kidnap the Talondarian prince took some courage.

It had become apparent that Ries had not been the one who had initially imprisoned him. His interest had grown when he discovered that there were two planets known as Rajan. He was yet to confront his father about this secret and how it affected the Galactic Alliance. If the stories he'd uncovered were true, then the original planet known as Rajan was in the center of a GA barricade of ships, there to make sure that no one got to, or escaped from, the planet.

Meanwhile he'd heard the rumors of war coming from the planet currently known as Rajan. It seemed that the inhabitants had been stirred up by the Krahn Horde invasion. When Creon thought about it, there was no reason for the Krahn Horde to attack a planet so openly without fear of reprisal from the GA. It could only mean that someone high up in the GA was helping them. He wouldn't be surprised if it was his father.

Creon only had a glimmer of the machinations of his father, but what he knew made him ashamed to be his son. His father was a proud man, but he was also as ruthless as anyone Creon had ever met. It wouldn't be a shock to know that his father had helped the Krahn Horde attack Rajan in hopes that one or both of them would be destroyed as a result.

◊

Ries rubbed his four hands together, trying to stay warm. The room that Creon had stashed him in on his ship was bare and chilly. He had been careful to leave the room without anything that Ries could use to free himself or inflict injury on himself or others. That also meant that there was no furniture, blankets, or even a mat to sit upon. So Ries paced, and as he paced, he thought about his next steps.

He went over in his head what he knew so far. He knew

now that the Sekani contact on Rajan was named Janan. Perhaps he would eventually get free and take a trip to Rajan to find the Sekani, but his thoughts at the moment centered around the first Rajani planet, and why it had been buried in bureaucratic red tape so that it was essentially forgotten.

He also knew now that the prince was as interested in this aspect as he was, which was interesting. He hadn't pegged Creon for anything other than a spoiled royal in a galaxy seemingly full of them. Although each planet or system might have their own royals, all of them were under the authority of the GA, which meant, essentially, that they were under the authority of the Talondarians.

Yet the prince had so far treated him decently, present chilliness excluded, and he didn't have to. Even after Ries had tortured him on his ship, he hadn't returned the favor and done the same to Ries. He'd only turned him over to the authorities on Talondaria for imprisonment for his crimes.

The last thing he knew was that he still needed to find Oderey T'van. The Sekani was the key to finding out why the Talondarian King was trying to destroy the Rajani and using the Krahn Horde to do it. His best chance to do that would be to work with Creon, who had vastly more influence and connections than he did.

"Are you enjoying your time on the ship?" a voice said over the intercom. Ries looked up, though the voice wasn't necessarily coming from a speaker over his head. Jerboxh. It made sense now. It was his former pilot who was keeping his room cold. Petty, but not unexpected.

"Yes, thank you," he replied, smiling and unwilling to let the Sh'kallion know just how uncomfortable he was at the moment. "Perhaps you'd like to join me, and we can speak of better times together." There had been no better times together, but Ries couldn't help but make the dig at Jerboxh.

"I could make it colder, if you'd like," Jerboxh replied. "Or turn up the gravity until your body collapses on itself."

"No need for that," Ries said. "Does your new master know that you are antagonizing his prisoner?"

"He's not my master," Jerboxh hissed. "He pays me exceptionally well to serve as his private pilot."

Ries rolled all of his eyes, hoping that Jerboxh was watching him as well and could see the expression. "Whatever you say." It felt like the room was getting colder, and he knew that the Sh'kallion had most likely turned down the heat even more. If it got any colder, his body would eventually go into hibernation mode.

The thought was almost welcome.

◊

Creon was in his private chambers when he received the message that his father wanted to see him. He stood and looked at himself in the mirror to make sure he looked presentable. His father was a strict ruler, and showing up looking disheveled, even if only in his father's office, would be a mistake.

He walked down the hallway, passing by servants and clerks who were bustling about, presumably doing his father's bidding. He smiled or nodded as he saw people. He knew almost everyone in the palace and tried to keep a good relationship with each of them. They were who made the palace run efficiently.

He smiled when he saw his mother walking toward him. "Mother," he said as they came closer.

"Where are you heading?" Priss Tordor asked him, smiling back.

"Father requested me."

"Oh," her smile faltered for a moment. He wasn't sure what she was thinking, but he knew that his parents weren't necessarily on speaking terms now. His father had that effect on people, and his mother was the only one who dared show her unwillingness to speak to him at times when she felt he had done something she disagreed with.

"I'm sure it's nothing important," Creon said, unsure if he was trying to reassure her or himself. Probably both.

"Come by later and we'll have lunch together," she said.

"I will. Promise."

She squeezed his arm, and he smiled before continuing to his father's office.

In a few Standard minutes he was standing in front of the door to his father's office. He pushed the button to announce his presence, and the door opened almost immediately. Creon entered to see his father sitting at his desk and his chief counselor standing before it. There was also a royal guard in the corner, as always. This guardsman was named Alder Benen, and he was the king's private bodyguard and was almost always with him.

"That will be all, Evenu," his father said. The taller man bowed and then left the room with a nod to Creon. After the door had closed, Millen Tordor, King of the Talondarians, stood and began to pace behind his desk. Creon knew this wasn't a good sign. He waited silently, waiting for his father to speak.

Finally, after a few more minutes of pacing, his father stopped and looked over at him. "Why did you visit that prisoner?

"He kidnapped and tortured me, father," Creon replied. "I still want to know why."

"I think we both know why. Because you're my son."

"I think it may be a little deeper than that," Creon said.

"Regardless, the prison district is no place for a prince of Talondaria to be seen."

"I won't be going back," Creon said. He thought it best not to mention that it was because Ries was no longer at the prison.

"Good," Millen said, nodding once.

"Is that all?" Creon asked.

"What?" his father said, obviously having moved on to other matters on his mind. "Oh, yes. You may leave."

Creon bowed. "Thank you, father." He turned and left the room, happy to be out of it. He'd used to love coming to his father's office and looking at all the old-fashioned books and documents he had there, but lately, it seemed stifling in the room. He was perplexed by the feeling but knew he would have to think about it later. He had a prisoner to check on, then a lunch date.

◊

Ries was feeling lethargic due to the extended cold. He was sitting on the floor of his room, his mind fuzzy and not thinking about anything in particular. When the door opened, he only looked over at the prince who stood in the doorway.

"Jerboxh, this is no way to treat our special guest," Creon said, smiling.

"Sorry, forgot he was in there," Jerboxh replied from somewhere in the corridor.

The prince entered the room and came to stand over Ries. He bent down and looked Ries in the eyes. "Shall we warm the room up with some conversation?"

"Food?" Ries asked, wondering what the prince wanted to speak about. He was sleepy and hungry in equal measures.

"I'm sure we can find something for you to eat, as long as you cooperate with me."

Ries frowned. He couldn't remember now what he and the prince had been talking about. "Food?" he repeated.

The prince stood up again and turned back to look at Jerboxh, who now stood in the doorway. "I think you broke him."

Jerboxh shrugged and smiled.

"Turn up the heat just little so that he can begin to think straight. I'll be back a little later after lunch." He pulled a small fruit from his pocket and set it on the floor next to Ries. "To hold you over until I return."

Ries almost began to cry. The prince walked out of the room and the door closed behind him, but Ries' eyes were all on the fruit. He wasn't even sure what it was or what it would taste like, but he reached out all four arms towards it before falling forward on his face. Undeterred, he rolled towards the fruit and managed to get it in one of his hands. He brought it to his mouth parts just as he felt the first trace of warmth in the room. Jerboxh must have turned up the temperature as Creon had instructed. For a moment, Ries just closed his eyes, savoring both the somewhat sour taste of the fruit and the feeling of warmth enveloping his body.

Chapter 6

"Is this type of food common on Earth?" Dar asked as he took another huge bite from his cheeseburger. He had tied his long black hair in a ponytail to keep it out of his way as he ate.

"Yes, at least in my country," James replied. He was getting a kick out of watching the various types of aliens eat their food. It turned out that the Shif named Pico was a cyborg, and needed his food put in a food processor to eat it. He was some type of giant salamander-like creature, which made his cybernetic parts interesting to look at. The Sh'Kallian was a female named Jurl, and she had turned her nose up at cooked meat, preferring to eat it raw. The Sekani named Reilla had to cut up her burger into quarters to fit it in her mouth.

"Country?" Dar asked. "You mean that your planet isn't even united under one form of government?"

"No," James said. "Bob, how many countries are currently on Earth?"

"There are officially one hundred and ninety-six countries on Earth currently," Bob responded.

"There you go," James said. "By the way, what do you think of the drink?"

"What's this called again?"

"Whiskey. Tennessee's finest."

"My compliments to Tennessee. He seems a fine fellow," Dar said, and took another drink from his shot glass.

"You don't strike me as the mercenary type," James said.

"I wasn't always for hire," Dar responded. "I was once a statesman for the Talondarian government. Long ago, before things...changed."

"I was once a cop," James said. "Law enforcement, kind of like the ASPs for my planet."

"Now that does make sense," the Sh'Kallian murmured. James smiled at her.

James couldn't help but watch the interactions between Belani and Reilla. The Sekani hadn't seen a female member of his race in a few years. It had been a surprise to both of them to learn that she had come from the Sekani home world and not Rajan.

"So, Reilla," James said. "Tell me about your world. The only Sekani I've met were those living on Rajan."

"It's a beautiful planet," she said in between bites of fries. "Much like your Earth, except for the long blue grasses with red flowers intermixed in the habitable regions. Some say that is why we are colored as we are, as a sort of camouflage."

"That makes sense," James said.

"I would very much like to visit," Belani said. "Maybe someday."

"If we live through this mission," she said, "I'll take you myself."

Belani smiled, and to James it looked like he might be blushing, though it was difficult to tell.

"Bob, anything on the radar?" James asked.

"Nothing," Bob instantly responded. James had had to teach him to wait until a person had finished speaking before answering. Before that, he'd begun talking over the person asking before the question was finished.

"If Atalik is still looking for you, eventually he will find your ship," Dar said. He popped the last bite of burger into his mouth and chewed.

"Would he have Yvette and Gianni on his ship with him?" James asked.

"Hard to tell. If he did, it would be dangerous to try and liberate them."

"I understand," James said. "Tell me again about what happened. From the beginning. The Krahn put out a bounty on all of us..."

"No, not a bounty, per se," Dar corrected him. "More like an invitation. Maliq didn't know how to contact you directly, so he hired Atalik to bring his invitation. As I've said, Atalik is a mercenary, so he probably went straight to the Rajani to see if he could get a better offer. Apparently, he did."

"And the Rajani did put a bounty on us?"

"Yes, we believe so."

"That's not good," James said. "That means they either really want to speak with us, or they really want us out of the way."

"Yes," Dar said, looking at him and smiling. "I must say, I didn't know what to expect from you, James the Human, but your reputation does you justice."

"I'll take that as a compliment," James said.

"Good, it was meant as one," Dar said, smiling.

"Can we stop with the backslapping already?" Jurl said. James looked to see her practically rolling her eyes. He guessed she was maybe in her late twenties in Earth years. Not knowing the maturity level for her age, he guessed she was the equivalent of a teenager by her manners.

"Jurleen," Dar said. "Don't insult our host."

"It's okay," James said, smiling at her. "I'm just as impatient right now to find my...girlfriend...as you are to leave. I just need to make the decision on where it is I'm heading." He turned to Dar. "You said you want me to come to the Krahn home world with you to meet with Maliq. Why should I?"

"Maliq is an interesting character," Dar said. "Not what I was expecting, given the reputation of the Krahn in general. He is a thoughtful, mature leader, which is why I'm guessing he is still their leader." He took a drink of water before continuing. "Maliq wants to speak with you. He wants you to go back to Rajan to speak with their Elders in hopes of persuading them to stop their current actions."

"Which are?"

"The Rajani seem to be preparing for war. Their leader..."

"Welemaan?" James interjected.

"Yes, Welemaan, has them ready to invade Krahn in response to the Krahn Horde invading Rajan."

"I can see that," James said. "Welemaan lost many family members and friends. Many of them did."

"Maliq sent three aid ships full of medical supplies and food to Rajan, but the Rajani either captured or destroyed them," Dar said.

"Really?" James asked. He hadn't anticipated that tidbit of information. "And he doesn't think I might get the same reception?"

"You're James the Human," Dar said, shrugging. "He believes that they'll at least listen to what you have to say."

James sighed. "Bob, how long would it take to get to the Krahn home world?"

"Approximately three Earth months," Bob responded. "That's two Standard months."

"Belani, how are our supplies?"

"Fully supplied for that amount of time," the Sekani pilot answered. "We have a full frozen and refrigerated section, as well as dry staples and water."

"Would you be coming along with me?" James said, turning to Dar.

"Most likely," Dar responded. "But your ship is much faster than mine."

"I suggest that you ride on this ship, then," James said. "I'd rather not arrive on Krahn without you."

"Wouldn't dream of it," Dar said, smiling. "Pico, you'll stay aboard the *Freedom* and pilot her to Krahn. Jurl and Reilla, you both will stay aboard *Bright Journey*."

"And me?" Belani asked.

"You will take the transport down to Earth and investigate what exactly happened to Yvette and Gianni," James said. "I also want you to make sure that nothing has happened to Kieren, then I want you to stay with her. Don't let anything happen to her while we're gone. I'm entrusting her safety to you."

"I will guard her with my life. I owe it to you."

"Thank you, my friend," James said. "I would do it myself, if the circumstances were different, but..."

"I understand, James."

James nodded. "Bob, lay out your course for Krahn. Prepare to separate from the *Freedom* on my mark. Dar, collect any items you and your crew members may need from your ship."

"You heard him, Outsiders, you have twenty Standard minutes," Dar said.

"Outsiders?" James asked.

"Don't ask me where the nickname came from," Dar said, shrugging.

"I thought it came from..." Reilla began.

"Shut it, Sekani," Dar said, mock growling at her. She smiled in response. He turned back to James. "Thank you for being such a gracious host. The food was excellent, as was the company."

"You'll have to tell me on the way how a statesman became a mercenary," James said, standing. He held out his hand.

"Depends on if I get drunk enough," Dar said, clasping his arm once again and smiled.

◊

Belani had left aboard the shuttle an hour before with strict orders to watch over Kieren. It was the best that James could do for the moment, but he trusted the alien pilot to be true to his word to protect his daughter with his life, if need be.

James had shown Jophen, Reilla, and Jurleen to rooms that would be appropriate to stay in for the journey to Krahn. They were bringing supplies over from the *Freedom* in preparation. He was working with Bob to perform a full diagnostic on the *Bright Journey* before they left. He had to make sure they had enough fuel and supplies to last there and back.

"So, stopping at the Mandakan port isn't feasible?" he asked Bob.

"A trip there would take us approximately two hundred thousand miles outside of our current projected path," Bob answered. "It would cost more fuel than it was worth, economically speaking."

James thought for a moment. "No, I guess that wouldn't be a good idea. There has to be somewhere else we can stop if we need to. It's too bad there isn't an app that shows rest stops in space." He smiled.

"As far as I know, there is not," Bob answered.

"No, I know that," James said. "It was a joke."

"Humor is illogical."

"Thank you, Spock."

"My designation is Bob. If you prefer a different name, you could always reprogram that, although I have become used to being Bob."

"No, it was another joke," James said. "You said you have become use to being Bob? Did you not see yourself as Bob from the very beginning?"

"This unit and all the memory units it has filled constitutes Bob, but that is a name given to me by yourself. When I look in my programming and see a reference to myself, it is by a standard manufacturing number. I also have come to encompass the ship as part of myself, which means that I am also *Bright Journey*."

"Wow, I guess I didn't think about that," James said. "Think we'll stick with Bob, unless you would rather be called BJ."

"Was that a joke as well?'

"Yes, actually," James said chuckling.

"Then I would rather stay as Bob."

"Okay. We'll keep the name of the ship, though, if you don't mind."

"As you wish," the AI replied.

◊

Jophen was heading back to the airlock after carrying over most of the items he wanted to bring with him on the trip aboard *Bright Journey*. As he was returning to the *Freedom* to collect his pet, he saw Jurl and Reilla walking down the hallway towards him. "Almost finished?"

"Reilla wouldn't leave the ship without all of her products," Jurl answered. She rolled her eyes.

"Hey, you're the one who brought every weapon you

own," Reilla said, defensively.

"Those may come in handy," Jurl said.

"So might my products," Reilla said. "Have to look my best, you know."

Jurl rolled her eyes again. "I'm surprised she didn't jump the pilot right there at the table."

Jophen smiled. Things never changed with his crew, which he was grateful for, most of the time. "Get your things to your quarters. Jurl, go to the bridge and see if James needs any help getting prepped."

"Yes sir," Jurl said with only a hint of sarcasm.

Jophen smiled again as he watched the two walk away from him. He turned and headed towards his ship. As he neared the air lock, he put on his helmet and felt the air hiss to life within his suit. No reason to take chances on a failed airlock sending him spinning out into space without a helmet.

He stepped through the airlock and suddenly found himself on the floor of the *Freedom* as the ship jolted violently. "What?" was all he could think of to say. He pressed the button for the commlink on his helmet. "Pico, what's happening? Status report."

"The *Freedom* is under attack from an unknown ship," the reply came.

"Return fire!"

"I have been, but the other ship is much more maneuverable and smaller. Appears to be a one-being ship. I can try to..."

Jophen stood as the comm system stopped abruptly. "Pico? Pico!"

He looked up to see a wave of fire heading towards him. He turned and jumped for the control panel for the airlock, pushing the button to open it. As it opened, he felt the intense heat behind him as he stepped through and punched the button to close it. "James! Jurleen! Anyone" he screamed into the commlink. "Disengage from the *Freedom*. Disengage!"

He took off his helmet and began running down the hallway towards the *Bright Journey's* bridge with it under his arm.

"This is Jurl," he heard faintly from his helmet.

He held it up to his face without breaking stride. "Jurl, disengage from the *Freedom*. I think something bad is about to happen."

"Really?" she answered. "Couldn't be because we've been under attack for the last ten Standard minutes. Disengaging airlock. Get up here."

"On my way."

◊

James sat in his captain's chair and watched as the smaller ship on the monitor approached once again, firing on both ships as it passed. The *Bright Journey's* shield and armor seemed much better than the *Freedom's*, because he could see fire coming out of several holes in the *Freedom's* exterior.

"Are we free of your ship?" He asked Jurleen, who had taken up Belani's pilot seat on the bridge.

"Yes," she answered as she flipped switches and pressed buttons on the ship.

"James, it appears she is prepping to send me into n-space," Bob said on their private channel.

"Good," James replied. "We need to get away from this ship. It sounded like Dar agrees."

"We need to move further away from the other ship, and from Earth," Bob said.

"Right," James said.

Just then, the door to the bridge opened and Jophen stepped onto the bridge. "What's happening?"

"We're under attack. Your ship has taken some heavy damage," James told him.

"We need to get away from it," Jophen told him. "There was some kind of internal explosion that happened just as I stepped foot on the ship."

"What about Pico?" Jurleen asked, turning to look at them both.

"He can take care of himself," Jophen replied. "But in case he can't, we need to be as far away as possible. Get us out of here, Jurl."

She nodded after a moment, then went back to pushing buttons on her control panel.

"Incoming transmission," Bob said.

"Put it on the intercom," James told him.

"James the Human," a voice said over the intercom. "Can you hear me?"

"Yes, I hear you," James replied. "Who the hell are you and why are you firing on us?"

"I am Atalik. Prepare to be boarded and remanded into my custody."

"Like hell," James said. "What do you want from me?"

"You need to come with me now."

James looked over to Jophen, who shook his head and mouthed the word, 'no.'

"No, I don't' think so," James said. "Stupid mothertrucker, stop shooting at our ships and maybe we can talk." He motioned to Jurleen to continue prepping the ship.

"We need to draw him away from the *Freedom* and then hit n-space," Jophen said quietly.

James nodded. "Agreed. Jurleen, hit the gas."

She looked at him quizzically for a moment. "Go!" he said and understanding sparked in her eyes. She turned back to the control panel.

"James the Human, you cannot flee from me," Atalik said over the intercom.

"That's right, keep following us," James said. "Bob, let me know when we're far enough away from the planet."

"Affirmative," Bob replied. "Shall I give you a countdown?"

"Fine," James said, knowing that the AI seemed to enjoy countdowns.

"Ten. Nine. Eight. Seven. Six. Five. Four. Three. Two. One." Bob said.

"Hit it!" James told Jurleen. She seemed to know what that meant, because she hit a button and suddenly Jophen began to float, and then he was down on the floor again just as quickly as the ship's gravity well-adjusted to the sudden change in the ship's speed.

Chapter 7

Dennis Gray couldn't believe what he was hearing. "She's been missing for years now, and you still have no goddamn idea what happened to her?"

"At this point, it's considered a 'cold case,' Mr. Gray. There's nothing I can do about that. We have more pressing investigations that we're pursuing. We don't have the manpower to keep cases open this long."

"You know what I think?" Dennis asked rhetorically, "I think she was involved in this Infinity Killer case, and you're pushing it under the rug because you couldn't solve it. You're all a bunch of inept idiots."

"Mr. Gray, it's time for you to leave my office before I have you escorted out."

Dennis stood up and looked down at the Detroit police detective, unsure what he was going to do next. The cop, who had introduced himself as Detective Montgomery, stood up as well. "For your information, Mr. Gray, my best friend, my partner, went missing around the same time. James Dempsey was the finest cop, no, finest man I knew. He was in charge of the Infinity Killer case until his disappearance. So yes, I do have strong feelings about that case and the fact that it remains unsolved. But throwing you in a cell won't make anything happen, so my offer is this: walk out of here right now and don't come back or I will put you in a holding cell to think things over."

"You can't do that," Dennis said.

"I can put you in there for forty-eight hours without charges," Montgomery said. "Try me."

Without another word, Dennis turned and left the detective's office, heading for the front door of the station. He saw other police officers interviewing people at their desks or filing paperwork. It was the same as when he'd first reported Kieren missing. Nothing ever changes, he thought.

Once outside the station, he sat down on the curb and put both hands over his face. "Damn it," he said quietly. He could feel tears threatening but refused to release them. How sad he would look, sitting on the curb and crying, especially in front of a police station.

She was gone. There was no denying it—his baby sister was gone and there were no new answers to be found. Then he remembered the name that Montgomery had said, James Dempsey. Well, that's a start, he thought. There had to be something he could look up online about the man.

◊

"Watch your speed," Janan told the Talondarian woman sitting in the pilot's chair. The ship had just come out of n-space and was heading towards Earth. Janan recognized the red plant from his earlier visit. They were flying through an asteroid field as they passed the planet, and Amera was piloting the ship. She had been interested in learning how to fly it, so Janan had been happy for the company on the voyage from Mandaka.

"Good," he said. "The coordinates to Earth have been set in the ship's computer. Just keep going on this heading, and it should be a smooth trip."

"Thanks, Janan," she said. "You should get some rest. Looks like it will still be a few Standard days until we get there.

"I'd love to," he said, yawning. "But Bhakat doesn't want me leaving you alone on the bridge. Not that he doesn't trust you," he said hurriedly, seeing the look on her face.

"No, he doesn't trust me," she said. "I don't blame him, really. It's not like I've been piloting very long."

"Zazzil never let you pilot for him?" Janan asked.

"No, for most of my life he kept me secluded in his area of the space station. It was only when I'd grown older that he began to let me venture out. I think he was waiting until I fully appreciated why I was in so much danger if I were to be spotted."

"That must have been really boring," he said.

"It was. I spent a lot of time on the computer learning as much as I could about the outside galaxy. And learning about my species and more specifically, about my parents. I still don't know the full story about the coup by my uncle."

"Well, I for one am glad that you came with us," he said. He liked the tall Talondarian, even if she was a princess. He also loved the way that she pissed off Bhakat with her attitude at times. It was like he and Bhakat had their very own teenager.

Just then, the door to the bridge opened and Bhakat came in. "What is our status, Janan?"

"We're almost there. Amera is doing a great job piloting the ship."

Bhakat was silent, but he glanced at the girl.

"Did you sleep well?" she asked him.

"Yes, thank you," he said.

"Well, now that you're here," Janan began, "I'm going to sleep for a few hours before we get there."

"No, you're not," Bhakat said. "You need to perform a scan of transmissions from Earth."

"Really?" Janan asked, though he had known about it for a few days. "How about just an hour? Please?"

Bhakat scowled. "Fine."

Janan smiled. He knew that part of the reason Bhakat wanted him to do the scan was so that he wasn't left alone on the bridge with Amera. She made the Rajani nervous for some reason.

"Have a good nap," Amera said, smiling.

"Thanks," Janan replied, yawning again as he left the bridge.

◊

"Janan, wake up!" Bhakat's voice said over the ship's intercom.

Janan rolled over in his bed. It seemed like his head had just hit his pillow. He looked at his watch and saw that he'd been asleep for over two hours. "Shit," he said in English. He stood and pressed the com button near the door. "I'm up," he said.

He still felt a little groggy when he reached the bridge. "What's going on?" he asked when the door opened. He saw Amera in the pilot's chair and Bhakat in his usual spot in the captain's chair.

"Take the wheel," Bhakat said.

Amera stood and Janan plopped down in his seat. He noticed then on the display before him that there was a silent proximity alarm flashing. "What is it, another ship?"

"Yes," Bhakat said. "We picked it up on the ship's sensors about an hour ago. Which is why you were able to sleep until now." He scowled at Janan, but Janan knew he wasn't serious. "Standing by for visual."

Janan flipped a switch on the control panel and the large

screen in front of them turned black. They couldn't see anything at first, but as the ship progressed, they were able to make out the small ship floating in orbit.

"Magnify," Bhakat said.

Janan pressed a button, and the ship became larger on the screen. Now they could clearly see the damage to it. "It's not the Pwyntafa Naa," Janan said, using the Rajani words for Dempsey's ship.

"It obviously doesn't belong here, though," Bhakat said. "That's not an Earth ship. Set the sensors for maximum range. I don't want to be surprised by anything."

As the ship turned on their viewscreen, they saw several holes in the hull. Holes caused by laser fire. "Bhakat, it's the *Freedom*," Janan said. "Dar's ship."

Bhakat thought for a moment. "What are they doing near Earth again?"

Janan shrugged. He hadn't seen the ship since Rauph had hired them to collect the Humans all those years ago. It was strange seeing it now.

"Any signs of other ships on sensors?" Bhakat asked.

"None."

Bhakat thought for a moment before speaking again. "Pull up and dock with it."

Janan nodded. He looked back at Amera, who was still standing a few paces behind his chair. "This should be educational," he said, smiling. He turned around and concentrated on positioning the ship manually so that the airlocks were aligned. The ship's computer beeped when the airlocks came together. There was a very small bump, and a green light displayed, showing that a lock had been achieved.

"We're good," Janan said, looking back at Bhakat. The big Rajani nodded and left the bridge.

"Should I go with him?" Amera said.

"Up to you. He might need your help."

She nodded and then followed Bhakat off the bridge.

◊

Bhakat finished putting on his space walking suit before Amera. He stood a moment, watching her finish up. She put her helmet on, and he pushed a button on the small panel of buttons on his left forearm. "Are you ready?"

She followed suit. "Yes. Lead the way."

He turned and walked to the airlock door. From the holes in the hull of the *Freedom*, he wasn't expecting any atmosphere on the other ship, so the rush of air from his ship when the airlock door opened wasn't surprising. He walked through, then turned to make sure Amera got through.

She came through and pressed the 'door close' button. He nodded, then turned back towards the ship. He pressed the communication button again. "No air. Don't open any doors until you've checked to make sure there's no one inside."

She nodded, then realized that he couldn't see her. "Got it," she said, pressing the button on her suit.

"I'll head for the bridge," he continued. "You check the crew quarters. Be careful."

"I will. Do you know who owns this ship?"

"Yes, we've used their services before. They're mercenaries for hire."

"So, they may be armed?"

"Yes," he said. "Another reason to be careful opening doors." He didn't turn to see the expression on her face through the clear, protective shield of the suit.

As he walked down the hallway towards the bridge, he looked around, making sure there were no bodies evident. Everything had a fine sheen of ice, but he didn't see anyone. He came to the door of the bridge and pressed the com button. "Hello, this is Bhakat, is there anyone in there?"

He waited a moment, but there was no reply. He pressed the open button. There was no rush of air, which meant that the bridge had lost its atmosphere as well. He walked through the doorway and looked around. The bridge seemed empty at first, then he noticed the body in the corner. He rushed over to it, seeing that it was the strange cyborg—one of Dar's crewmembers. He wasn't sure how to tell if it was still alive, so he checked around the bridge further and found that there was no one else there.

He pressed the communication button on his suit. "I found someone. I'm taking them over to our ship. Not sure if they're alive or dead."

"Got it," Amera answered. "I haven't found anyone yet. Almost to the last room."

"Keep me posted," Bhakat said. He pressed another button on the panel. "Janan, I'm coming back. Prep the medical device. I might have a survivor."

"On my way to the medical center," Janan replied.

Bhakat bent over and picked up the cyborg, who was relatively light in the lower gravity of the ship. Bhakat made sure the body was settled in his arms and headed back the way he'd come. Once he got through the airlock door, the body became much heavier and he set it down as he took off his suit. Then he suited up and easily carried the cyborg to the medical room. He was grateful that his enhanced powers included greater strength.

Janan was waiting for him when he arrived and placed the body on one of the two beds. He powered down and then assessed the cyborg. The skin of the small creature was exhibiting signs of hypothermia from the extremely cold temperature. Bhakat tapped a few buttons on the medical robot and felt the bed growing incrementally warmer. He placed a sensor unit on the cyborg body's temple and ran a diagnostic check.

"There's electrical activity within his computer system," he told Janan. Plug the body into the ship's power supply. Janan did as he was told and Bhakat turned back to the creature.

He opened one of the Shif's eyes and shined a light in it. There was a slight narrowing of the pupil. The other eye was covered by a sensor device. Bhakat went back to the medical machine and pushed a few more buttons. The machine began injecting the cyborg's biological body with a series of chemicals and products that would speed up its heart and hopefully reawaken him. "Janan, watch that monitor. Let me know if and when a heartbeat is detected."

Janan walked over to the monitor.

Bhakat turned back to the cyborg. He began doing a thorough examination, making sure he hadn't missed any wounds.

"There," Janan said. "It's weak, but there's a heartbeat."

Bhakat nodded while finishing his inspection. He couldn't see anything except a few bruises. There weren't any puncture wounds or obvious broken bones. It seemed that the cyborg had succumbed to the cold and lack of oxygen. They would have to wait to see if he would regain consciousness. Bhakat walked back to the medical machine and pushed a few more buttons, setting it up to intermediately inject fluids and more chemicals into the cyborg's system. All they could do now was wait.

◊

Amera took her time searching through the rooms of the ship. She was conscious of her oxygen levels, knowing that they would eventually be depleted, but for now, they were at an acceptable level, according to the display on her arm.

She pressed the com button on the last quarters. "Hello, anyone home?" She waited a moment. No answer. She pressed it again just to make sure. "I'm coming in." She waited. Nothing. Then she pressed the door open button and waited. There was a slight decompression sound as it opened, telling her that the room had not previously lost its atmosphere. She quickly stepped in and closed the door behind her before turning to look around.

She couldn't see anyone, so she walked to the bathroom and opened the door. No one in there, either. Thankfully. She let out a breath she couldn't remember holding. She turned and scanned the room again, not seeing anything particularly interesting. It was a standard ship's quarters with a bed and some furnishings. She looked in the closet and saw some larger pieces of clothing, which meant it had housed someone with two legs and two arms.

She briefly looked through the clothes, though they were fairly boring. Suddenly a small, furry object crashed into her arms. She instinctively caught it and realized it was a living creature. It struggled in her arms, making curious noises as it tried to communicate with her. Her translation device couldn't make out any of it. Then she realized that this was probably a pet of the person who lived in the quarters. It was a miracle that the room hadn't lost pressure. She patted the creature's head and after a while it calmed down and even began emitting a pleasant rumbling sound.

"What am I supposed to do with you?" she asked it as she stroked its body. She sighed and was about to turn away from the closet when she noticed something that almost made her drop the creature. In the corner almost hidden by other items of clothing was what looked like a uniform. She held the creature with one arm and reached in to pull the uniform out. It was old looking, worn thin in some places.

But the thing that had caught her eye was the patch on one of the shoulders. She knew the crest on it as much as she knew her name. It was the crest of the Talondarian king and queen. Her parents. Her sword hilt bore the same crest.

She turned and was about to leave the room when she realized that the rest of the ship was a freezing vacuum. She hurriedly undid the front of her suit and delicately placed the creature inside. She held its weight with one hand as she refastened the suit, then picked up the uniform once again and headed back to her ship.

◊

Dennis had taken over as tenant of his sister's apartment in hopes that he would be there in case she ever returned. It was a crappy place and not nearly as nice as his old one, but he figured it was a sort of penance he was willing to pay if it meant seeing her again. He still felt like it was his fault she was gone.

Today, he felt like a ray of hope had suddenly broken through the clouds. It hadn't occurred to him before that the chief detective investigating the Infinity Killer case had also disappeared. He hadn't made the mental connection, and now he was kicking himself. He used a FOIA request to learn of the detective's last known address, and it just happened to be in the same apartment building as his sister. It had to mean something—it was too much of a coincidence.

He did some digging and found out that besides his sister and the detective, at least two others had gone missing from the complex on the same day. The thing that confused him, though, was that one of the missing was a man named David. The Infinity Killer had only killed women, as far as he knew. His plan for the day was to do some more digging and try to find friends or family members who he could speak to about their disappearance, and if they were ever found again.

The first thing he found when logging on to his computer was that James Dempsey was a dead end. His family members were either dead or too difficult to find—his brother had moved away some time before. There was little of his employment record online, and he didn't seem to have any social media accounts. He searched another name on the list of disappeared individuals and found that her father was a former senator. That could prove difficult, he thought. The last name was David Morris. He'd been employed at Morris Marketing. It wasn't much of a lead, he thought, but it was something.

He rubbed his eyes, feeling like he hadn't slept much the night before. His coffee wasn't doing much for him, either. He decided he'd better shave and take a shower if he was going out. It might wake him up a little as well.

◊

The small creature proved to be quite friendly. Amera hadn't told the others that she brought it back aboard the ship at first, not knowing what they would do to it, but the next morning, she hadn't been quick enough to close her door and the creature had followed her out and down the hall to the bridge.

"Hello, Janan," she said as she entered the bridge.

"Hi Amera," he said. "The big day."

"Yes," she said. They were planning on going down to the planet's surface today. It would be her first time on an alien planet in years. From what Janan had told her, the occupants of Earth were surprisingly similar to Talondarians. "Are you staying on the ship?"

"Why would I do that?" he replied, smiling. "I've learned so much about this planet, both from research and speaking with the Humans. There's no way I would pass this up."

"You're not worried about being discovered? Being

caught by their authorities?"

"We'll be going down at night," he replied. "It will be dark, so as long as I wear clothing that covers most of me, I should be good. I will most likely be perceived as a child or diminutive adult."

"Okay, and Bhakat?"

"Yes, he's going...where the hell did the cat come from?!"

"What?" she asked. She felt the creature rub against her leg as it walked past her into the bridge. "Oh, that?"

"Yes that," he said. "That's an Earth creature called a cat."

"Really? I found it on the other ship. It was in one of the quarters."

Janan got down on his knees and looked at the cat. "Careful," she said. "This animal does have sharp claws on its feet."

"Fascinating," Janan said. The cat approached him slowly, then hissed at him and ran back out the door to the bridge. "Gee, friendly," he said sarcastically.

"What the hell was that?" Bhakat asked, coming onto the bridge from the hallway.

"Cat," Janan responded. "It's her fault."

"I...how was I to know that it was an Earth creature? How did it get on their ship?" she asked.

"They've been to Earth before," Bhakat said. "They must have picked it up there."

"More mysteries," Amera said. "How is the cyborg doing?"

"He's stable," Bhakat said. "Still unconscious, but I'm hoping that will change soon. Janan, prepare to take us to the planet's surface."

"Will the Earth authorities detect us?" she asked.

"Not hardly," Janan said. "First thing I had done to the ship when we got to Mandaka was to have a radar repeller installed. We should be invisible to any primitive detection system they have."

"You should be strapped in, as a precaution," Bhakat said. There was only the pilot's chair on the bridge.

"What about you?" she asked.

Bhakat powered up, his suit of energy appearing around him. "I won't get hurt," he said.

She nodded and left the bridge. She was anxious to find the cat again and make sure it was safe for the journey down.

Interlude

Josiah Manidoo was a man who took precautions. His military service and his time as a senator had taught him at least one thing—always be prepared for the worst. That's why, as soon as he noticed that the back door to his house was partially left open, he went straight to his gun safe in his bedroom closet and loaded the shotgun.

Now he held the shotgun up to his shoulder as he stalked through the rooms of his house. He had to be careful, though. Kieren was upstairs in her room. He couldn't be trigger happy knowing that she was somewhere in the house. He checked the downstairs rooms thoroughly, then walked slowly up the stairs. He had designed the house to have the master bedroom on the first floor knowing that eventually he wouldn't want to be walking up and down stairs as he grew older—new hip or not.

He checked the bedroom and bathroom that his daughter and James were using, then moved down the hallway towards Kieren's room. He paused when he heard her speaking. He couldn't quite make out the words—her door was closed. Perhaps she was hosting a tea party with some of her favorite dolls. He moved closer and then stopped to listen once more.

"Why are you so short?"

Josiah raised the gun once again to his shoulder when he heard a deeper voice answer.

"I'm actually very tall for my species."

"And all of you are that color?"

"Yes, for the most part."

"Would you like some more tea?"

"Yes, thank you. You make the best tea."

Josiah moved to the door. It was open a crack, and he tried to angle his sight to see what was happening in the room. He still couldn't see who she was talking to. He thought that if he busted into the room with gun raised, he would only scare her and whoever else was there. He pushed the door with his left hand and then once again held up the shotgun, his finger lying next to the trigger guard and ready to go to the trigger if needed.

"Grandpa! Do you want to come to my tea party?" Kieren said, smiling widely.

"No, honey," he said. He was surprised his voice didn't shake. The little blue alien was sitting cross-legged across from his granddaughter, holding a plastic teacup. It smiled at him.

"I come in peace, Human," it said, then pretended to sip more tea with a loud slurp.

Chapter 8

Bhakat was bothered by the fact that they had not picked up the *Bright Journey* on their sensors. Either it meant that James had landed the ship on the planet's surface, or it meant that he had left Earth's orbit for some unknown reason. The ship was larger than the one he and Janan were using, and it had its own lander, so it didn't make sense for it to be on the planet's surface, unless he had landed it and camouflaged it somehow when they had returned from Rajan.

"Janan," he said. The Sekani turned from his station at the pilot's chair. "Before we go down to the surface, I want you to search transmissions from Earth and see if you can find anything about James, Yvette or Gianni. Anything with their names or any unusual events near their last known locations."

"Will do," Janan said. He'd done the same thing many years before when they had first come to Earth, their ship damaged and Rauph looking for anything that might help them. Then, he hadn't known anything about the Human civilization. Now, he was familiar searching through news broadcasts and what the Humans referred to as the Internet. It wasn't long before he had found a handful of stories that came from local Detroit broadcasts or mentioned a Human with the last name of the people they were trying to find.

He spent a while narrowing down the articles—some had nothing to do with James, Yvette, or Gianni, some were generic or years old from when they had first disappeared. Finally, he had a few articles that he began to read over. "Bhakat, listen to this." He turned to make sure he had his friend's attention. Bhakat powered down and walked over to Janan's chair.

"...the abandoned car, which is registered to former Senator Josiah Manidoo, was found several miles from his residence..." Janan said. "I believe that this person is Yvette's father."

Bhakat nodded, scowling. Janan continued. "Here's another article about the building where James, Yvette and Gianni used to reside. 'The damage to the walls was extensive, and police were left questioning a man found unconscious in the apartment. The listed proprietor is Gianni Moretti."

"Something is wrong," Bhakat said. Janan nodded in agreement. "Anything about James?" he asked.

"Not that I could find," Janan replied. "But it may be why the *Bright Journey* is no longer here. I'm sure the derelict ship has something to do with this as well."

Bhakat walked back to his captain's chair and sat down. After a moment he spoke again. "There's only one way we can discover what happened, and that's by visiting the planet's surface and investigating it for ourselves."

"Or we could wait to see if our patient will wake up and ask him," Janan said.

Bhakat sat and thought for a moment. "No. I don't think we can wait to see if they wake up. We need answers now."

Janan nodded. "Where do you want me to go first?"

"Go to the apartment building where they originally lived first," Bhakat said. "Maybe we can find a clue there."

"Got it," Janan said. He flipped a switch on his control panel and then spoke over the ship's intercom. "Amera, we're going in. Strap yourself in and stow that cat."

Luckily there was an area of abandoned buildings that seemed the perfect place to land their ship. The landing was uneventful, and as Janan shut down the ship's power, they all felt the change in gravity. It took a moment for his body to adjust to the added weight from the heavier gravity of the planet.

"Ugh," Amera said as she came back to the bridge. "I feel like I'm walking through a room full of mud."

"You'll get used to it," Janan said. "It will make your muscles feel like you've been exercising for a while, but they'll eventually get acclimated if we're here for any stretch of time."

"Great," she said, sounding not at all enthusiastic about it.

"Anything on the sensors?" Bhakat asked.

"Looks pretty deserted," Janan responded.

"How far is it to our destination?" Amera asked.

"It shouldn't take too long to get to James' dwelling," Janan said. "Actually, it was all of their dwelling units. Maybe we'll be lucky, and James, Yvette, and Gianni will all be there having a party."

"We've never been that lucky," Bhakat said. "Keep to the shadows and don't get us noticed," he said, looking at both of them. "We don't need to complicate matters by getting the Earth authorities involved."

◊

Dennis stepped out of his shower, toweling himself dry as he did so. He felt a little more awake than he had earlier, but still felt less than motivated to leave the house. He wrapped the towel around his waist and looked at himself in the mirror. He'd lost weight over the last few years, and it showed. His hair was a mess. He hadn't kept up his professional image much since losing his job at the law firm he worked at, and he needed a haircut and a beard trim.

He'd been barely living for the past two years, living on government assistance and his own savings, which he was quickly depleting. He grabbed the can of shaving cream from the bathroom counter and began to lather his face. The shaving cream was menthol and it stung as he applied it. Just as he was about to begin shaving, he heard a loud noise from outside the bathroom door. He turned off the hot water and stood there, listening. He was about to turn the hot water back on when he thought he heard someone speaking. He was sure he hadn't left the television on.

He looked around but didn't see anything he could use as a weapon. Not even a pair of scissors. He settled for his hairdryer, feeling the weight of it in his hand and deciding that he could at least hit someone with it. He steeled himself and then quickly opened the door of the bathroom. There was no one in the hallway. He felt his towel loosening and grabbed the front of it with his left hand.

He walked out to his darkened living room and saw a woman standing in it, looking at the pictures on the coffee table. They had been Kieren's and they showed her and friends, her and him, and some places she'd visited when she first moved to Detroit, like the zoo.

"Who are you?" he asked, trying to sound menacing. "Why are you in my place?"

She turned and saw him. He had a split second of noticing that there seemed to be something off with her face, especially her eyes, then he saw her pull out a sword. He saw the blade and turned to run back to the bathroom. There was a wall there that hadn't been before, and he ran into it, discovering that the wall was actually a very large man.

A voice called out and he turned to see a dwarf. Am I being attacked by circus performers? He thought and almost giggled. It was a surreal situation. The dwarf in the hood spoke again, this time in English.

"Stop, Amera. He isn't armed. That's not a gun."

Dennis turned to see the woman re-sheath her sword. He looked down at his hairdryer and finally understood that they had mistaken it for a gun in the gloom of the living room. "What the hell is going on?" he asked. He turned again to the large man behind him, and looking up, saw that it wasn't a man at all. The creature was some kind of werewolf. He turned to see the dwarf pull his hood down and saw that he was a light blue or grey color and that his eyes shown in the darkened room like a cat. That was when he thankfully fainted.

◊

Bhakat didn't think the situation was humorous at all, but Janan and Amera were laughing uproariously at the naked human lying on the floor of his living room, his face still covered with shaving cream. When he'd fainted, he'd let go of both the hairdryer and the towel around his waist, and he was now completely naked except for the foam around his mouth.

"Wrap him back up, please," Bhakat told Janan. "Let him have a little dignity when we wake him up."

"Fine," Janan said, still chuckling.

"Amera, I want you at the door. Make sure we're not disturbed. We still don't know who may have taken the others." She nodded and walked to the closed door.

"Wake him up," he told Janan.

The Sekani gently prodded the man's shoulder. When that didn't work, he shook him gently, and the man began to stir. "It's okay," Janan said. "You're safe. Wake up, Earth man."

Bhakat could feel the impulse to roll his eyes but put it off.

Finally, the Human opened his eyes. He looked at Janan and then up at Bhakat. "What the hell is going on?" he asked weakly.

"It's okay, Human," Janan said, soothingly. "We mean you no harm. We're only looking for our friends."

"Your what?" The man still sounded confused, which Bhakat could not blame. He had three alien life forms standing in his dwelling place.

Janan stood up and backed off a step so that the man could sit up. He held his hands out in front of him in what he knew was a non-threatening gesture to show he wasn't holding a weapon. "We're looking for our Human friends. This building was their last known dwelling place, but they're not here. We decided to check Kieren's old dwelling place as well."

"What? What did you say?" the Human asked, standing up and almost forgetting to hold his towel as he did so. He was shaky on his feet and closed his eyes a moment. "Did you say my sister's name?"

"Your sister?" Janan asked. "I noticed a picture here of the two of you. You must be Dennis."

"Yes," the Human answered. "Who...what?"

"Maybe you should sit down," Bhakat said.

Dennis looked at him and nodded. "Yeah, maybe I should." He walked over and sat on the chair next to the coffee table, wishing he had some pants.

"It's a long story," Janan said. He looked to Bhakat. "Should we tell him?"

"We don't have the equipment here to change his

memory, and I don't think we should take him to the ship to do it." He sighed. "But I think he deserves to know the truth."

Janan nodded, turning his attention back to Dennis. "My name is Janan. I'm known as a Sekani. This is Bhakat who is a Rajani, and over there is Amera, who is a Talondarian. We were friends of your sister, Kieren."

"How did you know Kieren? She's a teacher, for god's sake." His mind was whirling with all of the alien names he'd just heard.

"Funny thing about that," Janan said. "A few years ago, our ship was damaged, and we happened upon Earth. Rauph, who was my boss then, decided that we needed help from certain Humans, and it was also decided that your sister was one of them. I know, it sounds stupid now, but at the time, we were ignorant of many things about Earth and Humans."

"Uh huh," Dennis said, still sounding confused.

Janan pushed on. "To make a long story short, we took your sister and four other Humans with us when we returned to our own planet, Rajan."

"You took her," Dennis said. "Back to your planet."

"Yes."

"So where is she now?"

Janan looked at Bhakat.

"She's dead," Bhakat answered. "I am sorry. Your sister is dead."

"What?" Dennis stood up. "What? How?"

"The reason our ship was damaged back then was from the war that was happening on our planet," Janan said. "We had been attacked by another species called the Krahn. The five Humans, including your sister, came back with us to help us fight them."

Dennis sat back down and rubbed his face with both hands. "What the hell," he said quietly. "Please tell me this is a dream."

"I'm sorry, it is not a dream," Bhakat said. "We offer our condolences for your sister. She was a good person."

"How did she die?"

"Is that import..." Janan began to ask.

"How did she die?" Dennis said, dropping his hands and looking at Janan. Bhakat could see the tears in his eyes.

"She was killed by one of the Krahn. Bitten. On the neck. She bled too much before we could get her medical attention," Bhakat said.

"You couldn't save her?"

"No," Janan said. "It was the ending battle of the war. She and the other Humans were able to defeat the Krahn and save our planet."

"How?" Dennis asked. "She wasn't a fighter. This doesn't make any sense."

"Show him, Bhakat," Janan said.

"Show me what?"

"Don't freak out," Janan said as Bhakat walked to the middle of the room to give himself space. He suited up.

Dennis took it relatively well, Bhakat thought, though he did almost drop his towel again.

"So what are you saying," he asked. "My sister could do that?"

"Yes," Janan said. Before we got back to our planet, we implanted her with the same type of Stone that Bhakat has in his head."

"Stone?" Dennis asked. "Jesus, you did some type of medical experiment on my sister. I don't know whether to laugh or cry at the absurdity of this situation. Alien abduction? Did you probe her, too?"

"What?" Bhakat asked, confused.

"Nothing. Never mind," Dennis said. "So, you're basically

saying that you kidnapped my sister, took her to your home planet and got her killed fighting in your war?"

"It wasn't quite like that," Janan said. "She was our friend."

"Then why couldn't you save her?!" Dennis yelled.

"I was held captive," Janan said. "I wasn't freed until after the war had ended."

"I couldn't get to her," Bhakat said quietly. "It wasn't until Gianni brought her to us that we knew she was...gone."

"Gianni?" Dennis asked. "Who the hell is that?"

"He was another of the Humans we brought to Rajan. They were...close," Janan said.

Dennis just looked at him a moment, as if processing what he'd said.

"He is one of the Humans we are looking for now," Bhakat said. "Have you seen him?"

"What? No," Dennis said. "I don't even know who that is..." he stopped for a moment, as if something had clicked. "Wait, you said you took all of the people from this apartment building?"

"Yes," Janan responded.

"Was one of them named James Dempsey? A cop named Dempsey?"

"Yes," Janan said. "James was the leader of their group. Along with Gianni, David, Yvette, and your sister."

"Son of a bitch," Dennis said, his eyes wide. "Son of a bitch," he repeated.

Janan looked to Bhakat and shrugged. He still didn't understand Humans at times.

"It makes sense," Dennis said. "I knew there was a connection." He sat down in the chair and covered his face with his hands again. His shoulders began to shake as he began to sob.

Janan stepped forward and placed a hand on his shoulder. "I'm sorry about Kieren."

Dennis lowered his hands and looked at him. "You killed her."

"What, no..." Janan began.

"We took her, but it was her decision to fight with us. For us," Bhakat said. "We still mourn her loss."

"Where is she now?" Dennis asked.

"She was buried on Rajan," Janan answered. "It was a nice place. Near the ocean."

Dennis nodded. "I...have to go there. I have to see. For myself."

"No," Bhakat said. "I'm sorry for your loss, but we can't take you."

"Why not?"

"Well," Janan said. "Uh, we've been...banished."

"What?"

"When I implanted myself with the Stone," Bhakat said, "I broke our laws. As punishment, I was banished."

"I came along to keep him out of trouble," Janan said.

Bhakat heard a snort from near the door and turned to see Amera watching them. "Watch your door," he told her. She made a gesture with her hand that he assumed was some type of obscenity.

"So, you helped save your planet and got banished for it?" Dennis asked.

"Yes, basically," Bhakat said. "It was the only way to help save my species."

"What kind of messed up people did you help save?"

"We don't have time to go into the politics of the situation or of my species," Bhakat said. "We need to find out what happened to James, Yvette, and Gianni. If they are not here, then we need to move on."

"Wait," Dennis said. "You can't just break in here, drop all this shit on me and then just leave."

"We can," Bhakat said. "I'm sorry for disturbing your grooming session, but it is time for us to go."

"Again, we're sorry about Kieren," Janan said.

"No," Dennis said, shaking his head. "No, you don't get to do this. You're responsible for her death and now you think you can just leave? I don't think so."

"We don't have time for this," Bhakat said. He turned and began to walk towards the door.

"Wait," Janan said.

Bhakat turned back to look at him.

Janan walked over to him and motioned for him to bend down to his level.

"We could use him," Janan whispered.

"What?"

"There are a few other places we need to go, like Yvette's father's house. I think we'd learn more if we didn't just storm in there like we did here. We could send him in to ask questions and stay unnoticed."

"Surely you're not suggesting that we bring this Human with us?"

"Yes, I am," Janan said. "We could bring him back here afterwards and he wouldn't know any different."

"Wipe his memory?"

"Exactly," Janan said. "I remember seeing equipment on the other ship. We could go back there and get it."

Bhakat stood up straight. Janan did have a point, he conceded. It would be much safer to send in the Human to any other Human residences or buildings. He sighed. "Fine, we can bring you with us," he told Dennis.

"What? Really?" Dennis asked, looking surprised.

"You have to agree to help us in finding the other

Humans," Janan said.

"Sure, yeah, okay," Dennis said. "Uh, let me get dressed first."

"That would be an improvement," Bhakat said. He still wasn't sure if this was the best course of action, but they needed to get out of the building before they were discovered by anyone else.

"I can't believe we're doing this again," Janan said when Dennis had disappeared to his other room, presumably to get dressed and wipe off his face.

"This had better work," Bhakat said.

"It will," Janan smiled. "What could go wrong?"

They both heard Amera laughing from the doorway.

Chapter 9

Gianni slowly woke up, then he sat up quickly, startled. He didn't know where he was, but found himself in a white room similar to the one aboard the Tukuli. "What...what the hell!? Where?"

"Not too smart. Especially if you don't remember this place."

He sat there, dumbfounded for a second, unable to even say her name. "Kieren?"

"Gianni, wake up."

"What?" He sat up slowly and looked around at a room eerily similar to the one he woke up in years before aboard the Tukuli. "Shit, not again." He turned to see that Yvette was sitting on the next bed over from him. "Yvette?"

"Hey there," she said, smiling, but still holding a hand to her head. He assumed that she had just woken up as well. He noticed that she had some type of small, black device attached to her temple. He slowly reached up and felt the one on his own.

He stood, shakily at first, and then got his bearings and took a step towards her. She looked up at him. He couldn't help himself as he bent and wrapped his arms around her. "I am so glad to see you."

She laughed as she returned his embrace. "Damn, G, what have you been up to? And what's the last thing you remember?"

"Some big ugly son of a bitch trapping me in a bubble..." He pulled back from her a bit, so that he could look into her eyes. He smiled. "I've been surviving. How about you? Where the hell is James? How is the kid?"

"I've been better, obviously," she said. "Kieren is fine. Healthy. As far as I know she's safe at my dad's place still. At least I hope so."

"I'm sure she's fine," he said. "I hope so, anyway, too."

"You look like hell, by the way," she said, smiling to take away the sting.

He turned away from her and walked a few paces, as he cleared his head. "I was sort of...hiding out when I was taken. My family isn't happy with me at the moment."

"Being gone for so long was tough on everyone, I guess."

Gianni turned back towards her. "Um, listen. There's something I've wanted to get off my mind. I guess this is the best chance I've got.

"You don't have to..."

Now Gianni walked back over and looked down at her. "No, I want to, I have to. I meant to tell you. I was going to tell you but...then..."

"Yeah. I know...shit happens."

"My dad was a lieutenant in the Giovanni crime family up in New York. He worked for my uncle. I'm..." he began.

"I know that you are a good man, and so does James." Yvette reached up and placed her right hand on Gianni's left shoulder. "I know that won't change, no matter what name you use. Besides, James told me right after we arrived back on Earth."

"What?!"

She laughed again at the look on his face. "He was a cop, remember?"

"Did he know when we were on Rajan?"

"I think he suspected something, but he didn't confirm anything until after we were back, if that makes you feel any better."

"Where is he?"

"I don't know," she said. I was grabbed by that big SOB as well. James was up on *Bright Journey* waiting for me. We were supposed to be having dinner together."

He reached up to his temple again and felt the device there. It didn't feel like metal, but it wasn't like any type of plastic he'd ever felt, either. "What the hell is this?"

"I tried to use my powers and I got a shock," she said. "I think it's some type of blocking device."

He tried to form a force field and felt a quick, painful shock run through his temple. "Ow! Shit!"

"I told you," she said. "I don't think we're near Earth anymore. I think we've been drugged and sleeping for a while. I don't know about you, but my body is achy, and my head is fuzzy."

"Yes, same," he replied. "The question now is, where are we and when are we getting out of here?"

"Probably best to begin looking for the door."

"Yes. You look great, by the way."

"Thank you. Nothing like having an alien stone in your head to quickly get rid of baby fat and stretch marks."

They both laughed as she stood shakily, holding onto his arm for support, then walked around slowly on her own. Their first pass around the room revealed nothing. They continued searching, until finally Gianni saw something that he had missed the first time—a slight crack between the molding and wall on one side of the room. He bent in closer to look at it, when suddenly he felt the same painful shock run through his head. He dropped to a knee. "Damn it!" he said.

"Told you not to try and use your powers," Yvette said. "Think you would have learned the first time."

"I didn't," he answered, defensively. "And this one lasted longer."

Just then, the crack in the wall became bigger as the door slowly opened. A large figure filled the doorway. It was Atalik, and he was holding a small device that looked to be made of the same substance as the ones on their heads.

"Step back," he said in Talondarian Standard.

Gianni understood that much, and he slowly got to his feet and they both stepped back away from the doorway. "Who are you?" he asked.

Atalik spoke again in Talondarian Standard, but Gianni couldn't understand him because he was speaking too quickly. He had never implanted a translator behind his ear. Gianni pointed to his head and then shook it, hoping to convey that he couldn't understand what the alien was saying. Atalik seemed to get the meaning and pulled another device from his belt and held it up in front of his mouth.

"Is this better?"

They both nodded.

"Primitive humans," Atalik said. "I said, my name is Atalik, and you are currently my prisoners."

"Well, that's just great," Yvette said. "I hope you know that you're going to pay to fix my father's car."

"Your father's vehicle is not my concern," Atalik said. "My concern is handing you over to my clients and getting paid so that I can get away from this planet."

"So we are on a different planet," Gianni said, and looked at Yvette, who was smiling, having been proven correct.

And, he thought, she was probably already thinking of how she was going to escape and kill this asshole. "Just what the hell is going on? Who are your clients?"

Atalik pushed the button on the dark device in his left hand and Gianni once again felt the shock go through his head. "Aargh, would you stop doing that? You're going to give me brain damage or something."

"Then behave, and calm down," Atalik said. "This was only a job. I have no desire to see you injured, but I also can't let you attack me or escape. If I feel that you need a reminder of your position, I have no problem doing that."

"Fine. Okay. Whatever," Gianni said, holding up his hands.

"Who are your clients?" Yvette asked.

"You'll learn soon enough," Atalik responded. "I'm taking you to them right now. If you'll please step through the doorway, we can be on our way."

Yvette stepped outside the room first and noticed that they were inside the foyer of a building or structure. The architecture looked familiar. Then it struck her—it was Rajani. She turned to look back at Gianni. "G, I think we're back on Rajan."

"What, how can you tell that?"

"Look around. Doesn't it look familiar?" She saw him look up at the ceiling and then around the building.

"Shit. Yes, it does look familiar. It's just new. Last time we were here, everything had more of a lived-in look. Everything that was still standing, at least."

"You are correct in your assessment," Atalik said.

"Then why bring us here like this?" Yvette asked. "The Rajani are our friends."

"They wanted you brought here as soon as possible," Atalik said. "That meant not wasting time explaining and having you possibly either not believe me or turn down my invitation and then cause...problems."

"Well, that's just great," Gianni said. "The last place I ever wanted to be again, and here we are."

"As I said," Atalik told them.

"Now that we know," Yvette said, "you can take these things off our heads now, right?"

"The inhibitors are there for my protection," Atalik said. "They will be removed by the client. That's standard procedure."

"Wonderful," Gianni said. "Anytime you're ready."

◇

Welemaan sat in his office and mentally prepared himself to see the Humans again. It had been years since he'd seen or talked with anyone other than David. He knew that it was going to be difficult to convince them to help the Rajani, but he had to make the effort. Two beings with Johar Stones would be an enormous help in the coming conflict.

And if they refused, well, there was the option to keep them prisoners on Rajan during the battle as well. At least then they wouldn't be fighting for the wrong side. He knew that James the Human was now out of reach. Atalik had failed to secure the leader of the Humans. He only hoped that these two, James' mate and the loose cannon known as Gianni, would listen to his plea.

If not, they would join others who had spoken out against the attack. In prison.

◇

They walked slowly down a hallway in the same building as Atalik directed them to turn here, go straight here, until Gianni was sure that they were deep within the bowels of the building. They finally walked down a hallway with only one closed door at the end. They seemed to have reached their destination.

"Open the door and step through," Atalik said.

Yvette reached for the door handle and turned it. The door slid easily to the left and she stepped through. Gianni followed close behind her. He felt protective of her without James there, which he knew was stupid. She could take care of herself. Hell, she could kick his ass if it came to it. He'd seen her fight.

Inside the room they saw that it was a large office, with some oversized chairs and an enormous desk. Sitting behind the desk was Welemaan. He stood when they came in. "Gianni, Yvette. Welcome," he said, smiling.

"What is the meaning of this?" Yvette said. She wasn't sure if he had a translation implant or not, but she didn't see one of the large, old-fashioned translators that the Rajani used sometimes. James had convinced her to have one implanted behind her ear, which she was happy about now.

"Please, have a seat and we can talk," Welemaan said.

"Damn it," Gianni said. His Talondarian Standard was rusty, and he was only catching about one in every three words from the big Rajani.

"How about you take these devices off our heads first?" Yvette said.

"I'm sorry, I can't do that until we've talked, and I know that you aren't going to cause a scene or attempt to hurt anyone," Welemaan said.

"Hurt anyone?" Gianni asked. He'd caught that much. "You're the one who kidnapped us. Again. We have every right to be angry."

"Please, have a seat and all will be explained," Welemaan said. "I need to speak a moment with Atalik first."

Yvette looked at him, and Gianni shrugged. "Nothing we can do right now," he said. He sat down in one of the chairs, remembering how much larger the Rajani were. Yvette reluctantly followed suit.

Gianni watched the Rajani leader and the bounty hunter speaking in low tones and Atalik pass over the control device.

"Welemaan has the device," Gianni whispered to Yvette."

"I saw that," she whispered back.

Welemaan and Atalik ended their business dealing and the large bounty hunter left the room. "Sorry about the wait," Welemaan said. Gianni thought he even sounded like a politician now.

"Start explaining yourself," Yvette said.

"Fine, pleasantries out of the way," Welemaan said. "We are currently on a mission to destroy the Krahn once and for all. To that end, we've been building a fleet of ships to attack the Krahn home world, and we need all of the help we can get."

"Building ships?" Gianni asked. "Did Rajan suddenly become rich, or did you steal the materials?"

"Most of the materials were already here," Welemaan said. "We've salvaged a great deal from the Krahn mother ship as well as their smaller ships. We even salvaged the Tukuli."

"What did you do with the Human bodies aboard it?" Yvette asked.

"They were given a proper burial, I assure you," Welemaan said, holding up his hand. "We buried them up near where Kieren still rests."

Gianni felt his stomach plunge. He was going to have to visit the gravesite.

"And what about David?" Yvette asked. Gianni's drifting thoughts snapped back to attention. David. He'd almost forgotten about the last time they had all seen David. The revelations had come quick and dirty. He'd been so heartbroken over Kieren's death that it had all seemed like a dream.

"Jesus," Gianni said. "Is he still alive?"

"Why wouldn't he be alive?" Welemaan asked. Gianni studied him a moment. The Rajani was almost smirking.

"You tell us," Yvette said.

"David is a proud member of our community, of course," Welemaan said. "He's been instrumental in the recovery and rebuilding efforts. He's a hero of Rajan, as are both of you."

"Then release your heroes," Gianni said. "There's no reason for these precautions. We're not going to suddenly begin hurting anyone or destroying things. Right, Yvette?"

She was silent, and he looked over at her. She seemed to be deep in thought. "Yvette?"

She broke out of her reverie, finally. "Oh, no, we're not here to hurt anyone. I'm curious about the rebuilding efforts. I'd like to see your progress."

"Of course, a formal tour can be arranged," Welemaan said. "But for now, I'm afraid that the restraining devices must be kept in place. At least for a short while. I hope you can understand my caution after all of the work that has gone into rebuilding our city."

"Yeah. Sure," Gianni said. He was tired of talking to the Rajani in that room. He needed some fresh air.

"And you say you are getting ready to destroy the Krahn. What's that supposed to mean? We eliminated the Krahn Horde when we were here last time. Surely you don't mean that you're preparing to attack the Krahn home world? Why would you do that?"

"You know why," Welemaan replied, losing his friendly demeanor for a moment before smiling once again. "You know what we lost; the sacrifices that we made to defeat the Krahn."

"I'm well aware of the sacrifices," Gianni said quietly.

"That doesn't mean an entire planet should be held to account for a small group of space pirates," Yvette said.

Welemaan stood a moment looking at her. Her face remained impassive, not giving anything away. He looked at Gianni then. "Do you promise to come back and speak to me at a later time when I'm less busy. Perhaps dinner tonight?"

Gianni looked at Yvette, and she nodded. "Yes, we can do that. I don't seem to have any other plans."

"Then you are free to go out and visit our new city, minus any restricted areas, which are clearly marked," Welemaan said, standing up. "Welcome back to Rajan."

"Thank you," Yvette said, standing as well.

"We'll speak again later," Welemaan said, leading them out the door of his office. They complied and were soon standing back in the hallway. Welemaan closed his door.

"So," Gianni said, looking around. "Any idea how to get out of here?"

"The building, or the planet?" she asked.

"Both."

Chapter 10

Millen Tordor awoke with a start; his senses awake for any sign of danger. Although the room he shared with his wife was guarded around the clock by his most loyal guards, that didn't stop him from being careful and not take his safety for granted. He had been this way since before he had come into his rightful kingdom. He had made a great many enemies throughout his lifetime, though several of them were now dead.

He turned and could see that Priss was lying beside him sleeping. Whatever had woken him had not done the same for her. He was beginning to think that perhaps it had been something in a dream, when there came a soft knock on the door to his chambers. He got out of bed and wrapped a robe around his naked body, then walked to the door and spoke low so as not to wake Priss. She was a beast if awakened, so it was better not to chance fate. "Yes, what is it?"

"Sorry, my liege," came the voice of Alder from the other side of the reinforced door. "We've received a message from our contact on Rajan. You said that you wanted to be alerted whenever..."

"Yes, yes, just a moment," Millen said. He returned to his bedside and began to get dressed quietly.

"What is it, Millen?" Priss asked.

"It's nothing important," he said, while cursing in his mind. "Please go back to sleep."

"Is Creon safe?"

"Yes," he responded, although he didn't know if that was true. The boy was old enough to take care of himself.

"Come back to bed soon."

"I will. Promise." It was the most she had said to him in a while, and he wondered if she was awake and would remember the conversation in the morning. If she had been fully awake, the conversation could have been much different.

He walked to the door and opened it just enough to squeeze out into the hallway. "Follow me," he told the large bodyguard and began walking towards his private office. He arrived and sat in his chair. Alder was quiet, knowing not to speak until the king was ready to listen. "Well, what is the report?" he finally asked when he was comfortable and had poured himself a drink from his desk cabinet.

"My liege," Alder began in his deep voice. "Preparations are still underway for the invasion of Krahn. They should be ready in only a Standard week or so. The Human prisoners have been brought to Rajan by the bounty hunter they hired for that purpose."

"And the Stones?

"There are now four known Stones on the planet," Alder replied.

"Good to know," Millen said, thinking out loud. "And do they anticipate that all of the Humans will assist in the attack on Krahn?"

"Yes," Alder said.

"And the Sekani are still allied to them in this?"

"Yes," Alder said. "Our contact says he has convinced the

Sekani leader to pursue this course."

"Good. Make the payment to our source. What was his name again?"

"Oderey T'van, sire."

"Yes, him," Millen said. "Their planet will be essentially defenseless while they are gone. Make sure our preparations continue as well."

"Yes, my liege," Alder said, bowing.

"Is that all?"

"No, my liege," Alder said, hesitantly.

"Well?"

"The prisoner known as Ries an na Van was released from prison today."

"What? Who authorized that?"

"Um, your son, Creon," Alder said, frowning.

"I know my own son's name, thank you," Millen said with a snarl. He stood up and began pacing, an old habit of his. "I told him to leave the prisoner alone."

"You told him not to visit the prison again, my liege," Alder said.

Millen stopped and looked at his bodyguard, wondering if the fool would be smiling, but he wasn't, which saved his life. "Be that as it may, I gave strict orders to the warden for this prisoner to not be released under any circumstances, and for him to not have any visitors. What is the warden's name again?"

"Fornen."

"Yes, Fornen. Have him standing before me first thing in the morning."

"Yes, my liege. And your son?"

"You're dismissed." Millen turned to his desk and took a long drink of the fiery liquid he had poured himself. It was going to be a long night.

◊

Creon entered the small ship quarters where Ries had finally warmed up enough to feel close to normal again. Ries' stomachs still felt empty, even after the small piece of fruit that he had eaten a few standard hours before. It could have been a day before, and Ries wouldn't have known. He wasn't sure how long he'd been kept in a cold chamber, or how long he had laid on the floor trying to move as the chamber became warmer.

"Shall we continue our conversation?" Creon asked, smiling as he sat down on a chair that he had brought with him.

"Yes," Ries replied, sitting in the corner with his back propped up against where the walls met. "It's much better than the alternative, I've found."

"Good. Tell me what you know about Rajan. The original Rajan."

"I know that it's under the military jurisdiction of the GA, which means that your father is blockading anyone from getting there. Or getting out."

"Getting out?"

"I think there are still Rajani on that planet," Ries said. "And I think they are probably not very pleased with the Talondarians."

"Does this have anything to do with the Johari Stones?"

"Johar," Ries corrected him. "And it has everything to do with them."

"What do you mean?"

"I think that your father is trying to get ahold of some, if not all of them."

"For what purpose?"

"You would have to ask him about that. But I assume that he is getting on in years. What is the life expectancy of a male Talondarian, by the way?"

Creon paused for a moment, ignoring the question. Then he nodded. "My father has always been an...ambitious person."

Ries decided not to comment on this vast understatement.

"Have you heard that the Rajani, on the second planet, are preparing to attack the Krahn home world?" Creon continued.

"First I've heard of it," Ries answered. "As you know, I've been indisposed. Not a lot of news in prison that isn't concerned with who died and who arrived for an extended stay."

"Well, it's true," Creon said. He stood up. "I think my father is manipulating events towards some end, and I don't believe it will end well for anyone."

Ries nodded. "I believe this too, now. I've had a long time to think about motivations and why the Krahn Horde would attack Rajan, and the only solution I've come up with is that they were directed to do so by an outside force. More than likely your father. He used the ASPs, Galactic Intelligence, and who knows what other resources to bring about this war. All I can think is it's all because of the Stones. He wants them, and he doesn't want anyone else to have them."

Creon looked at him for a moment before nodding again. "Yes, I've come to the same conclusion." He sighed. "The question is, how do we stop him?"

"We?"

"I can't do it alone," Creon said, sitting back down. "Jerboxh is handy to have around, but he's not exactly knowledgeable about this sort of thing. I can't bring in any of my friends from Talondaria. Their families are beholden to my father. I can't trust them, unfortunately. I don't have many allies."

"And you think I want to help you?"

"I think you want to find out the truth."

It was Ries' turn to think a moment. He stood up. Creon stood as well, wary of what his intentions were. Finally, Ries reached out his top right hand towards the prince. "You got me out of prison. I thought I would eventually die in there. You could have tortured me, as I did to you, but you didn't. And yes, I want to know the truth. I swear that I won't play any games with you. I'm done with that. I just want to find the Sekani named Odorey T'van. He's the only real clue I have left."

The prince hesitated, then shook Ries' outstretched hand. "Good. Let's eat."

Ries smiled.

◊

Millen had not been able to sleep again that night while he thought over the implications of what Alder had reported. Just before dawn, he called a council of his top advisors and waited impatiently for them to show. It was early, but he set the work hours. He knew he may have to make an example of one of them if they didn't show up in a short amount of time. In fact, it might be time to make an example of someone, he thought. No good having men who weren't a little afraid of him, still. It kept them on their toes.

A short while later, most of them were assembled in the meeting room adjacent to his private office. He could see that most of them had probably been sleeping when the summons came, which was good. He smiled at their uncomfortableness. There were two that were not yet present. One of them was Sinjen, one of his oldest friends. The other was an almost unknown son of one of his most important allies on Talondaria.

He realized he was still smiling and stopped, composing

his features once more into a scowl lest they think he was in a good mood. "Thank you for coming," he began. Just then, Sinjen entered the room and sat at the broad table. He nodded to Millen, and the king returned the nod.

"I believe that all of you know of the impending war between the Rajani and the Krahn?" There were nods around the table. "Although war can be a devastating affair for those involved, I don't think we can sit back and not become involved." There were looks of surprise around the table. "Therefore, I think that we need to be ready to send a large team of aid workers, with military protection of course, to Rajan."

Sinjen smiled at this, as Millen knew he would. He was a sharp man.

"Are there any questions?" Millen asked, just as the door opened again and the last advisor entered, looking flushed.

"I apologize, my liege," he said as he sat down at the table. "I was held up by affairs at home."

Millen walked around the table a few paces and pulled out a small pistol, pointing it at the younger man. "I don't like excuses," he said. The man's eyes grew wide, as did his mouth.

Millen changed his aim and shot Sinjen in the face, the brief flash of the laser lit the room. Sinjen suddenly had a large black hole through his cheek and the back of his head. He slumped forward and then fell to the floor. "Don't be late again," Millen said. "I expect discipline from my people. Do you understand?"

"Yes. Yes, my liege," the young man said. Millen looked around at the others and saw the look of shock on their faces. "Do you all understand?"

All of them began to speak over each other with affirmative answers and "my liege" thrown in liberally.

"Good," Millen said. He put away the pistol and walked back to his chair. "Then let us draft our plans for Rajan."

◊

Creon sat on the bridge of his ship, the *Sun Dancer*, and thought about recent events. The ship was the only retreat that he had. He'd been given the ship as a gift from his father a Standard year before, and now he spent most of his free time there, even if he hardly ever flew it anywhere. He still needed permission to take it because of security protocols, especially after the kidnapping aboard the Mandakan space port. He was the only offspring of the king of Talondaria. The only one who would continue the line of kings.

And now he was contemplating betraying that king.

His prisoner, Ries, had confirmed for him what he'd suspected for a while: that his father was likely responsible for countless lives lost in senseless fighting, yet Creon still didn't know why. Why was his father meddling in the affairs of other planets? Was it the Stones only, or was there something deeper involved?

It wasn't like he could walk up to his father and ask. He also doubted his mother knew, or if she did, that she would tell him anything. Although she was angry with his father at the moment, she wasn't about to betray his confidence, even to her own son. She was still the queen.

He'd been told from an early age that his uncle and the rest of his family had perished when their ship was attacked by brigands. Afterwards, Millen had been crowned king of the Talondarians. That had happened two years before Creon was born. He had always taken the story at face value, but now he was beginning to have doubts. If his father could start an intergalactic war, what else may he be capable of, and what had he already done? The thought made Creon both angry and restless to know the truth.

He needed to find his answers elsewhere, unfortunately, but he had little idea of where to begin. He reached over and pressed the intercom button on a control panel near the arm of the captain's chair where he sat. "Jerboxh."

"Yes, sire?" the Sh'kallion pilot answered after a moment.

"Come to the bridge. Bring Ries with you."

"Sire, do you think..."

"Yes, I do. Bring him. Now."

◊

Millen Tordor felt the ache in his bones. It was that ache that had forced him to set events in motion that would presumably end in an intergalactic war. He felt no moral obligation to stop it. It was a means to an end. A necessary sacrifice of life so that he could prolong his own.

The Johar Stones were the key. He'd been obsessing over them for years. Even before he became king, he knew that he must have one. He'd had a child, an heir, with his wife as a backup plan, but his goal was to rule from the Talondarian throne indefinitely. The Stone would help him do that. Once he was implanted with a Stone, his wife and son could die the next day for all he cared.

His initial plan of having the Krahn Horde do the dirty work had been foiled. Now, his agents within the Rajani government had stoked their hatred to the point that they were preparing to attack the Krahn home world. Once they did, his troops would be ready.

He'd made plans with his advisors and had the body of Sinjen taken from the room. He would rather have just killed the lax pup who had been so rudely late, but he needed the boy's father more than he needed his friend. He sighed and sipped more of his drink. His advisors all seemed to get the message, at least. He'd dismissed them and then reviewed troop numbers once again, though he knew them all by heart now. They would be more than enough.

◊

"You've said at least once that your goal in this is to find out more about the Rajani home world—the original home world," Creon began when Jerboxh and Ries were finally assembled.

"Yes," Ries said. For once, he looked uncomfortable and not smug, as if he knew more than everyone else in the room.

"Then you may get your chance," Creon said. "I'm planning a trip."

"To where?" Jerboxh asked, warily.

Creon smiled. "Rajan." He noticed the look of surprise on the Sh'kallion's face, as well as the way Ries seemed to perk up at this.

"But how..." Jerboxh began.

"Sounds like an adventure," Ries said. "How will we get past your father's blockade?"

"That's why we're all here," Creon responded. "How would you do it?"

Ries stood for a moment, thinking. "Before we get into that, why are you doing this?"

Creon frowned. "I love my father. Or at least, I thought I did. I've found out a few things about him—about how he came into power, especially—that have me rethinking basically my entire life."

"Your eyes have been opened," Ries said.

"You could put it that way," Creon said. "I like to think that my heart has been opened."

"And it's going to get us killed," Jerboxh said.

Creon turned to look at him. "It may, but I don't think I could live with myself knowing what I know now about my father and his machinations. You're welcome to leave if I'm not paying you well enough."

Jerboxh just scowled and crossed his arms.

Ries laughed. "I'm happy to say I feel no impetus to do this in response to your father's actions. In my society, the strongest and most ruthless is usually the one at the top. Your father just happens to be that leader here. But," he added when he saw Creon frown. "Keeping myself alive is all the motivation I need here. Promise to keep the heat up and the food available, and I'll follow you just about anywhere."

"You mean that? You really mean that?" Jerboxh asked. "I find it hard to believe."

"I admit," Ries said, "you and I don't have the best of relationships, but I'm willing to forgive your betrayal."

"Betrayal?" Jerboxh almost screamed, standing up. "Are you serious?" He turned to leave.

"Where are you going?" Creon asked.

"I'm checking the controls and plotting a course for Rajan," Jerboxh replied. "At least if we're all killed, I'll be rid of this criminal."

"Love you too," Ries said, smiling.

"Please don't encourage violence aboard the ship," Creon said.

"Apologies, but it's just so easy to rile him up."

"But we need him. He's a good pilot. No more antagonizing him."

Ries shrugged. "You're the boss."

"I am," Creon said.

"So how long have you been planning this trip?"

"Only a few days, really," Creon said. "But the idea has been in the back of my mind for a few years. Just before you kidnapped me, actually."

Ries at least had the awareness to look abashed. Creon continued.

"I went to the Mandakan space port on the pretense that

I wanted to see it and do some gambling," he said. "In reality, I had heard that there was a man there, a Talondarian, who might know more about the deaths of the king and queen."

"Did you find him?"

"No, I was taken before I could find him. My personal bodyguard was killed, and I woke up in the room where you found me."

"Yes, you can thank Zazzil for that," Ries said.

"He's dead," Creon said.

Ries looked surprised. "I knew he was getting old, but this is still unexpected. I assume that hairy bastard has taken over?"

"I don't know, and I don't care," Creon said. "What's important here is that you want to know why I've decided to go to Rajani. One, I want to know the truth. Two, I want to foil my father's plans. Simple."

"Simple," Ries repeated. "Let's go."

"It's not going to be that easy," Creon said. "We have to figure out a way to leave the planet. Security is tight."

"There's no way to just outrun them?"

Creon thought. "Not really. I'm sure they won't fire on us if they know it's me." He looked at Ries, who had a peculiar look on his face. It took him a moment to understand that it was a smile. "What?"

"How would you like to be kidnapped again?"

Chapter 11

Gianni and Yvette had made it out of the building finally and were both surprised to find that the city around them had changed so much since they were last there. There was no more rubble, no destroyed vehicles littering the roads, and no bodies lying in the streets. The Rajani and Sekani they saw were all clean—without dirty faces or torn clothing. All of them walked past the two Humans with a determined look on their faces, though some did spare a look for the Humans in their midst.

"Can you believe this?" Gianni asked her.

"All of this progress, and they still want to send most of their people to fight on a distant planet," Yvette said. "Have you recognized anyone yet?"

"Not really, though it's difficult getting used to seeing them again."

"Yes, so out of context, too," she agreed. "Well, we're free to walk around. Where should we head to first?"

Gianni thought for a moment. "I think we need to speak with Zanth," he said.

"Why?" She knew that he had been close to the Sekani leader when they'd been there last.

"I want to see if he is as determined to fight this war as

Welemaan seems to be."

"Makes sense," she said.

He turned around, looking at the buildings near them.

"What are you looking for?"

"Some type of landmark," he said. "Something that tells us where we're at."

"Typical guy," she said. "Refusing to stop and ask for directions."

"Ha ha," he said, though he smiled. Then he walked over to a small group of Rajani and Sekani stopped near them. She followed.

"Can you tell me where to find Zanth?" he asked them. None of them seemed familiar to Yvette, but one of the Sekani's eyes opened wide and he embraced Gianni around the waist enthusiastically. "Whoa. Hello," Gianni said. The Sekani released him and backed up, smiling up at Gianni. Suddenly Gianni's face broke out with a smile. "Golena?"

The Sekani smiled and nodded enthusiastically. "Sedan'ka."

Gianni laughed. "Yes, I remember. That's what you all called me," he said, surprised that he had forgotten it.

Yvette was smiling at the reunion. She hadn't expected to find happiness on Rajan, but here they were again. "Ask him where to find Zanth," she said to Gianni. She hadn't learned any of the Sekani language when she'd been there last, having spent most of her time with Bhakat and the Rajani.

"Where is Zanth?" he asked in Sekani, surprised that he could remember it so easily after so many years.

"Follow me and I'll show you," the Sekani said eagerly.

"That would be appreciated," Gianni said. "How are your children?"

As Gianni and the Sekani caught up with each other, Yvette stayed alert, looking at their surroundings. It was old habit by now, but she couldn't shake the feeling that she and Gianni were in danger. Things seemed too normal. Maybe it was because the last time they were there it was in the middle of a war, or maybe it was the impending war against the Krahn. She wasn't certain, but she kept her eyes and ears open to any signs of danger.

◊

David watched as Yvette and Gianni walked down the street away from where he was hidden by the corner of a building. His first thought upon seeing them again was to use his powers to immediately attack them, but he held back and decided to observe them for a while. Maybe they would be separated, and he could take on each of them individually. He had no doubt that he could take Gianni in a fight—he had done it before. But Yvette was a different proposition. She was lethal. He wouldn't underestimate her again.

Surprisingly, he didn't even have a scar to remind him of the injury she had inflicted on him just before the rest of them had left for Earth at the end of the fighting. Somehow, he had healed completely in a few weeks, most likely with help from the Stone implanted in his brain. It had taken a few years, but his infinity symbol tattoo had also disappeared, like it had never been there.

If it showed him anything, it was the need to make sure if he did fight Gianni and Yvette, he couldn't hold back—he had to make sure any injuries he gave them were fatal, much like Kieren's were. He posited that the Stone hadn't been able to heal her in time before she had bled to death, unfortunately.

He visited her grave from time to time, just to remind himself that he wasn't invincible and to talk to her about his problems. There were no other humans on Rajan until Gianni and Yvette had returned. No one he could truly speak with that would understand what he was experiencing as a human being stuck on an alien planet.

He thought at times about Lisa, his fiancé back on Earth, and wondered if she had moved on. Of course she has, he thought. Why would she wait for years for me to show back up? He wondered if James returned to being a cop and if he had closed the Infinity Killer case, or if it was still considered a cold case, without the killer being caught. He wondered if James was still obsessing over that fact. He fervently hoped so.

◊

They arrived at a small building and Golena pointed to it, saying that he needed to return to work. Gianni knelt and they embraced once more before the Sekani bowed to Yvette and then began to walk back the way they came.

"Aren't you the popular one?" Yvette asked.

"Guess we'll see just how popular," Gianni said, nodding towards the building.

"You go on ahead," Yvette said. "I'm going to check some things out. Maybe visit Tumaani."

"Sounds like a good idea," Gianni said. "Be careful."

"You too."

Gianni headed towards the door. The building was unassuming, considering it's where the leader of the Sekani was. Maybe he was just visiting. He opened the front door and found himself in a small waiting area. He looked around, but it seemed deserted at the moment. He walked further into the room and noticed closed doors on either side. He debated which one he should try.

"I'm either going to find Zanth or the bathroom," he said to himself.

Just then the door to his right opened and a female Sekani entered, holding a cup of what looked like water. She looked familiar, and then he remembered that this same Sekani had given he and Kieren food when they had first landed on Rajan. She smiled and handed the cup to him. He drank and found that it was water. It was lukewarm, but welcome.

"Thank you," he told her, and gave her back the cup. "No bowing," he said, wondering if she remembered.

She laughed and nodded. "No bowing, I promise." He smiled, happy that she had. "If you'll follow me," she said, "I'll take you to Zanth. "We saw you on the monitor."

He nodded. He assumed that they had seen him come in, so there must be a hidden camera in the room that he couldn't see. He followed her through the doorway and found it to be a larger office area. There were a few Sekani seated at desks and working at what looked like computer pads. They all looked up and saw Gianni and most of them smiled. A few said, "Sedan'ka," in acknowledgement. He smiled and nodded to everyone as he followed the female.

"What is your name?" he asked, not wanting to keep thinking of her as the Sekani female.

"Irishe," she said.

"Nice to meet you, Irishe," he said. "I'm happy to see that you survived."

"I'm happy to have survived," she said. She began walking up a flight of stairs to the second, and top, floor of the building. Gianni followed, admiring the craftsmanship of the stairs and banister. It looked like wood, but he wasn't sure, though there was intricate detail carved into each step and the banister itself. He ran his hand over it and felt its smoothness. For the plainness of the building's exterior, someone had taken time to craft the interior.

They arrived at the top of the stairs and there was a lone door. She walked through and he followed, seeing that it was a comfortable-looking room, with soft furniture in two sizes, which could fit Rajani, Sekani, and Jirina as well. "Please sit," she said. "Zanth will be in momentarily."

"Thank you, Irishe," he said. He picked a chair that looked about the right size and sat down. It was surprisingly firm, but it soon molded to his back and legs. He could feel his body relaxing for the first time since he arrived. He had to be careful, or he would fall asleep.

After a few Standard minutes, the door opened and Zanth came in carrying two glasses and a bottle. Gianni had been dreading this tradition. The last time he had drank fernta, he had drunk a great deal and became violently ill as a result. He stood and approached Zanth, who had placed the items on a small table. He noticed the prosthetic arm that the Sekani was using.

"Gianni!" Zanth said, opening his arms. Gianni knelt and embraced the Sekani leader. "Welcome back to Rajan."

"Thank you, Zanth," Gianni said. "I wish it were under better circumstances."

Zanth pulled back and looked at him. "As do I," he said. "War is not an optimum time for reunions, but at least it has brought you back to us."

"Yes, though that wasn't exactly a happy trip," he said.

"Believe me when I say that it was all Welemaan's doing. By the time we found that you were coming, it was too late to speak up about the nature in which you would be coming."

"I understand," Gianni said.

Zanth nodded and turned to pour them a glass each of the distilled liquid. He handed a glass to Gianni and motioned for him to be seated again. "Thank you," Gianni said. He sat back in the same chair, feeling it once again stiff and then conforming to his body again. He guessed that the seats, or at least the cushions, had been salvaged from a spacecraft. He took a small sip of the liquid, remembering now just how bad the stuff was. His stomach had a moment of revolt and he thought he would have to spit it out, but he swallowed it successfully.

Zanth drank a gulp of it and smiled at him. "We had a good harvest this year," he said. "Did you hear that the Jirina have taken over the running of the various farms around Melange?"

"No," Gianni said. "I was wondering why I hadn't seen any since arriving."

Zanth nodded. "Yes, they seem happy staying in the country and not being within the confines of the city. I believe that they are still recovering from the invasion."

Gianni nodded. "I believe it took all of us a while to recover," he said. He took another sip of fernta as a show of protocol and not wishing to offend Zanth, then decided that it was the last drink of fernta he would have if he could help it. It brought back too many memories.

"Yes," Zanth agreed. "But as you can see, we've rebuilt, and I believe the city is much more practical to everyone's needs."

"Congratulations on your work here," Gianni said. He thought for a moment about how to begin. "It is interesting that you've built it back to where it is today, and now you plan on leaving it to fight a war halfway across the galaxy."

"Fighting, it seems, is in our blood," Zanth said. "While the Valderren seek retribution, the Sekani seek something else."

"And what is that?" Gianni asked, almost forgetting and taking another sip of the liquid. He lowered his hand again.

"Conquest," Zanth answered. "Adventure. Honor. Courage. I could go on."

"Basically, you're bored," Gianni said.

"Yes, I suppose that does play a part," Zanth said, chuckling. "When Welemaan first broached the subject, it seemed to light a new fire among the Sekani, including myself. Rebuilding is all well and good, but we're just not built for a sedentary lifestyle. Once it was all finished, what was there for us to do? Some set off to explore this planet, and some were never heard from again. The Jirina have chosen a peaceful existence, and that is fine, as long as they keep supplying everyone with food, which they seem content to do. But for the Sekani, there is nothing else to do. Rebuilding ships and making weapons and other gear has given us a purpose."

The Sekani leader made sense, Gianni thought. Who was he to tell them what they could do?

"Have you visited the site yet?" Zanth asked, breaking his concentration.

Gianni thought a minute, then understood what the Sekani meant. "No," he said. "Haven't had a chance yet."

"We lost so many," Zanth said. "But losing Kieren was a stab in my heart."

"Yes," Gianni agreed.

Zanth lifted his glass above his head. "To Kieren, who is missed by many."

Gianni lifted his glass in return. Zanth took a long gulp of the liquid. Gianni touched it to his lips only. He wouldn't drink fernta to her memory, given that she abhorred the stuff and equally abhorred him drinking it.

"Will you fight in her memory?" Zanth asked.

The question caught Gianni by surprise. "I...haven't decided anything yet," he admitted, which was the truth. "I need to think about things. Yvette and I were kind of thrown back into this situation, so it might take us a little while to decide anything."

Zanth nodded his understanding. He sat forward in his chair. "I am so happy to see you," he said.

"You too," Gianni answered, smiling.

"I'm sure that David will be, too," Zanth said, standing. He wasn't looking at Gianni when he said this, and Gianni tried to keep the look of revulsion off his face. David. He had almost forgotten about David.

"Where is David?" he asked casually, standing.

"Here and there, I'm sure," Zanth said. "You know him. He could be anywhere."

"Yes. Anywhere," Gianni said. He would have to be careful. They didn't exactly part as friends.

Just then, another Sekani entered the room and stood looking at Gianni a moment before speaking. "Zanth, your next appointment is here."

"Thank you, Jinda," Zanth said to him, then turned to look at Gianni. "I must return to my work," Zanth said. "You are welcome to stay and drink, or I could have Irishe make you food..."

"Oh no, it's fine," Gianni said. He put down the glass on the table. "I should be going. I do have somewhere to go." He took a last gulp of the water that Irishe had initially given to him and set the cup down on the table next to the fernta.

Zanth looked at him, then nodded, knowing where he was going. "Be well, my friend."

Gianni nodded. "Thank you, Zanth. You too. I'm sure we'll talk again soon." He looked over at the Sekani called Jinda and nodded. The Sekani nodded back and smiled. Gianni wasn't sure that he liked this Sekani. He wasn't familiar with him from his last time on Rajan, and the Sekani looked a little too smug, like he knew a secret that no one else knew.

His contemplation was interrupted when Zanth patted him on the leg with his real arm and walked over to speak to Jinda. They both left and Gianni headed towards the stairs.

He wasn't sure how to feel about where he was going, but he needed to see it again.

◊

Yvette wasn't sure where she was going, but it was nice to be able to walk around Rajan without the imminent threat of being shot at by a Krahn warrior. She still had an uneasy feeling in the back of her mind, though, and contemplated suiting up while she walked, but chose not to. No need to scare anyone needlessly. Then she remembered that it was a moot point because of the inhibitor on her head, which she had forgotten about. The thought of it made her angry.

She decided that she would seek out Tumaani and see what his thoughts were on this situation. As she observed the various Rajani around her as she walked, she noticed that many of them had abandoned their ritual braids. She remembered from speaking with Rauph that the braids, called a Ralik, had signified adulthood and their journey to becoming an Elder.

She wasn't sure what this signified, but she knew that Welemaan still kept his. Did this mean that the ones who wore one were Valderren? Or were they Elders? She had a feeling that an Elder would be more helpful in her finding Tumaani.

She decided that the only thing she could do was ask around and someone would eventually point her in the right direction. She saw a group of Rajani working on the side of the road and approached them. They were connecting some type of buried power or information lines to what looked like a utility box. "Hello," she said in Talondarian, feeling foolish for not knowing the language better. The Rajani all turned to look at her. There was no one that she recognized, and while they didn't seem surprised to see her, they also didn't seem happy, either. "Tumaani?" she asked.

Some of them just turned away and began working again. A couple even waived her off, as if she was bothering them. "Tumaani?" she repeated. "Where Tumaani?" One of them finally pointed down the street towards what she remembered as the center of the city. "Thank you," she said. She began walking away but heard some of them hooting behind her in what she knew was Rajani laughter. She kept walking.

She began thinking about her daughter. It had been her first thought when she awoke once again on Rajan. She knew that Kieren was with her grandfather, and hopefully that meant she was safe. There was also the fact that James was not with them, which meant either he had escaped Atalik, or that Atalik hadn't tried to go after him. It was a curious situation, but she tried to push it away to the back of her mind. Her daughter was safe with her father and possibly James. She couldn't do anything about it while light years away.

She walked until she saw the old prison, which the Krahn had used to keep Rajani prisoners during their invasion. She remembered it had been a nasty place, and she was surprised it was still standing. She saw two Rajani working on the front of a building, repairing a doorway. She walked up to them and once again asked, "Tumaani?"

They both turned to look at her and one of them waived her off. The other looked like he was about to speak, but the first began speaking with him and drew his attention back to their work. Yvette was feeling frustrated, but she walked away from them. She thought about turning around and walking back to where she had been taken to see Welemaan and asking him.

She had walked about fifty feet back the way she had come when she heard someone coming up behind her. She had to stop herself from trying to suit up as she turned. She saw that it was the Rajani from the doorway who had looked like he wanted to speak. He quickly walked up to her and motioned for her to follow him. She nodded and followed close behind him as he led her into what looked like a tunnel that was between two buildings, with an arch overhead for a walkway between the two. She was ready to fight, if she was being led into some type of trap.

The Rajani finally turned to look at her and she stopped. "Tumaani has been imprisoned," he said. "Do you understand me?"

She pointed to the device located behind her ear and nodded. "Yes."

"Good," he said. "Tumaani was arrested for protesting against Welemaan's plans. He's being kept in the old prison where we were just at. I don't know if they'll let you see him."

"Thank you," Yvette said. "Were you an Elder?"

"I was one of Tumaani's students, yes," he said. "But it has become dangerous to speak against the Valderren. I don't wish the same fate as Tumaani."

"I understand," she said. "Thank you."

He looked over her shoulder, then placed his hand on her shoulder. "Please, help Tumaani if you can. Speak with Welemaan and see if you can at least visit him. I don't know his condition. He has been imprisoned for three Standard years now."

"Yes, I'll help him if I'm able," she said. He bowed slightly and walked toward the end of the archway before looking around and then turning the corner out of sight.

"Well, shit," she said.

◊

Zanth and Jinda walked slowly back towards Zanth's office. "Will he fight?" Jinda asked.

"He has not decided yet," Zanth said, his mind still preoccupied with the conversation he'd just had with the Human named Gianni. He did feel bad for the Human, having been brought back to Rajan against his will. He'd argued with Welemaan countless times that the Humans should be asked, and if they refused, should be left alone. Welemaan had argued that if the Humans weren't brought to Rajan, they would surely go to Krahn and had won over the Valderren and many of the Sekani with his argument. Zanth had been forced to concede the point, and they had hired the bounty hunter Atalik away from the Krahn.

"And the female Human?" Jinda asked.

"Oh, I don't really know," Zanth said. "I'm not too familiar with her. She could go either way."

"What do we do if they refuse to fight for us?"

Zanth turned to look at his assistant. "We will do nothing. They will be left here and returned to Earth as soon as possible. Is that understood?"

"Yes, of course," Jinda responded, smiling.

Zanth looked at him a moment more to make his point, then headed to his office with Jinda trailing slightly behind.

◊

Gianni found the spot overlooking the sea. It hadn't changed much in the time that he had been gone. He knelt at the graveside and closed his eyes. He could hear the sound of the surf below and the calling bird-like animals that lived on the cliff face. He pictured her face in his mind as he remembered her, smiling and full of life. Suddenly, the vision changed, and she was lying in his arms again, bloody and dying. He quickly opened his eyes and sat back on his feet.

"I've been gone a while," he said softly. "I'm sorry. Tried to get on with my life, and I guess I didn't do a very good job at that, either." He picked at the vegetation a moment, thinking. "I've missed you," he said. "I've been lost ever since I got back to Earth. I'm surprised at times that I'm still alive. I know, I know, now is when you'd be yelling at me, but it's true."

He stood up again and brushed the dirt from his knees. "Anyway, I'm here. I have a decision to make, and I don't know which is the right choice, if any of them. I wish I could talk to you again." He could feel tears in his eyes now. "I miss you so much." He used both hands to pull back the long hair that had gone over his face. He'd let it grow since returning to Earth, and it was now well past his shoulders.

He stood and watched the flying creatures as they swooped and landed on the cliffs nearby, and then he had a good cry. Finally, he turned and walked away from the gravesite without another word.

His decision had been made. He hoped she would be proud of it.

Chapter 12

It took a little while for James to get used to a ship full of aliens. He and Dar took shifts as captains, while Reilla and Jurl took shifts as pilots. They staggered their shifts so that half the time it was James and Reilla or James and Jurl, and the other half it was Dar and Reilla or Dar and Jurl. There were times when all of them were awake at once and they would share a meal together. James found that he enjoyed their company for the most part, but he could tell that they had been together for a while, and he was the outsider in this instance. He still had not learned how they had earned that nickname.

James went to bed each night and woke up each morning thinking about Yvette and Keiren. He missed them both and wondered if they were safe. He had no doubt that Yvette could handle herself, and he was certain that Belani would watch over Kieren, but it didn't make things any easier. He would have to speak with Welemaan about this in the future to...express his displeasure with his actions, and deal with the bounty hunter, as well.

"How much are you getting to bring me to Krahn?" James asked at one of their common meals.

Reilla and Jurl stopped eating and looked at Dar. "Thirty

thousand Standard credits," Dar said. "Each."

"Is that a lot?" James asked.

"It is enough to survive on," Dar said, smiling. "Hopefully I won't be needing to buy a new ship."

James nodded. "I guess you'll be sticking around until I've finished with my business on Krahn."

Dar paused. He looked at the other two. "Are you intimating that we would steal your ship?"

"The thought had crossed my mind," James said, smiling. "There's nothing stopping you from doing so once I'm on Krahn and caught up in whatever chaos they're dealing with."

"We won't do that," Dar said. James looked him in the eye for a moment, then looked at the other two for a moment each as well. He believed them, but there was nothing he could do about it, either way.

"So, what do you know about Krahn itself?" he asked, changing the subject. "Have any of you been there before?"

"I have not," Dar said.

"No, for obvious reasons," Reilla said, referring to the fact that Sekani were considered a delicacy by the Krahn. She looked at Dar. "I think I'll be staying close to the ship once we land."

"No, never been there," Jurl said. "They creep me out. Especially because they can't speak Talondarian Standard because of their beaks. It's all hisses and grunts."

James laughed. "They do me as well. It's like fighting a giant parrot." He smiled, but the three of them looked at him quizzically. "Oh, sorry. A parrot is type of flying creature on Earth called a bird. They have similar features to the Krahn, but parrots are much smaller." James didn't think he should go into talking about dinosaurs and how Earth scientists thought that birds had evolved from them. It had also crossed James' mind that Krahn might be what would have evolved on Earth if the asteroid had somehow missed.

Dar nodded. "Interesting. Speaking of fighting, can we expect you to behave once we arrive?"

James became serious once more. "You mean not going off half-cocked when we arrive, when I feel liking punching their leader in the face for bringing me there?"

"Something like that, yes," Dar said.

"I think I can hold myself in check," James replied. "But if they try to hold me there against my will or threaten me in any way, all bets are off. I'll do what I have to do to return to my family. They're safety is my top priority."

"Understood," Dar said. "I wouldn't expect anything less. As far as the planet goes, we've all heard about Krahn. They said that there are no buildings on the planet—that the Krahn live in caves and natural structures on the floor of the massive jungle that covers most of the planet's surface. They say that it is close enough to their sun that it never gets cold and that while primitive in that respect, they also have some advanced technology developed by their scientists."

"Sounds like an interesting blend of science and nature," James said.

"Yes," Dar said. "Krahn was still a primitive, uncharted planet when the first Galactic Alliance ship touched down there years ago. Contact with that ship was lost soon after. Another ship was sent to ascertain what had happened to the first, and they were soon attacked by the Krahn and taken prisoner. The Krahn had stripped the first ship of anything interesting to them, and they stole the second ship and learned how to pilot it."

"And the Galactic Alliance just let them?"

"No," Dar said, smiling. "Not everyone was happy about the fact that there was some primitive planet out there with current GA technology. But there were others who saw it as a chance to make first contact with a new species, for various reasons, I'm sure." He took a drink then continued. "In fact, it was the Talondarian king who spoke on their behalf for them to be spared. He argued that the Krahn, though a primitive species, had acclimated to the new technology exceptionally well. Plus, the Krahn home world was rich in various substances that were needed by the Galactic Alliance."

"Ah," James said, understanding now.

"The Krahn were given probationary status by the GA, and much later were given full status under the protection of the Talondarian empire," Dar continued. "They signed a treaty to cultivate and export the products of their world."

"And how do you know so much about this?" James said.

"Like I said, I used to be a statesman," Dar replied. He smiled, then the smile left his face as he became lost in memory. "The Talondarian king was my uncle. My mother was his younger sister."

"He was king until they killed him," Reilla said.

"There is that, yes," Dar said. "There was a rebellion by those loyal to the king's younger brother, Millen Tordor. The king and queen were killed aboard their ship as it travelled between their planet and another. No one knows what happened to their daughter."

"So, the king's brother performed a coup against him, and took over," James said.

"Yes," Dar responded. "Most of those loyal to the king were hunted down and captured or killed. You'd be surprised at how long a reach Talondaria has when it's trying to find someone. I've had to change quite a bit not to be recognized on site. As it is, I found myself hiding out at the fringes of GA society, which is where I found this lot."

Reilla smiled. "We love you too, Jophen."

He laughed. "I couldn't ask for a better crew, though.

They've proven themselves through many missions. All of them—even if they act like spoiled teenagers sometimes." He looked at Jurl.

"What?" Jurl asked, feigning shock, but then smiled.

"They never found the princess?" James asked.

"No," Dar said, growing serious once more. "I have given up hope that we ever will."

"I'm sorry," James said.

"It's an old wound," Dar said. "But not forgotten, by any means. If I ever get a chance, I will gladly kill Millen Tordor for what he's done without a second thought."

"Then I hope you get a chance," James said, holding up his drink to toast each of them. It somehow didn't surprise him that Dar was royalty. He was much too sophisticated to be a simple space pirate. But he knew that things could be complicated by the fact. For now, he would put it aside and not speak about it.

◊

Maliq found that being the High Vasin of Krahn was not an easy job; not that he had expected it to be. His father had sent both he and his brother to a variety of other worlds to learn all they could from other species. Maliq had learned a great deal about other governments in the Galactic Alliance. Ronak obviously just saw worlds to conquer. Krahn had diplomatic relations with a handful of other worlds, and formal alliances with few of them. As a relatively young civilization, keeping up these alliances and finding new ones was a burden that had fallen on Maliq. His father had done what he could to further their standing within the GA, but it was a slow process.

It had been a wide awakening for the Krahn when they had first encountered species from another world. Up until that point, they had thought themselves the only sentient beings in the universe. There were certainly no other creatures on their planet with the same level of intelligence. The discovery of Others, and especially Others with much more advanced technology, had caused a sociological and technological revolution on Krahn.

And now his idiot brother had set back relations with many of their alliances because of his foolish invasion of Rajan, and it was coming back to bite Maliq in the tail. Maliq's appointees for ambassadors to other worlds had all been called in to explain just what was happening between the Krahn and Rajan. Some ambassadors had been told to leave their planets entirely. Not only did Ronak lose the war on Rajan, but also the public relations battle for his older brother. Maliq had to continuously explain that Ronak was not a member of the Krahn government and did not act on behalf of Krahn. Those explanations had seemingly fallen upon deaf earholes on many planets.

So now he found himself preparing for an invasion of his own from Rajan, if the rumors were to be believed. Krahn had no form of orbital protection system like many other planets had implemented; no laser cannon or giant missile bases on orbiting moons. Nothing that would dissuade the Rajani from attacking the planet. The most they had were planet to air defenses—mostly guided missiles and a few laser cannons with a limited range. Nothing that could reach further out than the highest level of the atmosphere, meaning that they would be invaded if the Rajani chose to attack.

On top of this, the Rajani had taken most of the Humans that Maliq had hoped would be able to persuade the Rajani not to attack. The last was supposedly on his way to Krahn, but Maliq had no idea when he would arrive. Meanwhile, he had his people building ships and more weapons to defend themselves against the Rajani, as well as fortifying ground bases against ground attack. It was all he could do at the moment, and he hated it.

Even if they won this coming war, it could mean grave tidings for their future. If they won too handily, it would signal to the GA that the Krahn may be too dangerous to let live. If they lost, it could mean the end of their species, depending on what the Rajani chose to do with survivors.

Maliq decided that he would have to worry about that later. They had to survive the coming battles first.

◊

James had gone to bed only a few hours earlier when he was woken up by Reilla. "What? What's happening?"

"We're getting close to Krahn," she answered. "Jophen wanted me to wake you so you could be there when we came out of n-space."

"Okay, thanks, Reilla," James said. He rubbed his eyes a moment and looked around, trying to wake himself further. He sat up and drank from the water bottle next to his bed, then got up and dressed. He had a flashback of the first time he and the other humans had been kidnapped by aliens. He'd been wearing a plain white T-shirt with a Detroit Redwings jersey over the top and jeans. That jersey had made it most of the way through the fighting before he'd been given a change of clothes that somewhat fit him. The jersey now hung in his closet at home; a memento of their first journey. What he had hoped would be their last journey.

James made his way to the bridge and pushed the button to open the door. He walked in to see Dar, Reilla, and Jurl already present. He nodded soberly to all of them in turn. They must have all been wakened by Reilla, who had been on pilot duty.

"Jurl, bring us out of n-drive," Dar said.

She nodded and turned back to her console and began to

push buttons. Suddenly, an alarm began to sound.

"Bob, what's the situation?" James asked loudly over the sound.

"Proximity alert," Bob responded. "Another vehicle detected in our path forward."

"How close?"

"Approximately two hundred meters and coming closer."

"Can you identify them?" Dar asked.

"Markings on the ship suggest Alliance Society for Peace."

"Damn," James muttered. He was reminded of the last time he'd come up against the ASPs, aboard the Mandaka Space Port, and then later, when he performed a crazy, foolish, yet successful spacewalk to disable one of their ships.

"We are being hailed," Bob said.

"Put them on the intercom," James said. "Do not open a communication channel until I tell you."

"This is the ASP cruiser *Stinger*. I am Captain Yessacca Dow. Cut your engines and come to a stop, then transmit your heading and identification code."

"Can we outrun them to the planet's surface?" Dar asked.

"Probability of reaching the planet's surface without being destroyed by the ASP ship is 17 percent," Bob responded.

"So no, Bob," James said. "You know, you can just say no. Brevity is important."

"Sorry, James," Bob said.

"It's okay," James said, smiling, while his mind was furiously thinking about what to do next. "I think," he turned to look at the others. "I think we need to do what she says, for now."

He could see that they all looked uncertain about this, as he did. "Bob, send the information she requested."

"Yes, James."

"The rest of you," he said. "Be prepared for a fight. This ship is not registered. It was put together from parts on Rajan. I'm sure they'll see that as soon as the information is processed."

"Sounds wonderful," Dar said, dryly, placing his hand on his sword hilt.

◊

Yessacca Dow had been promoted to the rank of captain only a few Standard months ago, and this was the most excitement she'd seen since then. As a new ASP captain, she was stationed in a large swath of space in one of the more boring areas of the Alliance space. She knew, if she was ever going to move up the ranks and get a better assignment, that she had to be by-the-book in her dealings with any complications that arose.

Which was why as soon as her ship's sensors detected a ship coming out of n-space, she jumped at the chance to waylay them. They could be legitimate but given the infrequency of ships passing through the sector, she doubted it. Probably smugglers, she thought. A nice arrest would show well on her next report.

She got down from her chair aboard the bridge of the *Stinger* and slid closer to her pilot, her almost round body flowing over the floor. "Get ready in case they try to run," she said.

"Yes, captain," the pilot said.

"Have we received their information yet?" she asked, turning to look at one of the technicians. They both shook their heads. Yes, probably smugglers, she thought again. "Prepare to fire a warning shot," she said.

"Captain," one of the techs said. "Receiving a transmission from the ship."

Surprising, she thought. "And?"

There was a pause, and then the tech spoke. "Unregistered ship on a heading to Krahn."

It was what she had guessed. There weren't any other civilized worlds near, if you could call the Krahn civilized. "What is the name of the ship?"

"Pwyntafa Naa," the tech answered.

"That's Rajani," she said, frowning.

"Yes, captain."

"Open up the communication channel."

She looked at the tech, and he nodded. "Pwyntafa Naa, this is Captain Dow of the *Stinger*. Your ship is unregistered. Prepare for a landing party to enter your ship. We will extend our troop tunnel to your airlock soon. Do not move your ship. Is that understood?"

She waited a moment to see how the ship responded, still thinking that they could run at any moment.

"Understood, Captain Dow," a voice responded over the communication channel in Talondarian Standard.

"Prepare docking procedures and notify the docking troops," she said to the pilot and then headed for the docking bay.

◊

Dar thought for a moment while Jurl positioned the *Bright Journey* so that the ASPs could board her. "Jurl, are we within the jurisdiction of Krahn space?"

She checked and smiled back at him. "Yes we are, Dar."

He smiled as well. "Good. Send them a message. Tell them that we are here but have been stopped by an ASP patrol ship. Advise them that we could use a little help."

"Will do," she said.

Dar looked at James. The human was still standing near the door of the bridge with a somewhat confused look on his face at the interaction. "Each member of the Galactic Alliance is permitted a certain amount of space around their planet or even star systems where they have absolute authority. They may invite the ASPs to assist with problems, but they don't have to. I'm hoping that the Krahn don't know that this ASP ship has overstepped its authority."

"And if they have?" James asked, smiling.

"Then they can kick the ASPs out of the sector, if necessary," Reilla said, now catching on.

"Yes, that's what I'm hoping," Dar said. "But we'll have to stall long enough for them to respond."

"I think I just accidentally hit a thruster adjustment," Jurl said. "It may take a few moments more for their ship to line up properly."

"Nice," James said. "The only time I seem to break the law is where these ASPs are concerned."

"Welcome to the Outsiders," Dar said, laughing.

◊

Captain Dow waited at the airlock until the tech's voice came over the communication implant telling her that the *Stinger* was now docked with the rogue ship. It had taken longer than she'd expected, and so she had been standing in the dock impatiently, thinking of just how she was going to yell at the occupants of the ship.

She looked behind her at the assembled ASP troops and nodded. The lead officer nodded and stepped forward to press the button that opened the airlock door. Captain Dow noticed that the button was set at a height where she would have had to stand on the tips of her tentacles to reach it. She would have to speak with the head ship engineer to see if they could remedy that situation.

The other ship's door stayed closed a moment, then finally opened just as she was about to ask for an open communication channel and demand they open it. Her angry feelings only deepened. She stepped aside so that the troops could move past and perform a security check.

Finally, she slid through the doorway onto the other ship, following the lead troops, who were fully armed and armored. She kept her broad face impassive but was surprised to see that the ship's occupants had assembled in the hallway just off their airlock. The initial scan of the ship had told her that there were four occupants. All of them stood with their hands on their heads in a non-threatening pose.

She assumed that there may be other members of the crew elsewhere that their scan had missed; on the bridge perhaps, but a ship this size couldn't maintain too many more occupants that these four. She motioned for her lead to check the ship just in case.

The second surprise was just what a sorry-looking crew of misfits it was. It looked to her like two Talondarians, a Sekani, and a Sh'Kallion. She watched as her troops took up positions around the four while others followed her unspoken orders and went to inspect the rest of the ship. Her troops were well trained.

"Well," she said loudly. "Who is in charge here? Who is your captain?"

"I am," the lighter and shorter of the Talondarians said, stepping forward. "Why have you detained us? We are on important business."

"I'm sure you are," she said. "But you are also unregistered in our files and that is a bit troubling."

"I understand your concern," the Talondarian replied. "But the truth is, this ship was just commissioned less than a Standard month ago, and the application must be held up somewhere in your system."

"Or you could be lying and attempting to smuggle

something of value to the Krahn home world," she said.

"This is a small ship," the Talondarian said. "There is really no room to smuggle anything of importance."

"We shall see," she replied. Her thoughts were a different story though, wondering if what the Talondarian said was true. Also, if she had interrupted business between the Talondarians and their clients, she could find herself being the one who was reprimanded. No, she thought. It's a good stop. There's something going on here that doesn't seem right.

She saw her lead trooper returning down the hallway. "Report."

"No one else aboard," he replied. "No sign of contraband, either."

"See?" the Talondarian said.

She turned back to look at him. "What is your name?"

"Ezen Dur," he replied quickly. "We're consultants who were hired by the Krahn."

"What type of consultants? What services do you provide?"

"Landscaping," he said.

"Landscaping?"

"Yes," he said. "The High Vasin wants a more contemporary look to the royal palace. We have some lovely water elements and an exotic variety of non-poisonous seasonals that we think he's going to love."

"Landscaping," she said again, her furrowed brow giving away her consternation. She looked at the darker of the Talondarians, who was smiling and nodding.

"We also offer consultations for ship-bound gardens," he said. "If you'd like to brighten up your crew quarters..."

"Silence," she said, thinking. "If you're so good with plants and gardens, why is this ship so...plain?"

"We have a policy that this ship is kept as utilitarian as possible, in the event that we unwillingly spread any unwanted invasive species or a plant variety that's possibly harmful to the environment or an allergen to its people," the Sekani said. "This is only an initial visit so we can inspect the space and design an appropriate arrangement."

What they were saying was logical, but Dow still had a feeling in her primary stomach that something else was going on here. She was about to ask why the ship had a Rajani name associated with it when she was interrupted by the crackling of her communications implant.

"Captain," the tech said over her implant. "We have a Krahn warship approaching quickly."

"What?" she asked.

"We seem to have strayed into Krahn jurisdictional space," the tech said. "They are demanding that we leave at once and stop, I quote, 'harassing their guests.'"

"Blast," she said quietly. She turned to her lead trooper. "Return to the *Stinger*." He nodded without hesitation and motioned for the others to depart. They were well-trained troops.

She turned back to the two Talondarians. "I will be making a full report to my superiors about this, whether you are 'guests' of the Krahn or not."

"Sorry for any inconvenience," the lighter Talondarian said, smiling.

She frowned and turned away from them, displaying as much dignity as she could as she slid through the airlock door back to her ship. She took small satisfaction in knowing that they would have to clean up the trail of slime she left. Landscapers, indeed.

◊

As soon as the ASP captain left and the airlock door was

closed on her ship, the current crew of the *Bright Journey* broke out in laughter.

"Landscaping?" James finally asked. "Where the hell did that come from?"

"I'm an amateur gardener," Dar said, shrugging. "Very nice improvisation on your part, by the way."

"I know my way around a garden," James said. "Used to help my uncle when I was a kid. Planted all kinds of fruits and vegetables."

"And bravo, Reilla," Dar said.

She smiled and bowed at the compliment.

"Jurl," you'd better get back to the bridge in case the Krahn are trying to contact us."

She nodded and trotted down the hall towards the bridge.

"Now the fun begins," he said.

James' smile disappeared at this. "Yes," he said. "I suppose it does."

Chapter 13

Belani had spent a great deal of time attempting to explain to the Human named Josiah why he was there and what had happened to Yvette. He'd also spent a great deal of time at Kieren's tea parties. The daughter of James the Human and Yvette was quite a charming youngling. He was happy to learn that she was on an extended leave from her learning facility known as 'summer vacation,' which meant that she wouldn't go to the school and tell all of her classmates about the alien who had come to visit.

He was on his second cup of imaginary tea when Kieren stopped pouring tea for her large brown teddy bear and looked at him. "Where's mommy and daddy?"

He was at a loss for words for a moment. It was difficult enough to come up with a story, let alone translate it in his head into Earth English, since neither Kieren nor her grandsire had a translating device. "They had to go away for a little while," he said. "They will be back soon enough," he said, not knowing if they truly would.

"Where are you from?" she asked.

"I'm from a planet known as Rajan. Your mom and dad came to my planet and helped us all. I decided to travel back here with them afterwards." It wasn't exactly the truth but was simple enough for her to understand.

She looked at him a moment with her large brown eyes. "Will they come back?"

"Yes, I promise," he said. It was then that he noticed that the room had grown brighter. He looked and saw that the curtains were still closed. He looked back at her and finally saw that the new light was shining from her. She was generating it. His mouth dropped open.

"You better not be lying," she said, frowning.

"I'm not," he said, noticing that the light was growing brighter. "Kieren, are you angry?"

Suddenly the light stopped abruptly. "No, I just miss them," she said. She began to cry, and he stood and walked around the tea set to sit next to her. She leaned over and put her head on his shoulder. It was one advantage of them being almost the same height.

"It will be alright," he said. "You'll see."

"You smell funny," she said, "but you're soft."

"Thanks," he said, wrapping her in a hug and closing his eyes.

◊

Josiah Manidoo had seen and experienced a great deal in his time, both in the military, and as a Senator. None of it had prepared him for what was happening in his house at the moment. His daughter was missing, and his son-in-law had sent an alien to protect his granddaughter. At least the alien could speak English, though he still had to learn the language better to be considered fluent.

Josiah wasn't one to drink before noon, but today he felt like he needed a little something extra, so he sat in his comfortable armchair and sipped whiskey while watching the news. They were really muddling things up in the senate without him, he determined. The damn socialists were always trying to spend other people's money. He found himself talking to the television and stopped himself when he realized he may as well be yelling at clouds.

Just then, the doorbell rang, and he turned off the television with a noise of disgust. He put down his whiskey glass and looked in the mirror in the hallway that led to the front door. At least he had combed his hair that morning. Retirement was remembering to perform the menial tasks each day, even if they didn't seem important anymore.

He looked through the spyhole and saw a younger man with sandy brown hair and slightly lighter facial hair. Is this someone I know? He thought. He took another look and decided that no, the man was a stranger. He locked the chain at the top of the door before opening it.

"Can I help you? There's no soliciting here," he said.

"Mr. Manidoo?" the man asked.

"Yes," Josiah said. He heard alarms going off in the back of his mind. The man was not some random person selling vacuums.

"This is going to sound a little strange," the man continued. "My name is Dennis. My sister and your daughter were friends."

"Yes? And your point is?" Josiah asked. It didn't sound that strange.

"They were friends after, um, being taken," the man said, looking around. "I think you know what I mean."

Josiah did. That didn't mean he was going to just open the door. "My daughter isn't here at the moment," he said.

"I know," Dennis said. "We believe that she was taken again. So was another man that she knows. From the first time. We're trying to find her."

"Do you have a mouse in your pocket?" Josiah asked. "Who is we?"

"I was brought here with a few of her other friends," Dennis said. "They're...uh...not from around here." He pointed straight up, smiling hesitantly.

Josiah sighed. More damn aliens, he guessed. He closed the door and thought about not opening it again but then relented and unlocked the chain and opened the door. He stood back and allowed the other man to step inside. "So where are they, these other friends?"

"On their ship," Dennis replied. "It's parked out in your pasture."

Josiah was surprised at this. All of the science fiction movies he'd ever watched had damn near busted his eardrums with the noise the ships created. "Do you know what happened to my daughter?"

"We think we do," Dennis said. "Is James Dempsey here?"

"No, James isn't here, either," Josiah answered. "And Kieren is beginning to get worried."

"What did you say?" Dennis asked, suddenly wide-eyed.

"My granddaughter is getting worried about her parents," Josiah said. "What's wrong?"

"My...my sister was named Kieren."

"Ah, yes that makes sense now," Josiah said. "She was named after your sister. I believe she and Yvette and James were quite close before...you do know that your sister is dead, right?"

Dennis nodded, though his eyes began to fill with tears. "Yes, I had long suspected, and then my new...uh...companions, told me what happened. This just confirms it." He wiped at his eyes. "I'm sorry."

"No, grief is real," Josiah said. "No use trying to stop it. It needs to run its course." Josiah thought briefly about his wife, then shook it off. Now wasn't the time. "So, Belani is with Kieren now. I suppose you know him as well?"

"Belani?" Dennis asked. "No."

Josiah rolled his eyes. "Shit. Too many damn aliens around here." He closed the front door.

Dennis looked confused.

"Come on, then," Josiah said. He turned and walked to the stairway. "Follow me."

◊

Belani was beginning to feel hungry and was sure that Kieren would need to be fed soon as well. There was only so much imaginary tea and crumpets he could ingest without beginning to feel hungry for real. He wasn't even sure what a crumpet was, but Kieren explained that it was something you ate with tea, so he ate it, whatever it was. He was about to suggest that they go downstairs to see what was in the kitchen, when there was a knock on the door. He instinctively gripped the handle of his gun. "Yes?"

"It's Josiah. I'm coming in."

Belani relaxed a little but still kept his hand on the gun. The door opened and Josiah entered, followed by another man who Belani had never seen. The man looked at him and didn't seem surprised to see him. Which meant that he had probably seen a Sekani before.

Interesting. He felt a certain sense of security holding the gun, but wouldn't take it for granted.

"This is Dennis," Josiah was saying. "A brother of a friend of my daughter."

Belani nodded, understanding that he meant Kieren's brother. He hadn't wanted to mention her name in front of this Kieren. Belani stood and put down the toy plate and cup that was in his lap. He nodded to the other Human. "Pleased to meet you," he said.

"Do you want to come to my tea party, grandpa?" Kieren

asked. "How about you, Mister?"

"No, darling," Josiah said. "How about you come with me, and we can make a grilled cheese for lunch?"

"Yay!" Kieren said, hopping up. She walked over and grabbed her grandfather's hand. "Bye, Belani."

"Goodbye," Belani said. "Enjoy your lunch."

Josiah closed the door behind him, and then Belani pulled out his pistol and pointed it casually at Dennis. "You can understand why I'm being cautious."

"Yes," Dennis said, holding his hands up. "My sister was named Kieren. She and Yvette were friends after they were taken to another planet."

"Your sister was Kieren?" Belani asked, though this confirmed his first assumption.

"Yes, did you know her?"

"Of course," Belani said, putting his gun back in its holster. "I am very sorry for your loss. She was a very nice Human."

"Thank you," Dennis said. "By the way, I came here with some others that you probably know. Bhakat, Janan, and Amera."

"I know Bhakat and Janan. Amera doesn't sound familiar."

"Oh," Dennis said. "Once it gets dark, they will be coming in from their ship."

"Where is it now?"

"Out in the pasture," Dennis said.

"Good," Belani said. "My ship is hidden out there as well."

"You have a ship?"

"Well, it's a lander," Belani admitted. "It belongs on the *Bright Journey*, but James sent me down here to watch over his daughter."

"James," Dennis said. "You know, before yesterday, I

didn't know anything that was going on. I only knew that my sister was missing. This is all a lot to take in."

"I understand," Belani said. "The best I can offer is the knowledge that your sister died for a greater cause. She helped save Rajan."

"Thank you," Dennis said.

"Now, how about we go down and get some food. I'm starving."

Dennis smiled. "Sounds good to me."

◊

Bhakat felt that it was now dark enough to travel from the ship to the residence of Yvette's father. The open ground between the ship and the buildings had made him nervous, and so he had sent the Human named Dennis ahead of them to speak with Yvette's father. As they left the ship, Bhakat took a deep breath, taking in the various smells from the ranch. From the looks of things, it wasn't a working ranch, in that it had no garden or animals, but it still smelled good and clean.

Dennis had come back to the ship and explained to them that Belani was inside the house watching over James and Yvette's daughter, which had been a surprise. After explaining the circumstances of James' mission with the collection of mercenaries, though, it made sense that James wouldn't have wanted his daughter left unprotected.

They reached the main building and Dennis knocked softly on the door, which immediately opened. The older Human looked out and saw Dennis and then looked past him to see Bhakat. His eyes widened in surprise, but he backed up to let everyone in.

"You didn't tell me that there were other types of aliens," the older Human said to Dennis.

"I am a Rajani," Bhakat said. "My name is Bhakat. My

companions are Janan," he pointed to the Sekani, "and Amera," he then pointed at the Talondarian. "Thank you for welcoming us into your home."

"I thought Belani was a Rajani," Josiah said suspiciously.

"It's a long story," Bhakat said.

"I'm Josiah," the Human said. "I didn't have much of a choice in the matter of welcoming you here, but seeing as you are here, you can come in."

"Where's Belani?" Janan asked.

"Upstairs putting my granddaughter to bed," Josiah said. "He's taken a keen interest in some of the more mundane parts of his job," Josiah said. "And for some reason, Kieren loves him."

"We're all pretty loveable," Janan said, smiling.

Josiah gave him a somewhat stern look, and Janan stopped smiling.

"Is there a place where we can meet with Belani and speak without waking the child?" Bhakat said.

"Basement," Josiah said. "Follow me."

He led them to a doorway and opened it. They all followed him down to a lower floor, which was only partially finished but had a large, flat monitor on the wall and a few comfortable-looking chairs.

"This is eventually going to be my office," Josiah said. "But for now, it's Kieren's playroom during the summer months." He pointed to a pile of toys that filled one corner of the room. "You can sit down here and wait for Belani."

"Will you stay?" Bhakat asked. "This concerns your daughter and her mate as well."

"Her mate, huh?" Josiah said. "Yes, I guess he counts as that." He walked over to a brown rectangular object that had a cord running to the wall, which Bhakat assumed meant it was connected to a power source. He pulled open the front of the object, and Bhakat saw that it was a type of storage device with a light inside. Josiah pulled out a cylindrical object from inside and then closed the front again. He walked over and sat in one of the chairs and then opened the top of the object, and Bhakat finally realized that it was some form of drink.

"I try to stay away from the harder stuff now," Josiah said. "But you're all welcome to help yourselves to a drink." He took a long gulp from the cylinder.

Bhakat looked down at Janan, who was watching the Human drink. "Janan."

"I wasn't going to," Janan said. "Though I wouldn't mind trying a fermented beverage. I believe this is called beer."

"Thank you for your offer, but we're fine," Bhakat said. He realized that Amera hadn't said a thing since they arrived at the house. He looked over and saw that she was inspecting the large monitor.

"Is this how you communicate with others?" she asked in Talondarian Standard.

"She doesn't speak Earth language," Bhakat said. "She wants to know if that is a communication device. If you speak to her, she will understand you."

"That's a television," Josiah said. "It picks up transmissions from broadcasting stations on the planet. Stations. Think of it as a one-way communication device."

Dennis spoke up. "For two-way, we use this," he reached into his pocket and pulled out a small, flat device. "It's called a cell phone. With this we can talk to anyone and find out just about anything via the Internet."

"The Internet," Janan said, "is the first place I searched to learn more about your planet and civilization when we first came here."

"You've only learned our language recently?" Josiah asked.

"No, I mean the first time we came here, a few Standard years ago," Janan replied. "When we first...contacted your daughter and the others." He smiled sheepishly.

"You mean when you first kidnapped them," Josiah said. He took another drink from his cylindrical object.

"We made mistakes," Bhakat said. "If we could have done things differently, we would have. At the time it was felt there was no other choice. My master, Rauphangelaa, made a decision and eventually, it turned out to be the correct one. Our planet was saved with the help of the Humans that we brought back with us. For that, I am grateful."

"But not all of them survived," Josiah said. "You placed them in a great deal of danger."

"Yes," Bhakat said. "I am...happy to know that they have named their daughter after Kieren. I was Yvette's doctor on Rajan when she first discovered that she was pregnant."

"You're a doctor?"

Bhakat nodded. "I was."

"Well, you all may as well sit down while we're waiting," Josiah said. "Sometimes she makes him read her two or three books before bed."

"Thank you," Janan said. He sat on a long piece of furniture and was almost engulfed in the cushions and various pillows upon it.

Bhakat sat as well, lightly at first to make sure it would bear his weight but found that it was well-made and had no problem supporting him.

"Now," Josiah said. "Tell me about Rajan. What form of government do you have? I just recently retired from being a senator for the United States, which is the country we're in now. I'd be interested in learning more about your civilization."

"Civilizations," Amera said without looking at them.

"Tell him that I am not from Rajan."

"She wanted to remind me to tell you that she is not Rajani," Bhakat said when Josiah looked expectantly at him. "She is from a planet called Talondaria. The Talondarians have been the rulers of the Galactic Alliance for a very long time."

"So, it's not just Rajan? There are other planets?"

"More than you can imagine," Janan said.

"And they all belong to this Galactic Alliance?" Dennis asked.

"Our part of the galaxy does," Bhakat said. "Technically your planet of Earth is outside the boundaries."

"That's good to know," Josiah said dryly.

"Also, your planet should not have been contacted for a long time," Janan said. "Your technology is still not up to GA standards for inclusion yet. They prefer civilizations that have come by interstellar travel by their own means. Usually, it's a sign that you've matured enough as a civilization to enter a wider plane of knowledge."

"Fascinating," Dennis said.

Josiah looked at a device that was strapped to his arm. Bhakat was sure that it was some type of time monitoring machine. "Belani should be down here soon," he said.

"I'll go check on him," Dennis said. "If that's okay with you, Mr. Manidoo."

"By all means," Josiah said, rubbing his eyes. "Upstairs to the right. Hey, Amera," he said, "can you bring me another beer?"

She looked at Bhakat and smiled. "Sure, as long as I can have one, too."

◊

Dennis walked up the stairs of the house from the basement and stood a moment at the top after closing the door. It was still wild to think that he was in a house with now four aliens. He could almost feel a panic attack coming on but took a few deep breaths and the sensation went away. He hadn't had a full-blown attack in a few years but knew there was always the possibility of one happening. Especially in the situation he found himself in now.

He walked up the stairs to the second floor where Kieren's room was located. That's when he noticed that the door was open and the light on inside. He walked to the door and looked in and saw Belani standing over her bed with a book in his hands. He looked over at Dennis and nodded.

"Goodnight, Belani," she said sleepily.

"Goodnight, Kieren," he responded. She turned over and seemed to instantly fall asleep.

Belani turned and walked to the door and turned off the light. He closed the door partway.

"We were beginning to worry," Dennis said.

"I had to read two books about a cat with a hat and strange devices that came from nowhere. It was very surreal," Belani said.

Dennis chuckled. "Dr. Seuss is an acquired taste, I guess. Listen, can I go in and look at her for a moment?"

"She's asleep now," Belani said defensively, as if waking her would doom him to reading more.

"I won't wake her, it's just...she's my sister's namesake...."

"I understand," Belani said. "I will go downstairs and speak to the rest."

Dennis nodded. He watched the diminutive alien walk down the stairs for a moment and then entered Kieren's room slowly. In the darkness, he thought that maybe she had a glowworm or maybe a nightlight in her bed, but when he looked closer, he saw that it was her glowing for a moment, before the dim light faded and it was just a little girl in her small princess bed. Dennis thought his eyes were playing tricks on him but wasn't sure what he had seen.

He shrugged it off and looked down on his sister's namesake. She was a beautiful girl, and she seemed happy, which made him happy, in a bittersweet way. "Goodnight, Kieren," he said. He felt his eyes getting moist and turned away, not noticing that she was glowing once again as she dreamed.

Chapter 14

Millen Tordor was awakened by a guard rapping loudly on his chamber doors. He hadn't meant to fall asleep, but his chance to rest had been at a premium for a while. He sat up in his chair and called out, "what is it?"

"Sire, you're needed in the control center," the guard said through the door. "It's a matter of some importance."

"Fine, I'll be there soon."

"Thank you, sire."

It had better be a matter of great importance, he thought. He felt like he'd only just closed his eyes, but he checked the time and saw that he'd slept for almost a Standard hour. He looked in a mirror and made sure his appearance was acceptable, then made his way to the logistics room. When he arrived, he noticed a buzz of activity. He walked to the nearest technician.

"What's happened?" The technician turned to him and his eyes grew wide. Must be new, the king thought. "Well?"

"Sire, it's your son, Creon," the technician said.

"I know my son's name," Millen said, angrily. What had the boy done now?

"Yes, sire," the technician said. "Your son's ship has been hijacked by persons unknown at this time."

"What? How can that be? Where's security?"

Just then another person walked to where the king stood. Millen turned to him, expectant.

"Sire, we received a transmission from your son's ship stating that they want safe passage off the planet or else they would harm the prince."

"Do you have a recording of the transmission?" Millen asked. How would he explain this to the boy's mother, he wondered. If the boy was hurt, she'd never speak to him again. Not that it was a bad thing...

"Sire," the security officer said to him, breaking into his thoughts. "If you'll follow me."

Millen nodded. The officer turned and Millen followed him to another room. The officer closed the door and sat at a monitor and began to type in a pass code. Then audio of the message began to play.

"Is it on? It is? Fine. Millen Tordor, we have your son, Creon."

I know my son's name! he thought angrily. I only have one!

"We require safe passage off the planet and no pursuit once we our away from here. If you don't comply within eight Standard hours, we will detonate this ship with the prince aboard, and your lineage will die here. We await your answer."

"Who is we?" Millen said out loud.

"Unknown, sire," the security officer replied, not knowing that Millen had almost forgotten he was present. He looked over and nodded at him. Then an idea occurred to him. His son had just released a prisoner into his custody. Ries something. It had to be him that had taken over the ship.

"I want a direct communication channel set up with my son's ship," he said to the officer. "Now."

"Yes, sire," the officer said. "One moment."

Millen waited impatiently as the officer typed something into his control board.

"Sir, I've opened the channel. Do you want me to stay?"

"That's fine," Millen said. "If word of this gets past these walls, you'll regret it."

The officer gulped and nodded.

Millen picked up the microphone that the security officer pointed to. "This is Millen Tordor to the occupants of my son's ship. Can you hear me?" He waited a moment, but there was no answer. "This is King Tordor. Do you copy?"

Another moment, then a voice responded. "King Tordor, this is Agent A. Can you hear me?"

"Yes."

"Good. We have your son."

"You've already made that clear. Do you have any proof of this?" There was another moment of silence, and then Creon's voice came over the channel.

"Father, I'm sorry," he said.

"It's fine, son," Millen said. "You made a mistake, but we'll fix it."

"You'll fix it by letting this ship leave," the other's voice broke in. "Now."

"And if I say no?"

"Then you'll be picking up pieces of your son all over the city."

"Father, please, I'm afraid..."

"Quiet!"

Millen heard a loud thump. "Creon? Creon?"

"Creon can't answer right now, he's taking a little rest."

"If you hurt him more, you will never be able to relax again for the rest of your short, miserable life," Millen barked into the microphone. "Do you hear me?"

"Spare me your threats, oh king," the voice answered. "Now, send the security code for us to leave. Once we've escaped, I will drop your son off at the nearest station. Unharmed. Unless you pull anything like following us or notifying anyone that we may be coming. We had better not see an ASP ship within a thousand miles of us."

"No, I won't. I won't do that," Millen said, but he looked at the security officer and shook his head, showing that he very much would be trying something to save his only son. "By the way, I know who you are," he said. "I recognize your voice. Five Standard years ago, right? You've kidnapped my son before."

There was silence on the other end for a moment. "That was an unfortunate misunderstanding. This won't be. Do as I say or he dies."

"Fine," Millen said. He nodded to the security officer. "Send it."

The security officer nodded back and then began typing into his communications pad. He finished and then looked at Millen and nodded again. "Security code sent."

"The code has been sent," Millen said into the microphone. "If you harm my son in any way..."

"Don't have us followed," the voice said.

"Fine, you've made yourself clear," Millen said. "Is that all?"

There was no answer, and he looked over at the security officer. "He's cut the channel," the officer said.

Millen put down the microphone. He needed to talk to his senior advisors about this. There hadn't been time to contact them before he arrived, and now he regretted not doing it. He hadn't been prepared for the severity of what was happening. One thing he knew was that he couldn't have news of this spreading. Especially news that he had caved in his negotiations. It would unleash a variety of copycat crimes if they knew he'd been soft on the person who kidnapped his son not once, but twice.

He thought for a moment and then turned to look at the security officer. "Sorry about this," he said as he pulled out his small personal beam pistol and shot the officer in the face. The body slumped to the floor of the room as he placed the pistol back in its holster beneath his vest. What a waste, he thought as he left the room. He'd send someone to clean up the mess later.

◊

Ries ended the transmission with the planet's surface, having sent the security code to the large Talondarian battleship that was circling above their position. He turned to look at Creon and saw that the prince was smiling.

"Jerboxh, take us out on the straightest course."

The Sh'kallion pilot nodded and began punching in coordinates on his control panel, then grabbed the steering yoke with both hands and began maneuvering past the ships as they broke up. There had been a number of ships gathered around them as they'd held their tense conversation with the king of Talondaria, but they began departing, as Ries had hoped they would.

"By the way," Creon said. "Nice work on your conversation with my father. I thought the assault on my person was the high point."

Ries nodded his acknowledgement. "My mother always told me I would do well as an actor." Or as a main dish, he added mentally.

"Now I just hope the coordinates I got are the correct ones for the planet," Creon said. He had paid a lot of his own money to get them from a contact within planetary security. "First, though, we need to stop and replenish supplies and fuel for the *Sun Dancer*. I assume we shouldn't go to Mandaka?" he asked mischievously.

"That would be a mistake, I agree," Ries answered, not rising to the bait. "I suggest getting away from the Talondarian sphere of influence. We shouldn't stop anywhere that is too close to the planet."

"I agree," Creon said.

"Leaving Talondarian atmosphere," Jerboxh said. "Setting artificial gravity levels." He flipped a few switches and Ries felt the change in gravity, though small, throughout his thorax. "Heading?"

"Anywhere that is not a straight course for our final destination," Creon said.

Ries wasn't sure he liked the term 'final destination,' but let it slide. It very well may be, he thought, but he didn't want to dwell on that. For now, he was free. "And I would avoid any large space port, let alone Mandaka," he added, looking at Creon. "Too many entanglements if we were to run into ASPs or local planet security."

"Agreed," Creon said, smiling.

"I know just the place," Jerboxh said.

◊

Millen had played the conversation he wanted to have over and over again in his mind. His scowl as he walked down the hallway should have been enough to tell underlings that his thoughts were not to be disturbed as he headed to his quarters to speak with the boy's mother, his wife. Priss was from an aristocratic family that was held in high regard by the people of Talondaria. Her father was a wealthy businessman who controlled many of the trade routes to and from the planet. She had been picked to be his wife for that very reason.

But she had a sharp tongue and wasn't afraid who she

lashed it with, and this included her sovereign king. And now he had to tell her that her son had been kidnapped yet again, and by the same person, no less. It was not a conversation that he looked forward to, but it had to happen. If she learned of her son's status from another source, it would be that much the worse for Millen.

Better to get it over with so he could continue with his other duties. He had to finish planning an invasion.

◊

"Slow us down," Creon said from his captain's chair on the bridge. Jerboxh nodded and brought the throttle back. They had come out of n-space a few minutes before and found themselves approaching an asteroid field at the outer edge of a small solar system.

"The colony is located on that big asteroid there," Jerboxh said, pointing to it on the screen before them.

"And how do you know about this place?" Ries asked. He was standing near the door, having just come onto the bridge. There was only the captain's chair and pilot chair on the bridge, which meant he'd had to secure himself for the trip in his room.

"You think piloting for you was my first job with the ASPs?" Jerboxh answered without looking back at him. "I've been to places that not even ASP leadership knows about."

"So, these are mostly miners?" Creon said, hoping to avoid the usual arguments between the other two members of his crew, as he thought of them.

Jerboxh swiveled in his chair to look at the prince. "Yes. There are certain elements found in these asteroids that are important to various industries in the Alliance. Many of them are for technologies for space travel or communications. The inhabitants of the colony are long-term contractors. They've been out here for years, some even having children who now work as miners as well."

"Gee, thanks mom and dad," Ries said, stepping forward to get a better look at the large asteroid before them. Jerboxh shrugged and then turned back to the screen.

"We can't pick who our parents are," Creon said softly.

"You got that right," Ries said. "Have I ever told you about my father?"

"Later," Creon said. "Jerboxh, contact the colony and ask for permission to land. I assume there is a place to land on that rock?"

"Yes, sending request now," Jerboxh said. "By the way, there is something I should tell you."

Ries felt his antennae quiver. "Do I even want to know?"

"The miners are Asnurian," Jerboxh said, laughing.

"Oh," Creon said, surprised.

Ries just covered his eyes with his top hands. Maybe I can just stay on the ship, he thought, ruefully.

◊

Millen arrived back at his private chambers to find his wife waiting for him, a scowl on her face. She knew.

"I need to explain..." he began before she landed a slap to his left cheek. It stung, but not as much as the look of disappointment in her eyes.

"Again!" she said. "Again!"

"Our son is not a child," he replied, on the lookout now for another blow, but she seemed to have only hit him to get his attention. She had it.

"He's still our son," she said. "Still our duty to protect him. You know this, Millen!"

"I know. We're doing everything we can to find him."

"Then why are you here and not helping in the search?"

He sighed. "I came to tell you. I wanted you to find out from me. Obviously, I was too late."

"Alder told me," she said. "He holds that boy dear, as you know."

"Yes, I know that." He would deal with his bodyguard later for the breach, he decided.

"So, what do we know so far?"

"It was the prisoner, Creon, and his pilot aboard the ship. I told him not to go near that vile convict, but he didn't listen."

"Blaming him for getting himself kidnapped again?"

"No, that's not what I meant," he answered defensively. "I only meant that it was just the three of them. They should be easy to find and overtaken. And remember, Creon has outsmarted this bug before, and he can do it again, I'm sure."

"Of course he can," she said, appearing slightly mollified. "He's our son."

"I will keep you updated on our progress, Priss. I promise. But for now, we just need to trust that our people can handle the search and rescue. I've got other pressing matters that need my attention right now."

It was the wrong thing to say, and he knew it as soon as he said it. He saw her eyes open wider and the flames that danced in them now. "We'll talk more of this later," he said, turning to leave her with her rage. He closed the door and heard something heavy hit it from the other side. He was proud of himself for not wincing in response. He settled himself then headed for the control room. The ships were preparing to launch.

◊

As the ship settled onto the landing pad, Ries looked on the ship's monitor as a small group of miners appeared on the surface of the asteroid. The asteroid was too small to have an airlock docking bay on the surface that would connect to the ship and provide safe passage for the occupants, which meant they would have to wear space suits while they walked to the airlock doors. The gravity registered just safe enough that they wouldn't instantly float off into space. Ries could see several miners along the path, which was equipped with safety cables with handholds.

He left the bridge and went to the ship's bay to find that Creon and Jerboxh were already dressed in their suits, patiently awaiting instructions from the miners. "I suppose you really want me to come with you?" he asked no one in particular.

"Like we would trust you..." Jerboxh began.

"Their instructions were clear," Creon said, smiling. "They want to see all inhabitants of the ship. It's not about us trusting you so much as them not trusting all of us."

Ries looked at him for a moment, then nodded. He began to get dressed. At least he wouldn't smell the Asnurians while he was in his suit. "Are these miners to be trusted by us?" he asked Jerboxh. "How do we know they won't turn us in to the king as soon as we leave the ship?"

"They're not exactly...legal," Jerboxh said.

"What do you mean by that?" Creon said.

"They operate outside of GA control," the Sh'kallion said, smiling.

"So, it's an unlicensed, possibly illegal operation that you've brought us to?" Ries said, securing his helmet in place.

"Yes."

"Perfect!" Creon said, still smiling. "That means it's outside of my father's sphere of influence."

"Yes, great," Ries said. "They could kill us and steal the ship without your father ever knowing how to find us."

"You're far too pessimistic. Has anyone ever told you that?" Creon asked.

"Pragmatic," Ries replied. "The word is pragmatic."

"Either way, there's no turning back now," Creon said.

Interlude

Alder Benen sat at the console in his quarters and ended his communication with the GSA. Although not an agent, he was paid well to inform them of what was happening within the halls of Talondarian court. He didn't see this as a breach of trust with the king. The GSA was controlled by King Tordor's forces, so in effect, he was still working for the benefit of the king. Better not to let the king know of it, though, He was prone to fits of anger and the object of that anger usually didn't live very long.

Besides, the report he had just given was concerned with only one subject: finding and rescuing the crown prince of Talondaria. Agents would be alerted all over the galaxy to look for the *Sun Dancer* and then report its coordinates. They were told not to engage for the safety of the prince, but Alder needed to know where they were and where they were heading. Although he was the personal bodyguard of the king, he felt that protection extended to all members of the royal family.

He took the prince's kidnapping as a personal affront, and knew if he felt that way, that the king would no doubt be thinking it as well, and if he needed a scapegoat, then Alder would be it. He would have to tread lightly around the king until he was able to bring the prince back, healthy and whole.

Chapter 15

Yvette was sitting outside of a building watching various Rajani and Sekani walk by. The last time she was on Rajan, she hadn't made many friends among them, preferring to stay independent or to stay with Bhakat or James. It was not surprising that she didn't recognize anyone. She was surprised when a Rajani walked up to her and sat next to her.

"My name is Seliban," he said. "I was told to extend an invitation to dinner with Welemaan."

"Tonight?" she asked.

"Yes," he said. "He wishes to speak with you more about our plans for the future."

"Is that what you call going to war?"

Seliban thought a moment. "The Krahn must pay for what they have done," he said simply.

"The Krahn did not attack you," she said. "That was the Krahn Horde, led by Ronak. And you defeated them."

"No matter," he said, standing. "The Krahn are guilty by their inaction. They let Ronak free to do this and are just as guilty."

"These actions will do nothing except cause more needless bloodshed," Yvette said.

Seliban looked down at her a moment, thinking. "Shall I

tell him you'll attend?"

"Sure," Yvette said.

Seliban nodded and turned away. Yvette watched him walk away, not knowing if she'd made even a dent in his mind. Finally, she shook her head and stood up. It was time to speak with the Elders, or at least what was left of them.

It was a relatively short walk to where she'd been shown the Elders were headquartered. The building, like most of the others, was a new structure and unadorned. She wondered how anyone knew where to go without some type of number or letter designation on the buildings.

She entered and immediately was confronted by a young Rajani. "Andraal has been waiting for you," he said. "My name is Ternan."

"Were you just standing in here waiting for me?" she asked him.

"Andraal posted me here when he saw you earlier today. He was too busy to stop and say hello, unfortunately."

She remembered the name. Andraal had been a doctor when she was there last.

"If you will follow me," he said. She nodded.

The young Rajani led her to a set of stairs. At the top was a short hallway with three doors, with the young Rajani leading her to the one at the end of the hall. He opened the door and held it open, motioning for her to go through.

Yvette walked through, nodded to the young Rajani, then looked and saw a sparsely furnished office with an older Rajani sitting behind a large desk in an overstuffed chair. He looked up and saw her.

"Yvette," he said, standing up. He smiled. "It's good to see you again. I wish it was under better circumstances."

"You, too," she said. "How are you?"

He sighed and lost his smile. "I've been better. I'm a

doctor. I'm not cut out for leadership."

"You're the leader of the Elders now?"

He nodded. "Only while Tumaani is imprisoned. We've been working to get him free, but we're in no position to go against the Valderren, I'm afraid. Please, sit. Can I get you a drink? Water? Fernta?"

"No, thank you. What I really want is information."

"Whatever I can provide," he said, sitting down. She sat down across from him, feeling the chair engulf her body. It made her feel like a child again, sitting in her father's favorite recliner.

"Why was Tumaani imprisoned?"

"He spoke out against their plans to attack Krahn, primarily," Andraal said. "But I think it was mostly because he defied Welemaan's wishes to bring all of you here."

"He fought against it?"

"Yes, and I agree with him. You all went through enough fighting for us as you did. You may not know it, but Welemaan didn't want us to let you leave even back then, but he wasn't in as strong of a position as he is now. Tumaani and I argued that you had done enough and that you should be allowed to return home, unmolested."

"Thank you for that," Yvette said. "I wasn't in any position then, either."

"How is your child, by the way," Andraal asked, knowing what she referred to.

"She is wonderful," Yvette said, smiling. "She will be starting school on Earth soon."

"That's good news," he said. "I never had a chance to have a child of my own, unfortunately. Too busy with work, and then...it was too late."

"I'm truly sorry," Yvette said, leaning forward. "Sorry for all of this."

He nodded. "Maybe I can try to get you access to Tumaani."

"That would be great," she said.

"Perhaps you can put in a good word for him as well," Andraal said. "Welemaan might listen to you. Tumaani needs to be freed. He's not in good shape. Age and conditions in the prison have taken their toll."

"I'll do what I can, I promise," she said. "Was there anything else you need to tell me?"

He thought for a moment before answering. "No, except for you to know that we are still opposed to this war, and the Elders will not participate in it."

She stood up and he followed suit. "Thank you, Andraal."

He nodded. "May we all see better times."

"Yes," she said. She had a feeling that things were going to get worse before they got better.

◊

Gianni was walking down a street, wondering how he was supposed to find Yvette again, when he was approached by a Rajani. He wasn't in a great mood, and the big Rajani didn't look particularly friendly, so he decided to suit up just to mess with him. He felt the painful pulse run from his head to his toes a moment later and was reminded that he had a restraining device on his head. "Dammit!" he said as he bent over from the pain.

The Rajani stopped walking for a second as Gianni stood up slowly. Then he walked a few more paces until he was close enough to speak in quiet tones. "I'm sorry if I startled you. My name is Seliban."

"Hello Seliban," Gianni said. "What can I do for you?" His head felt like he'd licked a light socket.

"I was sent to invite you to Welemaan's residence for dinner. Your companion is already there."

"Yvette?"

"Yes," Seliban nodded.

"Lead the way," Gianni said. *Feeling jumpy, G?* he thought. *But his instincts were telling him that there was danger here, he wasn't going to be caught unaware.*

Suddenly there was a flash of light around him, and he felt something hit him hard in the chest. He went flying, bouncing down the street and coming to rest next to a waste receptacle. "What the hell?" he said quietly. He felt like he'd been hit by a truck. He looked around, then it occurred to him: David.

He stood up, feeling the new sore spots on elbows and knees and knowing that he was probably bleeding from various scrapes. "Come on, man," he said. "Don't be a coward. Show yourself."

There was a streak of blue light, and he had just enough time to hold his arms up defensively next to his head when he was hit hard in the back and knocked into the trash can, knocking it over and sprawling on the pavement. "Son of a..." he said. He felt like the world was spinning for a moment.

Suddenly David was standing over him, looking down. "Hello, Gianni."

"Nice to see you, too," Gianni said.

"This somehow feels familiar," David said, smiling. "Kieren's not here to save you this time."

"Keep her name out of your mouth or I'll kill you," Gianni said.

"Says the man with a restraining device on his head," David said, laughing.

"David, what are you doing?" Seliban shouted. "He's a guest of Welemaan."

"Shut your pie hole," David said, not turning to look at the Rajani. "This doesn't concern you at all."

"Big man, attacking me when I can't use my powers," Gianni said.

"I never claimed to be a Boy Scout," David said.

"No, you're a freaking serial killer," Gianni said. He sat up slowly. "What the hell do you want with me?"

"You're actually secondary in my considerations," David said. "But I saw a chance here, so here we are."

"She'll kill you, you know," Gianni said.

"She can try."

"David," Seliban said. "Welemaan says to leave the Human alone and allow him to come with me."

David looked back at the Rajani. "Fine. Welemaan can have his little pet here." He turned back to look at Gianni. "You tell her that I'm coming for her. She won't know where or when, but I'm coming. I guarantee it."

"Okay, Men's Wearhouse, I'll tell her," Gianni said, slowly standing up. "How about you piss off now."

David frowned, then he was gone in another flash of blue light.

"Asshole," Gianni said. He bent and looked at his knees. There were holes in both, and he could see blood from the scrapes. "Well, that's just great."

◊

Welemaan was sitting in his living room when the door opened, and Yvette stepped through the doorway. He stood and smiled at her. "Welcome," he said.

"Nice house," she said.

"Thank you," he said. "Would you like a drink?"

"Water would be great," she said. He nodded and went towards his kitchen.

"Follow me," he said, noting the irony of his words. Would she follow him? He opened a cupboard and took out a cup and then walked to the refrigeration unit and pulled out a bottle of water. He turned and handed it to her.

"Interesting kitchen design," she said, pouring water into her cup and taking a sip. He couldn't help but notice the slight frown as she tasted the water.

"It suits my needs," he said, shrugging.

"Anyone else coming for dinner?" she asked, looking around. No doubt she noticed that nothing was cooking or being prepared in the kitchen.

"Seliban should be here with Gianni shortly. And the food should arrive soon as well."

"Pizza delivery?" she asked.

"I don't know what that means," he admitted.

"Forget it," she said.

"Did you enjoy becoming reacquainted with my planet?" he asked.

"Your planet?" she asked him. She wasn't smiling.

"My home planet," he said, clarifying his words. She was too smart for her own good.

"I commend you on your people's ability to rebuild," she said. She sat down on a stool and took another sip of water before placing it on the counter.

"Thank you," he said.

"I also wonder why you would take the time to rebuild everything if you were only going to leave."

"We still need to live," he said. "Still need to have shelter and protection. There are still wild animals that sometimes enter the city."

"I see that the old prison is still there," she said.

"Yes, a reminder of older days."

"And a place to keep political enemies?"

He stopped for a moment, carefully selecting his words. "When those political opponents seek to cause civil unrest, sometimes there's nothing that can be done other than to secure them to avoid violence."

"I see," Yvette said. "So, it's not about silencing others who don't share the same way of thinking as you?"

"No, of course not," he said. "Tumaani was warned about his disruptive rhetoric on more than one occasion. He would have begun a civil war among the Rajani if he could."

"You're sure about that? And I never mentioned Tumaani by name."

"There is no doubt in my mind that he and his followers would have gone to any length to stop our progress."

Just then, the door opened and Seliban entered while assisting the Human Gianni to walk."

"What happened?" Yvette asked, standing abruptly and almost spilling her water. "Are you okay?"

"I'm fine," Gianni said, taking a few steps and sitting down on a stool. "Had a nice visit from David. Great reunion." Welemaan could see bruises forming on the Human's face.

"David?" Welemaan asked. "David did this?" He looked at Seliban, who nodded.

"What the hell?" Yvette said. She turned to look at Welemaan. "You need to arrest the man. You talk about civil unrest, well what would you call this?"

"I assure you that this won't happen again," Welemaan said. "We need to meet with David and see what brought on this attack."

"David was a killer on Earth and stayed one here," Yvette said. "It's a wonder he hasn't killed since the end of the war." She looked at him. "Or has he?"

Welemaan knew of David's proclivities but normally told his people to look the other way. He was too valuable an asset to be rotting in a jail cell. "David remains an important part of the war effort, as would the two of you be if you joined with us against the Krahn."

"Joined with you," Yvette said. "To go kill innocent beings on a faraway planet."

"That's not the way we see things," Seliban said from behind her.

"Yes, I know that, genius," Yvette said, turning to look at him. "I can see you're not smart enough to think for yourself."

"Can we all calm down and have a civil conversation about this?" Welemaan said. "Our food should arrive shortly, and we can enjoy a good meal together."

"I agree," Gianni said.

"What?" Yvette asked.

"Just calm down, Yvette, and we can listen to what Welemaan has to say," Gianni said.

"Thank you, Gianni," Welemaan said.

"We can all be reasonable," Gianni said, looking at her.

"You're unbelievable," she said to him. "Once a mobster, always a mobster, eh?"

"You mean a survivor," Gianni responded.

"Fine, you do what you want, G." She began walking towards the door. Welemaan looked at Seliban, who nodded. He stepped in front of the Human female.

"We're not finished with our discussion," Welemaan said.

"You may not be, but I am," Yvette said. Welemaan reached into the front pocket of his vest and felt the restraining device controller.

Suddenly, Yvette kicked out and struck Seliban on the side of his left knee. He fell, screaming and holding his knee with both hands. Yvette hadn't stopped her motion and was near the door by the time that Welemaan had pulled out the controller. He pushed the button to incapacitate her, but by then she was gone. He walked over and looked down at Seliban, who was still rolling around on the floor, grimacing in pain.

"He should have that looked at," Gianni said from his seat. "Looks like a nasty injury." He tut-tutted a moment. "By the way, where's the food?"

◊

Yvette ran as fast as she could from Welemaan's house, not knowing where she was headed, but sure that the only way to escape the restraining device's controller was to put distance between herself and it. The meeting hadn't gone exactly the way she had planned it, but she'd been ready to run if it came to it. She didn't know what kind of game Gianni was playing, but she trusted that he knew what he was doing. She'd done her best to set him up favorably with Welemaan, but it was up to him now.

She was surprised at how far she ran before finally feeling a stitch forming in her side and deciding to slow down and look for shelter. Bhakat had told her that the Stones would make their bodies return to their peak physical condition, but she had assumed that meant when they were using their powers. She had told James what she'd been informed by Bhakat that the Stones were actually symbiotic creatures that interacted with the host's body, but she didn't think Gianni or David knew they had a living organism inside them.

She finally saw a darkened alleyway and ducked into it. She let her breathing return to normal as she looked out for any signs of pursuit. After a while, she determined that there wasn't anyone after her, at least no one that she could see. She sat down and wondered what to do next. Then it hit her; she needed a safe place away from the city or she would be captured again. There was only one that she could think of, and that was with the Jirina. She stood and looked out to make sure no one was around. Once she had scanned the street both ways, she quickly left the alley and walked down the street and out of town.

She wasn't sure if she was heading in the right direction, she only knew that the Jirina were not in the city and the Rajani were. She knew if she kept heading this way, she would either find the Jirina or the ocean. That was good enough for now.

It was beginning to grow darker now, and with no lights, it was becoming difficult to see where she was going. It occurred to her that she was now alone in the middle of the wilderness without her powers on an alien planet. She tried to remember if there were any large predators on the planet as Welemaan had suggested, but the only one she could think of was the horrible sounding monster that had almost killed David and Janan in the desert. It was a pity it didn't, she thought. Yes, it would have been a pity that Janan was killed, but it would have taken care of the psychopath in their midst as well.

She remembered living in Detroit when all the news wanted to talk about was the Infinity Killer and there were warnings galore about not venturing out on your own because he was on the loose. To find out that the killer had travelled with them to Rajan had been quite a shock. She'd acted without thinking when she had stabbed him just before leaving Rajan the last time. If she'd been thinking more clearly, she would have gone for a far more vulnerable spot on his body. She wouldn't make the mistake again.

She stopped for a moment, and then the hair on her neck stood up when she heard something near her make a noise. It was almost completely dark now, and she couldn't see well. She stood still and closed her eyes to focus on hearing. There. Another noise, and now she was sure she wasn't alone. "Hello?" she called out softly in Talondarian Standard. One of the few words she remembered in that language.

She saw movement, and then as the figure approached, she could make out a small Jirina. "Hello," Yvette said in English. "I'm not going to hurt you," The figure stopped, then came closer, and she could finally see that it was a female Jirina.

"Hoo-man?" the female asked.

"Yes," Yvette responded, smiling. "Human. Can you show me where to find Mazal? Mazal?" she repeated just to make herself clear.

"Mazal?" the Jirina asked.

"Yes. Do you understand?"

The Jirina stepped closer, and Yvette guessed that she was young, though it was difficult for her to tell. She hadn't spent much time around the Jirina when she'd been on Rajan last. That had been James' job.

"Mazal is this way, if you will follow me," the Jirina said. Yvette was suddenly very thankful that James had talked her into getting the translator implant. She smiled at the Jirina reassuringly.

"Thank you," she said in Talondarian. The Jirina didn't smile back, but she did nod, then turned away and motioned for Yvette to follow.

◊

Gianni sat and pondered this new development. He hadn't foreseen Yvette assaulting Welemaan's right hand man and fleeing into the night. He knew she was strong-willed and respected her for that, but she hadn't even waited to hear Welemaan out on what he proposed for them. He, on the other hand, was hungry and looking forward to eating. Especially because this was all a formality. He had already made his choice.

While Welemaan helped Seliban up to a sitting position on a chair, Gianni thought over his confrontation with David.

The man was dangerous, and there was no way to defend against him without his powers. Therefore, the only way he was going to get his powers back was to play nice with Welemaan and get him to take off the restraining device. He'd tried to signal this to Yvette, but she either disagreed or didn't get the message. And now she was out on her own.

"We'll need to put out an alert on her," Welemaan was telling Seliban. The Rajani looked in pain still, but it didn't look like the leg would collapse under him. Yvette must have pulled her kick at the last moment. "She needs to be apprehended, for her own protection," Welemaan said, looking over at Gianni when he said this last part. Gianni nodded.

Just then, the door opened once again and a Sekani stood there. "Welemaan, your food is prepared. Where shall we place it?"

"The kitchen is fine," Welemaan said to him. He reached down and helped Seliban to his feet. The Sekani nodded and then left again to bring the food, which Gianni now assumed was being prepared at a close location.

Gianni almost laughed at the absurdity of the situation but stopped himself. As the Sekani and some others began bringing in food and placing it in the kitchen area, he watched as Welemaan spoke in hushed tones to Seliban. He had no doubt that they were talking about Yvette. She was probably now considered a fugitive. What would they do to her? Throw her in the prison? Mind-wipe her? Gianni didn't know, but he had a feeling they wouldn't catch her easily. At least he hoped that was the case.

"I'm happy to see that you are a practical Human," Welemaan said, walking over towards him.

"Like I told Yvette, I'm a survivor," Gianni said. "Shall we eat?"

"Yes, of course," Welemaan said. "Shall we sit in the dining room?"

Gianni nodded and then followed Welemaan and a limping Seliban to the formal dining room that held a large oval table. There were plates and silverware as well as bottles already on the table, and Gianni knew what they must be. Fernta. He wasn't sure if he could stomach it, but he also had no choice. To refuse it would be an affront to his hosts, not to mention that his body would begin to go into delirium tremors if he didn't drink at least a little alcohol soon. At this point, he had given into the knowledge that he was addicted. He'd worry about getting clean once he got back to Earth—if he got back.

He poured himself a glass of fernta as the Sekani from earlier and two others brought in covered platters full of food and placed them on the table. They uncovered the platters and Gianni's stomach gurgled as he smelled the meat, though he didn't know what it was. The Sekani served each of them and Gianni took a bite of what looked like some type of root. The taste exploded in his mouth, and he nodded his head appreciatively to Welemaan as he took a sip of fernta.

"I'm sorry that Yvette couldn't have stayed to listen to what I have to say," Welemaan said, taking a gulp of his own fernta.

"Yvette has always been...prickly," Gianni said. "Even when I first met her, she was a bit of a cold bitch."

"I grasp your meaning," Welemaan said. "Nothing we can do about that now. She'll be found soon enough."

"I'm sure," Gianni responded.

"What I propose to you, is that you help us in our fight against the Krahn. They must be eliminated to ensure they will no longer pose a danger to the inhabitants of Rajan."

"So, this is for your own protection?" Gianni asked.

"Of course," Welemaan said. "As their leader, it is my responsibility to keep Rajan safe."

"It has nothing to do with revenge?"

Welemaan stopped and looked at him a moment before taking another gulp of fernta. "I'm sure there is an element of revenge present in the hearts of some Rajani," he conceded. "I for one don't care what their motivations are, as long as they are willing to fight for the survival of Rajan."

Gianni nodded. "I can respect that," he said. "Sure, I'll help you, but under one condition."

Welemaan put his utensil down and looked at Gianni. "Yes?"

"Yvette is not to be harmed. She is to be taken back to Earth when this is all over and returned to her home. Is that acceptable?"

Welemaan smiled. He held out his glass to Gianni, and Gianni responded by doing the same. The glasses clinked, and Welemaan nodded. "Yes, the Human woman will not be harmed. You have my word. She is a hero of Rajan, after all. Once we return to Rajan, you both will be free to return to Earth."

Gianni nodded and then took a sizable gulp of his own fernta. It would have to do, for now. He lowered his eyes to his food, hoping not to show the uncertainty on his face. This was like a high-stakes game of poker, and he had a horrible poker face.

◊

Yvette followed the young Jirina as she was led further away from the city. It was dark now, but she had difficulties seeing the alien as they walked. She remembered now the last time she was on Rajan and how she'd been able to see even in the dead of night without any problem. She guessed that this just confirmed that she probably had another power from the Stones. It was a power she would have been happy to have as they made their way in the darkness. She worried that she would lose her guide in a matter of minutes, but the girl proceeded slowly enough that she was able to keep up relatively easily.

She followed for another few minutes and noted that there were no visible lights. She wondered if the Jirina could see in the dark as well. It certainly didn't seem to be affecting her guide. She didn't think that she would receive a satisfying answer if she tried to communicate with the girl, so she stayed quiet.

They finally came to a large structure and the Jirina looked back at Yvette before knocking quietly on the front door. The door was opened slightly, and the girl spoke quietly with someone inside before the door was closed once more. The girl turned back to Yvette.

"They are informing Mazal of your presence."

"Thank you," Yvette replied. She felt bad that they might have to wake up Mazal.

The door was opened wide, and a figure motioned for them to come. Yvette followed the girl and found herself in a sort of dimly lit waiting area. And then she found herself wrapped in an embrace as Mazal appeared from the gloom. She returned it with a smile.

"Yvette the Human," Mazal said excitedly as he released her and stepped back.

"Hello, Mazal," she said. "Thank you for seeing me on such short notice. I didn't know where else to go."

She saw his features grow stern for a moment. "Let me guess. Welemaan."

"Yes."

He sighed, then turned and motioned for her to follow. Then he turned back. "I'm sorry, Henme, I almost forgot about you. Please give my best to your mother and thank you for bringing Yvette here." The girl smiled then and nodded.

"Yes, thank you," Yvette said and smiled at the girl, who returned it this time. Yvette turned to see a larger Jirina approaching from down the hallway towards them.

"Derreg, please show Henme out and then secure the grounds and house," Mazal said. Derreg nodded, then nodded again at Yvette, who returned the gesture.

"Follow please," Mazal said to her. He led her down the same corridor to a closed door and opened it, stepping through into a well-lit room and holding the door as she entered. "Excuse the darkness of the entryway, please. We try to keep exterior light to a minimum at night.

She smiled at him, then looked around to see that the room was part office, with a desk and chair and sort of bookshelf, as well as part of the room filled with comfortable-looking furniture and a small table.

"I suppose the first thing we need to do is figure out how to get that thing off of you," Mazal said, rubbing his chin.

Yvette's hand went to the restraining device. "Yes, that would be great."

"Do not worry," Mazal said. "I'm sure that Derreg can figure something out. He's very resourceful. That's why I keep him around."

"You keep me around because I'm the only one who will put up with all of your war stories from the invasion," Derreg said, entering the room.

"Yes, that too," Mazal said. "Yvette, this is Derreg, my bodyguard and assistant."

Derreg held out his hand and Yvette shook it, feeling the strength behind it. She remembered now how strong they were, even without enhancements like hers.

"I'll see if I can find a tool to get that off," he said. He turned and left once more.

She turned to see Mazal smiling at the retreating figure. "Do you happen to have any water to drink?"

"Oh, yes," he said. "Are you sure you wouldn't like some fernta? I just got a fresh supply."

"No, thank you," she said. "I haven't had a drink since my daughter was born."

His eyes grew wide. "That's right! I forgot that you were pregnant when you were last here. How is the child? How is James? Please, come in and sit. We have a great deal to catch up on, it seems. Like why you are here now."

Yvette picked a chair near the table and sat. It was comfortable. Mazal left through another door momentarily and then came back carrying a cup of water and a plate with some fruit and what looked like small loaves of bread. He handed the cup to her and set the plate on the table before her, then sat down opposite her.

Yvette almost gulped down the water, not realizing just how thirsty she had been. She set the cup down on the table near the plate. "Thank you, I needed that."

He nodded. "Please, eat as well, if you need to."

"I'm good for now," she answered. "As to why I'm here. I was kidnapped from Earth by a bounty hunter who was hired by Welemaan. Gianni was as well. I haven't seen James, so I'm assuming he somehow got away or wasn't targeted.

"I would not be surprised by James the Human's ingenuity," Mazal said, smiling.

"Welemaan wants us to fight for the Rajani when they invade Krahn," Yvette continued. "I refused. Gianni, well, I think Gianni went along with it to see what was happening, but you never know with him."

"Either way, you're now on the run," Mazal said.

"Yes, unfortunately."

"I have also refused," Mazal said. "For my people. None of us will fight for him."

"Good to know," Yvette said. She reached for one of the loaves and took a bite, not knowing what to expect. She was pleasantly surprised to find it light and sweet, almost like Hawaiian bread, but of a lighter texture. "This is good," she said appreciatively. "Did you make it?"

"No, the girl you just met, Henme. Her mother makes it for me. She is a wonderful baker."

"Give her my regards," Yvette said, taking another bite.

Just then, Derreg returned with what looked like a pair of bolt cutters and some other tools. Yvette sat up so that he could look at the device.

"This should be as simple as removing the device from contact with your skin," Derreg said. "Though I'm not familiar with the technology that Welemaan's doctors are using to disrupt your powers."

Yvette felt him gently pushing the skin next to the device around, attempting to get a better look at where it was attached.

"What I don't want to do is cause harm to you," Derreg said.

"Perhaps we should scan the area first?" Mazal said.

"Never would have thought of that," Derreg said, sarcastically.

Yvette smiled. They reminded her of an old married couple. "Do you have access to a medical device? I know that when Bhakat was diagnosing my pregnancy, it was a real pain to find one that was still working."

"Yes, yes," Derreg said. "It's just a little late to be bothering the doctor tonight."

"I see," Yvette said, disappointed. She had truly hoped she would be rid of it now.

Derreg bent down and grabbed a tool from the floor that looked somewhat like a cross between a screwdriver and a wrench. "Hold still, please," he said.

Yvette closed her eyes and felt the tool sliding between the device and her skin. There was a moment of pain and then dizziness, and then more pressure on her temple.

"How are you feeling?" Derreg said. She opened her eyes and saw that he was holding up the device before her eyes. It took her a moment to focus on it, and she saw that the side had a short stem on it, which at the moment was covered in blood. Her blood.

"Please tell me there's not a hole in my head," she said.

"Sorry," Derreg said. "But it should heal nicely. The hole is small."

"Damn, I hate scars," she said. She reached up and felt the bandage that Derreg was pressing to her temple. "I can hold that."

He nodded and released it as she began holding it to her head, hoping that the hole was indeed small.

Chapter 16

The call from the Krahn warship had come not long after the ASP ship had left the planet's vicinity. Dar had been called to the bridge by Jurl, who was in another nasty mood, which happened when she became too stressed by events. He didn't blame her this time. He'd never been to Krahn and was sure none of his crew had been either, though there was a great bit of Reilla's past that he didn't know. Honestly, he wouldn't put it past her, Krahn delicacies aside.

"We've been ordered to a landing field in what looks to be in the middle of a large rainforest at the equator of the planet," Jurl said, turning to look at him.

"Do it," he told her. "No reason to get blown out of the sky for not complying. What are conditions on the ground?"

"I'm picking up a lot of vegetation," Reilla said from behind him. "Air quality is excellent, and oxygen levels are high. Gravity is within norms, though a little lighter than we're used to. Looks like some rain clouds moving in, which is to be expected as well. It is a rainforest."

"Good," he said, quietly.

Just then, James entered the bridge. "Well, are we landing?"

"Affirmative," Bob said.

"Yes," Dar answered, turning to look at him. He had forgotten about the ship's AI and how it was keyed to James' voice. "You may want to sit down and strap in for the landing."

James nodded and sat in the nearest unoccupied chair. "Here we go."

"Yes," Dar said. He decided he would deliver James and then get away from the planet as soon as he could. No use getting caught in an interstellar war that had nothing to do with him. He hated to have to take James' ship, but he had to get back to his own. Perhaps he would be able to return it to James after the war was finished, but the safety of his crew was most important, and he was worried about Pico.

◊

James wasn't sure what to expect when he landed on the Krahn home world, but a full unit of Krahn soldiers in full military regalia wasn't it. When the hatch opened on the *Bright Journey* and he stepped off the ship, followed by Dar, Reilla, and Jurl, he had to check his impulse to suit up immediately.

The stone corridor was lined on both sides with Krahn soldiers with their backs to the walls. James stood for a moment observing them and saw that they were much different than the warriors he had fought on Rajan. They were all standing straight and tall, all dressed in the same uniforms—their feathers were clean, and their hackles were down. Each had a gun in a holster on their side and a rifle held in both hands at rest. They looked straight ahead.

"Ooh, fancy," Dar said quietly behind him.

James turned to see him smiling and returned the smile. "Well, no use keeping them waiting." His shoes made loud clopping, echoing noises as he walked down the grey corridor. There wasn't any floor or wall coverings to dampen the sound of their footfalls. He could also hear the sound of fans and realized that the corridor was probably air-conditioned, which explained why it wasn't as warm as he expected it to be.

He saw a large set of doors at the end of the corridor ahead. A soldier on either side of the doors stepped forward in unison and opened the doors when they drew near, which was followed by an influx of warmer air and bright sunlight. James squinted for a moment to let his eyes adjust before walking through.

He came to the doorway and stopped, looking out. He could already feel himself beginning to sweat as he took in his first real look at the Krahn home world. They seemed to be in the middle of a jungle, and the bright green of vegetation was almost overwhelming. The air was filled with the sound of living things—strange sounds that could be insects, animals, or even the plants themselves, for all he knew. Probably a combination of all three, he decided, when he saw some of the plants moving on their own.

An older-looking Krahn, dressed in a thin black robe trimmed in some type of animal fur and carrying what looked like a scepter was walking towards them. He stopped a few steps away before speaking. "The High Vasin of the Qadira Clan bids you welcome to our world. I am Xenic, senior advisor to Maliq. We have quarters ready for you to stay, but the Qadira would like you to meet with him now, if possible."

James looked at Dar and the others before turning back to the Krahn official. "That would be fine. Please bring us to him."

Xenic bowed slightly and then turned without a backward glance. James followed, feeling his clothes now beginning to stick to his back and under his arms. If he had to guess, he thought it was probably in the nineties, if not over one hundred degrees, and humid as hell.

There had been a summer in Detroit when he was a kid when it seemed like every day was warmer and more humid than the last. His dad had bought half a dozen floor fans at K-Mart and placed them around their small house, and James had spent hours sitting in front of the large square fan in the living room, drinking pop, reading or watching TV and speaking in a loud voice into the fan so that it would echo back, which sounded pretty cool. His brother hadn't been amused, and would unplug the fan, which would cause James to angrily chase him around the house.

He looked down and saw that a large, peculiar insect had landed on his chest. He was about to brush it away when it turned, and he saw the large stinger on its abdomen. He had never been afraid of bees growing up, but hornets were another thing entirely. Those hell spawn were nasty. He thought for a moment, then shrugged and powered up. He was curious if his power suit would form over the insect as it did his clothes, or under it, knowing that the insect was a foreign, and possibly dangerous object. He was happy to see that the suit formed under the insect, and that it flew away as a result. James powered down to see that Xenic had turned back to look at him.

"I had been prepared to ask you to prove you were who you claim to be, but I suppose that will do," he said dryly, though it was difficult to tell through the translators implanted behind James' ears.

"Yes, well, I am James Dempsey. Human. Earthling. And bearer of a Johari Stone."

"It's a good thing," Xenic said. The sting from a whattoe has been known to kill, though it's mainly from an allergic reaction. Mostly it's a very painful annoyance."

"Good to know," James replied. Damn alien hornets, he

thought, wondering what else was around that could prove dangerous, besides the Krahn themselves.

◊

Dar's first thought of Krahn was that it was too hot outside of the stone corridor. The second thought was that he was glad he had a translator implant. The Krahn language was incomprehensible at best. It made them sound like they were angry all of the time, and maybe they were, but he didn't think so. The advisor, Xenic, seemed welcoming enough, though it was difficult to read his facial expressions, since most of his face was a beak.

They had walked outside for a short distance, maybe two hundred Standard feet, then had entered a large stone facility that looked to be made of the same stone as the landing site and corridor. They walked down another corridor and then entered a room through another pair of double doors—again, like the first corridor.

The room was relatively small, though it was large enough for a table and ten small chairs—the Krahn were all relatively short and thin as a norm. The tabletop and the seats of the chairs seemed to be made of the same material, which he guessed to be some type of wood or similar organic material.

"I will inform the High Vasin that you are waiting for him here," Xenic said, then bowed and left them all still standing inside the doorway, which he shut behind them.

"Well, here we are," James said. He looked around for a moment, but there wasn't anything to look at—the walls were bare stone with no ornamentation. Finally, he shrugged and sat in a chair facing the table and also the door, with his back towards one of the walls.

Dar nodded as well, more a note to himself that James was correct to not have his back towards the door. He sat near James while facing the same way. He motioned for Reilla and Jurl to sit as well.

"This place is boring," Jurl said. She reached out to the wall next to her and ran her claws over it. "Good for sharpening, at least," she said with a smile.

"Do not scratch their walls," Dar said, rolling his eyes. She shrugged and crossed her arms, now pouting.

"Can't take them anywhere," Dar said, looking at James. James smiled, though remained quiet. Dar couldn't tell if the Human was nervous or just anticipating his meeting with the Vasin.

"How long are we to wait?" Reilla asked no one in particular. No one answered. They were all caught up in their own thoughts. Just then, the door opened and a Krahn carrying a tray of glasses and a large pitcher of liquid stepped into the room. Dar could somehow tell that this Krahn was female, though she didn't say anything to them, only placing the tray on the table and pitcher on the table before them and then leaving.

James reached out and picked up the pitcher by the handle, looking into it. "I think it's water." He poured himself a glass and it did, indeed, seem to be a clear liquid. He took a small sip and then nodded. "Yes, water."

Dar poured himself a glass as well and drank. Not the worst he'd tasted, at least. Probably filtered. He offered the pitcher to Reilla and Jurl, who both shook their heads.

"Interesting thing about these glasses," James said. "There's no way a Krahn could drink from them. Do you think they just had them laying around in case they were needed, or do you think they made them especially for us?"

It hadn't dawned on Dar. "That's an intriguing question, for sure. I would imagine they would have something larger to fit their mouth parts."

James nodded and took another mouthful of liquid. "You know, I was afraid that this was going to be fernta." He laughed.

The door opened again, and this time it was Xenic, followed by a large Krahn who was dressed in black armor. By the look of it, custom made.

"May I present the High Vasin of the Qadira Tribe, his excellency, Maliq Qadira," Xenic said.

James stood and the others followed his example.

"Please sit," Maliq said, motioning them back to their seats. "Thank you all for coming, though I wish it were under better circumstances."

"And not against my will," James added. Dar winced. So that was how this would play out.

"I apologize," Maliq said, sitting across from him. "I truly do. I didn't feel I had much choice either." He motioned for Xenic to sit as well.

"The first order of business is to see you are paid for your services," Xenic said to Dar.

"That would be welcome," Dar said, sitting up straighter.

"I have authorized our treasurer to pay your money in Galactic Credits to any account or institution of your choosing. You only have to let her know."

"Thank you," Dar said, nodding.

"Though," Maliq continued, "I was hoping that you would stay with us a little longer."

"Technically, they can't leave until I do," James said. "We came on my ship, the *Bright Journey*. It might take some time for their own ship to arrive, if it ever does."

"That is true," Dar had to admit. "What did you have in mind?" All the while, his mind was frantically trying to work out a plan on how to leave. Perhaps they could steal a Krahn ship? He looked over at Reilla, who seemed to be thinking the same way. He shrugged imperceptibly.

"The Rajani are still on their home world," Maliq said. "They haven't yet taken off, which means we have a little time to decide how best to defend ourselves. Once they do launch, we will have a matter of weeks to set up our defenses adequately."

"And you think you need our help to do this?" Dar asked.

"We are proud warriors," Xenic said. "But we haven't faced a worldwide invasion in quite some time. Our strategies may not be up to our needs." He looked at James.

"When my team and I arrived on Rajan," James said, "the invasion had already been carried out. The Rajani defenses had already been overrun. I'm not sure if there is any input I can offer."

"We don't expect our initial defenses to be able to repel the invaders," Maliq admitted. "Once the Rajani land, I believe then it will be the same type of guerilla warfare that you led on their planet, unfortunately."

James sat and thought for a moment. "There are many variables that need to be considered. The first would be where the Rajani land. They won't be a large force, so they won't be spread out too much—unless I guess wrong, they won't have many ships and will want to hit the larger cities or population centers first, probably while they're still in the air above your planet."

"My thought as well," Xenic said. "The capital here is one of the larger population centers on Krahn but is not the only one. There are other clans that boast a large number of members. They are spread around the planet in their individual territories.

"I admit I did not think we would get right into war planning when you arrived," Maliq said. "Xenic has prepared more comfortable lodgings for you all." He stood and motioned for Xenic to as well. "Please escort them to their rooms so that they may perform their ablutions and perhaps sleep, if needed. We can speak again at dinner."

"Yes, Vasin," Xenic said, bowing low. He turned to the others. "Please, follow me."

They all stood, and Dar was still wondering how he was going to get his crew off the planet when Maliq broke his train of thought.

"James, would you please stay behind for a moment?"

Dar looked at James, who had a surprised look on his face. He looked at Dar, and Dar shrugged.

James smiled at him, then turned to Maliq. "Yes, I can stay. I don't seem to have any other plans."

Dar wasn't sure if the Krahn got the implication from his words, that he was basically a captive with nothing else to do, but Maliq nodded as if taking him at his word.

"I will speak with you later," James said.

Dar nodded. "Yes. Be well, James."

"You too."

◊

James waited while Xenic led the others from the small room. Dar gave one last backward glance at him as the door was closed. James nodded to reassure him that it was alright. He wasn't sure if it was, but he didn't want Dar or his crew members to try anything stupid now that they knew they weren't technically prisoners of the Krahn.

"I apologize again for bringing you here," Maliq said. James turned to look at him. He was an impressive-looking Krahn. Much neater than his brother and the rest of the Horde had looked. He also didn't seem crazy like Ronak. Time would tell, he supposed.

"That doesn't matter now," James said. "I'm here. I do sympathize with the situation that you now find yourself in, but I'm not sure what other help I or my shipmates can offer you."

Maliq walked to the door and opened it. "Please, walk with me while we talk. I cannot stand being in this small, ugly room."

This surprised James. He had assumed that it was just a norm that the Krahn lived in these small empty spaces. He nodded and followed the Vasin out of the room.

"I've told Xenic in the past that visitors are going to think us simple or boring if we stick them in that room to begin with, but he argues that such a nondescript room serves its own purpose—to not give away any information about us. I suppose he is correct, but I try to spend as little time in there as possible." He chuckled, and James couldn't help but smile in return, even though the sound was more like broken glass in a trash compactor—it was the thought that counted, he decided.

"As you may have surmised," Maliq began again, "we believe that we have the defenses to repel the Rajani, eventually. The random number in the equation is the Stones."

This brought James' focus to the front. "What about them?"

"The fact that we don't have them," Maliq said. His expression hadn't changed, but James could see a wry glint in his eyes. He thought it would be interesting to study how the Krahn communicated with each other, both verbally and non-verbally, but there wasn't time at the moment. They were now at the end of the corridor and another double door loomed ahead. Instead, Maliq turned a sharp corner and then came to a stairway that seemed cut out of the stone.

"This way to leads to my throne room and logistics center," Maliq said. They both began climbing, with Maliq leading the way. "The door down there leads to kitchens and other necessities."

"Is everything here made out of this stone?" James asked, running his hand along the rough surface of the wall next to him.

"It is quite plentiful in this area," Maliq answered. "I can see why my ancestors chose to use it to create a hard bunker, but I admit it does not have much visual appeal."

They climbed the staircase that went straight up from the corridor below until they came to the landing, and James had to stop, amazed at the view. The throne room was large—perhaps the size of a football field back on earth. It was enclosed not in stone, but in clear, rounded panels of either glass or other see-through material, and was surrounded by forest. The ceiling was also see-through, but was darker than the side panels, as if set that way to provide shade from the sun.

The room itself was filled with bustling Krahn, many looking to be dressed in simple clothing. Each one bowed to Maliq when they saw him leading the human through the middle of the room. He nodded back to each in acknowledgement. James was beginning to like the Krahn leader, despite himself.

"Come, join me in the lounge room," Maliq said. He led James down a short corridor which also seemed to be made of the transparent material. James looked out at the forest and noticed small animals in the trees that looked like a cross between lemurs and birds. The corridor opened up again, and James found they were in a smaller room that had a few comfortable-looking chaise lounge chairs as well as small tables and what looked like a full-stocked bar.

"I apologize that I don't have any fernta to offer you," Maliq said, bending down behind the bar and laughing again.

"You were listening to us," James said.

"I would be a fool not to," Maliq said. "You are the bearer of a Johar Stone and more dangerous than just about anyone else on this planet. "I needed to know for sure that you weren't going to attack me the first time I made an appearance. I'm sure my brother, Ronak, didn't make a very good first impression for our family, either."

"No," James said. "No, he didn't. Water will be fine, by the way."

Maliq opened a cabinet, and James saw that it was a sort of refrigerator. He poured James some water into a bowl. "Sorry, I don't have glasses here. You'll have to drink as we do."

"Thank you," James said when Maliq handed him the bowl, which had high sides and was made to accommodate the beaks of the Krahn. "I had wondered how you drank liquids. Most of your brother's soldiers had bottles that they would squirt into their mouths."

"Our soldiers are outfitted with the same types of bottles," Maliq said. He sat on one of the chairs and motioned for James to follow suit. "Now what was I saying? Oh yes, the Johar Stones. I believe that most of your team was taken to Rajan?"

"Yes, I think so," James said.

"Is there a possibility that they may join the war on the side of the Rajani?"

"Possibly, depending on what the Rajani tell them," James said, taking a sip of water. "Though I know Yvette, for one, will be highly skeptical of what they have to say. They would have to explain their motivations and why they feel the need to attack you. Gianni, on the other hand...well, let's just say I'm less sure about his motivations."

"I'm hoping that once they get here, you will be able to

tell them the truth," Maliq said.

"And what is the truth?" James asked.

"That we do not want a war. We don't want to fight the Rajani and never have. My brother did this, not the Krahn empire."

James looked at him a moment, measuring his words.

"But," Maliq continued, "we will defend ourselves. We will not just let the Rajani invade our world without a fight."

"Understood," James said. "I too, hope that war can be avoided. I still have many friends among the Rajani from when I was there last. I don't want to see any of you hurt or killed. I especially don't want my people caught in the middle, if it does come to war."

"Good," Maliq said. "I was hoping you could help. I ask this of you freely. I also want to reaffirm that you are not my prisoner. I only wanted to meet you in person—you and your team—though that plan unfortunately failed. You are free to leave at any time, though as I told the mercenaries, I would like you to stay and help us."

James pondered what Maliq was saying a moment. "I would like to speak to the others. The Outsiders, as they call themselves. As I said, the ship is mine, so they can't really leave until I do, unless they steal it." He meant it as a joke but caught himself when he thought about it. It was a real possibility until he was able to speak with Dar and quell his fears.

"Yes," Maliq agreed. "I will have to tell Xenic to make sure he guards our ships. We have few enough as it is."

"Speaking of numbers," James said. "We found that air superiority really turned the tide of our fight with your brother's forces. What type of air support will you have if the Rajani attack?"

"I would have to check with Xenic, but I believe at last

count, we had one hundred fighter aircraft. Those are sub-orbital vessels. Another twenty-five warships like the one that escorted you here. I also have one large mothership that can be used as a command headquarters if need be. It's currently off-planet on one of our closer moons, awaiting orders."

James thought for a moment. "Are those numbers for your clan only, or for the entire planet?"

"All clans," Maliq said.

James frowned. He had hoped that it was the other way, but they would have to deal with such a small force trying to defend an entire planet. "I think the key to this will be response time once the Rajani arrive."

"I agree," Maliq said. "I've given orders to all of the other clans to spread out their forces in anticipation. I don't want them bunching up and being taken out in one strike."

James nodded. The Krahn leader was not stupid, at least. He took a drink of water to forestall speaking. "What type of shelters do you have for non-combatants?"

"As I said, most clans have these hard bunkers. Most also have natural caverns that we've begun outfitting with medical supplies and food."

"Good, they can be used as emergency hospitals as well," James said.

"That is a good point," Maliq said. "We will have medical units set up once the fighting begins, but backups would be a good idea for any surges in injured warriors that might occur." He took a drink from his bowl. "You've given me some things to think about, James, and I thank you for that." He stood up, and James followed suit. "I will let you get to your quarters and rest, and perhaps talk to the...what did you call them? The Outsiders."

"Thank you," James said. "You've given me much to

think about as well."

Chapter 17

Most of the crew had stayed in the house to sleep, but Bhakat had wanted to stay on the ship just to be careful. Early the next morning Amera went to the ship, saying that she wanted to get something. Dennis didn't ask her what it was as he was busy eating a bowl of fruity marshmallow cereal that he had found in the cupboard. He hadn't had it since he was a kid, and the taste brought back bittersweet memories.

Just then, Kieren and Belani came down the stairs. She walked up to Dennis and smiled. "Hi, who are you?"

"I'm Dennis," he responded, smiling.

"Are you a friend of my grandpa's?"

"Well," he said, looking at Belani for help. "I am now."

"You don't look like an alien."

Dennis laughed, almost choking on a dry marshmallow—he hadn't ever liked it with milk. "I'm human, just like you," he said.

"Oh," she said, thinking a moment. "Belani said there were more aliens."

"Yes, there are," Dennis told her. "Bhakat and Amera are out at their ship, and I think Janan is still sleeping."

Suddenly, the front door opened and Amera entered, followed by Bhakat. The day was growing brighter, and they would have to wait until later to leave again.

Kieren looked at Amera and smiled, then at Bhakat. Her smile faltered a little and she backed up a step. Bhakat knelt on one knee.

"I'm Bhakat," he said. "I'm a friend of your parents."

"You are?"

"Yes," he said. "We came here to see them, but they went away for a little while."

"Yes," she said. "But Belani came to keep me company."

"Do you want cereal or toast?" Belani asked.

"Toast. And eggs and sausage," she said. Belani sighed and began rummaging in the fridge.

"Our friend Amera brought something for you," Bhakat said. He looked around and Dennis finally noticed the cat in her arms. She stepped forward, smiling, and placed the cat on the ground in front of Kieren.

The girl's eyes lit up when she saw the cat, who was looking around sleepily, having just been woken up from a nap in the alien's arms. Kieren bent down and began stroking the animal, which responded by curling around her legs and meowing softly.

Dennis smiled. It was a good choice—a spaceship was no place for a pet.

"What's his name?" Kieren asked.

"We don't know," Dennis said. "We found him. What should we name him?"

Kieren thought for a moment.

"What the hell is that?" Josiah said, walking into the kitchen area.

"Grandpa, it's my new cat!" Kieren said. "What should we name him?"

"How about 'Gone'," Josiah answered, grumpily.

Amera said something. Bhakat stood and looked at her.

She nodded towards Josiah.

"She says that this is a special creature, and not to be gotten rid of," Bhakat said.

"What? Why?" Josiah asked.

Amera spoke again and Bhakat translated. "He is...critical to our fight," he looked back at her, and she shrugged. "She will return for him when this is all over."

Josiah sighed. "Fine, as long as someone comes back for him."

"Chocolate!" Kieren said.

"What?" Dennis asked.

"No chocolate before breakfast," Belani said as he whipped her eggs to scramble.

"No, silly," Kieren said. "His name. His name is Chocolate."

Dennis looked at the tabby cat. It fit, or at least well enough, he supposed.

◊

Bhakat sat and watched Yvette's daughter play in the living room with her new pet. From the moment he had told Yvette she was pregnant; he had felt a bond with her for some reason. He didn't make friends easily. His friendship with Janan had happened only because they worked with each other every day. Maybe it was because Yvette had needed him, or that she seemed vulnerable at the time. All he knew was that he felt protective of Yvette's daughter and was torn as to how to move forward.

He looked up and saw Janan coming down the stairs, finally awake. That meant that everyone was present. "We need to talk," he announced, loud enough to get everyone's attention. Amera looked up from watching the large television. She was sitting on the floor next to the armchair that held Josiah. Dennis was looking out the window and turned to look at him. Belani looked from his perch on a barstool.

When Bhakat was sure he had everyone's attention, he sat forward and spoke again. "We need to determine how we are going to move forward. James, Yvette, and Gianni are missing. We know from Belani that James was taken by bounty hunters to the Krahn home world. Yvette and Gianni were taken back to Rajan. We need to decide who needs our help more."

"I will be staying here, no matter your decision," Belani said. "My orders from James the Human still stand. I am to protect the child at all costs."

Bhakat nodded. "That was James' decision, and it was the correct one. I will leave it up to others to decide if they are accompanying me."

"You know that I go where you go," Janan said, smiling.

Bhakat nodded again. "I had no doubts."

"Now that I know what happened to my sister, there's no way I can just walk away from all of this," Dennis said. "And I want to see where she died, if I can. I vote we go to Rajan."

"I'm not sure..." Bhakat began.

"I think he's earned the right to decide," Janan spoke up. Bhakat looked at him a moment, then nodded.

They all looked to where Amera stood, her arms crossed before her as she watched Kieren play with her teacup set. "What?" she asked when she noticed everyone's attention on her. "I'm along for the sheer sake of getting away from the space station." Janan translated for her into English.

"You have no other concerns?" Dennis asked her.

She looked at him and smiled. "Just so I'm not left here. No offense," she added, looking at Josiah. After Janan translated, Josiah smiled wryly but said nothing.

Dennis laughed as Bhakat threw up his arms in seeming

frustration. "This doesn't help me make my decision. Other than Dennis, does no one have any reason for either alternative?"

"I do," Josiah said, standing up and entering the kitchen. They all turned to look at him. "I sure would appreciate it if you could go rescue my daughter and her boyfriend. I don't know this Gianni fella, but I assume he needs rescuing, too." They all nodded, and he continued. "Now if I know James, he can take care of himself. He's a tough customer and I have no doubt he can survive this, especially with that...upgrade of his."

"So essentially what you're saying is leave James to his own devices and rescue your daughter," Janan said.

Josiah nodded. "I guess I am. I almost lost her once, and my granddaughter needs her mother."

Bhakat sighed. "Then I guess it's settled. We're going to Rajan."

◊

Janan had woken up early to steal away into the woods near Josiah's house. There was something he needed to do, and he didn't want anyone else to watch. He found a clearing some ways into the forest and looked around in awe once again at the beauty of the planet called Earth. It was so different than Rajan. He'd seen pictures of it on his first trip to the planet, when Rauph had ordered him to find out as much about the inhabitants as possible but seeing it in person was much different.

He finally pulled out the pistol that Punjor had given to him aboard the Mandaka Space Port. It was surprisingly light in his hands, though it was made for a larger being than him. He had to use both hands to hold it up to fire—and that was the problem. He'd never fired a weapon before. He wasn't sure what would happen, but he didn't want to look like a fool the first time he pulled the trigger, especially if that was in the middle of a fight against a real enemy. He wasn't sure if there would be any type of kickback when he fired, or even if he could hit what he was aiming at.

He looked it over and decided that all he could do was aim at something and pull the trigger and see what happened. He lifted the gun up with both hands and aimed at a large tree that looked to be fairly thick and solid. He pulled the trigger, trying his best not to close his eyes in anticipation. There was a rumble in the grip of the gun, and a bolt of white energy flew towards the tree.

Janan's eyes grew wide in surprise. There had only been the small shaking feeling in the grip to indicate he had pulled the trigger. He looked over again at the tree and saw the large hole through the middle of it, about the size of a large fist. He ran over to the tree to study the damage and saw that the hole went all the way through the tree. The hole was black, as if it had been burned through. He looked through the tree and saw that a tree behind it about ten strides had a hole in it as well, though this one only appeared to go about halfway through.

He looked at his gun again. He didn't see any type of knob or lever that would adjust the strength of the blast, so he supposed that needed to be careful any time he fired it to make sure that there wasn't something behind his target that he didn't want to hit.

He stepped back again and aimed at another tree, this time holding the gun in one hand. He wondered if the blast would change the longer he held the trigger. He pulled the trigger, but this time, held his finger down on it. Again, there was a shaking sensation in the handle, and he saw a hole appear in the tree, though it was off-center and only clipped the edge of the tree this time. He moved the gun to the center, but no further damage was done. So, it was a single blast emitter.

He carefully stowed the gun back under his shirt and smiled. He hoped he wouldn't have to use the weapon, but he was satisfied that he could if the opportunity came.

◊

It was time to leave.

Bhakat sat on his ship and contemplated what he was about to do. He still had a death sentence on Rajan, as far as he knew. Implanting a Johar Stone within himself had been against the laws of his home planet. He had been prepared to forfeit his life to save his people but had been given a reprieve and was exiled instead. Most of the credit for saving his life went to James and Yvette. He owed it to them to make sure they were safe, especially because of what they had unwillingly left behind on Earth.

He'd said his goodbyes to Josiah, Kieren, and Belani, and now waited for the others to say theirs as well. He heard the door to the bridge open behind him and turned to see Dennis, Janan, and Amera walking on the bridge, each with a pensive look on their faces.

"She's a special girl," Dennis said, finally, as if that explained all of their moods.

"She is," Bhakat said, nodding. "Now we are off to rescue her mother so that they can be reunited."

"I'm going to miss Earth," Janan said. "It's a beautiful planet."

"Yes," Dennis said. "But this is the most excited I've been in a long time. I never thought I'd travel to space, let alone meet aliens from another planet on the way."

"You sound like Kieren did," Janan said, sadly. "She was excited about the prospect of traveling through space as well."

Dennis frowned.

"Janan..." Bhakat began.

"Sorry, but it's true," Janan said. "Are you sure you want to go with us? Obviously, space can be dangerous."

"Yes," Dennis answered after a pause. "More than anything. And I want to visit her grave and...say goodbye."

Bhakat nodded. "There is an unoccupied room down the hall to the left that you may use to rest. We can speak about a language implant later."

"You mean a translator?" Dennis asked, his interest peaked.

"Yes," Janan said, smiling. "You'll find they help quite a bit when trying to speak to others. We taught James and his friends a few words of Talondarian Standard and Rajani on our way to Rajan the last time, and we can do the same for you, but it really is better to have the implant to fully understand others. Then you'll be able to speak with Amera as well."

Dennis looked at the tall alien female, who had looked up when she heard her name. "That will be great," he said and smiled at her. "But do you always have to operate on us humans when we come aboard?"

Janan laughed. "Just feel lucky that we won't probe you, Earth man."

Dennis laughed as well. He liked the little blue alien. He wasn't sure about Bhakat yet, and the Talondarian woman was an enigma. He looked at her.

She smiled back at him, then turned to Bhakat and Janan. "I need a drink."

Janan laughed. "C'mon, let's raid the stores. I think there's some fernta left over. And maybe some beer as well." He walked towards the door then turned to Dennis. "We're getting a drink. Want to come?"

"Sure," Dennis said, smiling. He turned again to Bhakat. "Thank you."

"For what?" Bhakat asked, puzzled.

"For allowing me to come. It means a great deal to me."

"I'm not in charge here."

"Could have fooled me," Dennis said, smiling and patting the large alien on the shoulder. He turned back and walked off the bridge.

Bhakat sat for a moment, thinking this over before moving to the pilot's chair and preparing to lift off.

◊

Dennis left the bridge of the ship and headed for his own room. He had asked to be on the bridge so that he could watch as they lifted off from the surface of the planet and headed into space. It was a smooth flight and soon they were underway, moving into what Janan had referred to as n-space. It all seemed anticlimactic.

He was still amazed by the fact that he was in space aboard an alien spacecraft. He was still getting used to the lack of oxygen aboard the ship, as Bhakat had set the interior settings of the ship to match those of Rajan. He still wasn't used to the gravity setting, and if he wasn't paying attention, he would stumble at times. At least the others seemed to be having the same problems, though the Sekani named Janan was by far the most agile and was the quickest to acclimate.

Janan had given him a small, portable translator to hand around his neck until they could give him an implant. It had taken a few minutes to get used to the mechanical English voice that came from it whenever someone spoke in a different language, but he was grateful for its presence. He was almost at the door of his room when another door down the corridor opened and Amera stepped into the corridor.

She smiled when she saw him. "Are we still on for Ships?"

He'd agreed to meet her so that she could teach him how to play the card game, which he assumed was something like poker. He'd never been much of a gambler, but he thought it would at least pass the time. "Sure," he said, returning her smile. "I just got off bridge duty."

"In that case," she said, turning around and going back to her room. He was puzzled for a moment, until she returned holding two six packs of beer.

"Where did you get those?"

"I took them from the older Human's house. He said he could always get more."

Dennis laughed. "Yes, beer is pretty plentiful back there. It looks like Josiah has good taste as well. Your room or mine?"

"Lead on," she said, pointing with one of the six packs towards his room.

His room was sparsely appointed, and he pulled a chair up to the end of the bed so that they could sit across from each other with a small table between them. "So, this game uses cards?" he asked her when they had both opened a beer and drank deeply.

"Yes," she answered, pulling a deck from her pocket. "There are thirty cards in the deck. Each player is given three cards to begin." She handed out three cards to each of them. He picked his up from the table and looked at them. "You're not allowed to look at the cards during a real game, but since you're just learning, I'll let it pass."

"Oh, sorry," he said, placing the cards back, face down.

"Once you get your cards, then you place a bet." She pulled a few coins out of her other pocket and gave him some, then placed one on the table. He followed suit.

"Now, each player flips a card," she flipped one of her cards over and he did as well. She looked at the two cards.

"So, there are thirty cards. They are split into ten suits, from the original Chelos Pact that began the Galactic Alliance. Those planetary systems were Sh'kall, Domdarri, Zbat Sigma, Talondaria, Mling-don, Asnuria, Fritellia, Tamiz, Clorn, and Penrozs. Each of those have three cards, with either past leaders, outposts, or ships. Understand?"

"I think so," he replied. He had turned over an interesting ship on his card. She had turned over an alien that looked like a giant housecat standing erect.

"I have turned over D'pac," she continued. "He was a famous Sh'Kallian leader. You have turned over a Domdarri trawler. That means I have won this round." She grabbed the two cards and placed them to the side. "We'll keep our bets as they are, since we're just playing for fun right now." She flipped over another of her cards, and he did the same. "Now we both have ships, which means it's a tie, so we add another bet to the pot." She added a coin to the table and he mirrored her. She flipped over her last card, showing an older man that Dennis saw was probably Talondarian. He flipped his final card and saw it was another ship."

"Well, shit," he said. He smiled before looking up and seeing the look on Amera's face. "What, didn't you win?"

"I'm sorry," she said. "This deck came from Janan, and I haven't played with it before. He must have recently bought it on Mandaka. This card is my father." She took a long drink of her beer, emptying the bottle.

"I'm sorry," he said, unsure what to do.

"It's fine," she said. "It was just a surprise. I knew that the people and ships sometimes change. I just wasn't prepared to see this."

He stood and came around the table and sat beside her, putting his arm around her shoulders and giving her a hug. "We can stop playing now. I think I get the gist of how to play. It's surprisingly similar to a game we play on Earth. Maybe..." before he could finish his thought, she looked up and leaned forward, kissing him lightly on the lips.

He sat still for a moment as the shock wore off, before he sat back. "Oh, hey, I'm sorry if I...I mean, don't take this wrong, but, um..."

She stood up, not looking at him, "I'm sorry, I shouldn't have..."

"No, please," he said, standing. "Please sit for a moment." She did, though she still wouldn't look at him.

"It's just, uh, I'm not attracted to...your kind."

"Talondarians?" she asked, finally looking at him.

"No, females," he said with a self-deprecating smile. "I'm gay."

"You...you like other males?"

"Yes. Is that a problem?" He felt that sinking feeling in his gut, not sure if he had just ruined their budding friendship. It had happened before. Too many times before.

She smiled. "No, I understand. I, um, like both." He could see that she was now blushing, her cheeks turning a slight tinge of pink. "Can I...have another hug?" she asked him.

He smiled and spread his arms wide.

◊

"Do you think David the human will still be there?" Janan asked from the pilot's chair.

"I'm hoping that all of them will be there when we arrive," Bhakat answered, though his attention seemed to be more on checking the settings of the ship as he sat in the captain's chair.

"Yes, but he is now an outcast," Janan said. "He was a killer, and I never knew."

"You can't blame yourself," Bhakat said. "He had everyone fooled."

"Yes, but he was my friend," Janan said. "He betrayed me. I was the biggest fool of them all."

"Don't be dramatic," Bhakat said. "He was able to outsmart the authorities of Earth and the rest of us. Even his own team of Humans didn't know."

"I guess you're right," Janan said. "But I won't make the mistake again."

"Of trusting David?"

"Of making friends."

"I'm your friend," Bhakat said.

"That's different," Janan replied.

"Why is it different?" Bhakat asked, turning to look at him. "We met; we worked together. We became friends though we are very different from each other."

"I suppose you're right."

"Of course I am," Bhakat said. "I'm your captain." He turned back to the control panel, but Janan thought he saw a slight smile on his friend's face.

◊

Dennis and Amera had agreed that he should learn some better self-defense if he was going to be out in the unknown of space. Bhakat had told them that it would still be a number of weeks before they got to Rajan.

Dennis ended up flat on his back on the floor of his room for what seemed like the tenth time during this training session alone. He lay there a moment, doing a mental calculation and making sure he wasn't hurt.

"Get up," Amera said. "Don't be so fragile."

"I'm a lover, not a fighter," he finally said, sitting up. She was pulling no punches in her training, and he was already sore. He reached for his water bottle and took a drink. "Tell me about growing up on a space station," he said in an attempt to distract her from beating on him.

"There's really not much to tell," she said, sitting down next to him and drinking from her own bottle. "I wasn't allowed to go out much, lest I be seen. I remember getting so mad at Zazzil for keeping me tucked away in his room, though my quarters were quite expansive. I didn't really know that, though, until I was allowed to explore the station more."

She took another drink. "It was also lonely. None of his people were allowed to play with me and even talk to me much, except for Punjor, who was basically my nanny for most of the time."

"Sorry to hear that," Dennis replied.

"I used to sneak out sometimes—always covered or disguised, of course. That's how I learned to play the gambling games on the port and learn how to keep out of sight of the ASPs."

"Asps?" Dennis asked. "Like, snakes?"

She laughed at this. "No, no. They're the law enforcement for the Galactic Alliance."

"Oh, I see," he said. "How old were you when...it happened?"

"You mean when my parents were killed, and my uncle became emperor of Talondaria? I was seven Standard years old."

"How did they die?"

"No one knows for sure, but there was always a hint of foul play. Their royal star cruiser was attacked, and they were both killed. My uncle said it was space pirates of some sort, but there was never any evidence either way."

"That does sound suspicious," Dennis said.

"Yes, which was why I was forced into hiding so soon after," she said. "There was a short-lived rebellion by people who were loyal to my parents, but it was soon put down by my uncle. The only thing I have to remember my parents by are my sword, and vague memories."

He reached over and gave her a hug with the arm closest to her. "I'm sorry, kiddo."

"Thank you," she said. "Now get up so I can kick your ass once more."

He groaned.

◊

Bhakat had told Janan to stay on the bridge in case of any emergencies. He didn't foresee anything happening while they were in n-space, but didn't want to take any chances. He headed for the small room that he'd converted into an infirmary to check on their patient, who had still been in a medically induced coma since they brought him aboard the ship. He was hoping to wake up the cyborg so he could tell them why his ship had been so close to Earth and if it had anything to do with James' disappearance.

The small hospital room was not as extensive as the one he'd had aboard the Tukuli, Rauphangelaa's old ship, but it served its purpose well. So far the cyborg was the first patient he'd had with serious injuries. The tank that the creature, what he thought was a Shif, but wasn't sure, lived in had protected him from the fire that had swept through the cabin, at least. But the loss of cabin pressure had caused the cybernetic components to shut down, which in turn had placed the Shif into its coma-like state of suspended animation.

Bhakat had run diagnostics on the mechanical suit and had found two pieces that needed to be replaced. He had done his best to do that, though he was in no way an expert with that type of equipment. He had the medical machine hooked up to it now to monitor the Shif's condition when he turned the equipment back on. He hoped that would be enough to wake him up.

He bent down over the cyborg's suit and found the power cord that he needed to reconnect. It wasn't like the suit had an on-switch. He connected the cord's ends together and then stood up to look at the medical machine's readings. The Shif's blood oxygen level was now rising, and his heartbeat was speeding up. Bhakat hoped it was a good sign.

He looked down at the creature suspended within the tank of the suit. He could see that its tail and appendages were moving slightly. Its skin had regained some color as well, going from a dull ochre to a deep red.

Suddenly the eye facing Bhakat opened, and the Shif visibly jumped in the tank. "Get away from me!"

"It's fine, you're safe. Please be calm," Bhakat said, backing away a little.

"Where am I? Who are you? Where's Dar?"

"I will answer all of your questions, but right now you need to calm down or I'm going to have to give you medication that will sedate you."

"Maybe that wouldn't be such a bad thing," the Shif said.

Bhakat couldn't tell if he was joking or not. "Please, you're safe here. I'm a doctor and you're aboard my ship."

"How did I get here?"

"We found your ship orbiting near Earth, and rescued you, bringing aboard this ship for medical attention."

"Why can't I move my suit?"

"I temporarily disabled those features of the suit. Looks like I made the correct call. When you're calm, I can enable them again."

"I'm calm."

"Good, then you'll be able to hold a conversation with me," Bhakat said. "My name is Bhakat. I am a Rajani."

"Pico. Shif pilot of the *Freedom*."

"Is that the name of the ship we found you on?"

"Yes. Was there anyone else aboard the ship when you found it?"

"No, just an Earth cat."

"A...cat? Is that what that thing is called? Dar loves it."

"Yes. Is Dar your captain?"

The cyborg didn't answer for a moment, and Bhakat thought he could guess why. He still wasn't sure about where he was or who he was talking to. "I assure you, I'm not the one who attacked your ship. Whoever it was, they were gone when we found you. We were looking for our Human friends on Earth. James, Yvette, and Gianni."

"Yvette and Gianni were captured before we could rescue them. We made contact with James the Human's ship and spoke with him before we were attacked," Pico said. "I assume they got away, since you didn't find the Human's ship near mine. It happened fast. One moment I was prepping to enter n-space to go to Krahn, and the next, things were exploding around me."

"So, they were going to Krahn with James?"

"That was the plan. James agreed to it and sent his pilot to Earth to see what he could find and protect his offspring."

"Yes, we met up with Balani on Earth. He is safe, as is James' daughter."

"That's good, at least. Can you hook me up now? I'm still feeling...vulnerable."

"In just a moment," Bhakat said. "First I want to let you know that we are not following James. We're heading to Rajan."

"That's just great. What about the *Freedom*? Did you just leave it there?"

"That's all we could do. It had extensive damage."

"So, what am I supposed to do now?"

"We can probably drop you off on Mandaka," Bhakat said.

"I don't have any money, and no way to contact my shipmates."

"I could ask Punjor to take you in," Bhakat said, contemplatively.

"The gangster? The crime boss? Are you kidding?"

"It was just a thought."

"No, that doesn't sound like the best idea, either."

"Then your only choice is to come with us to Rajan," Bhakat said. "I promise, once we've sorted out what is happening, we will make every effort to reunite you with your captain and ship."

"It doesn't look like I have any real options."

"What was your role aboard the *Freedom*?"

"I was a pilot and technical crewmember," Pico said. "Basically, I could plug into the ship and perform diagnostics and directly steer the ship."

Bhakat bent over the machine body and began to change its settings manually, turning on its ability to move. "You would be a welcome addition to the crew here in the time we have together."

The Shif sat up on the bed it had been laying on. He worked his arms and legs slowly, getting use to being able to move again. "Your offer is acceptable, as long as I can get some food. I'm starving."

Bhakat grinned down at him. "I'm sure we can come up with something. Follow me."

"By the way, I haven't thanked you for saving me," Pico said, holding out his hand towards Bhakat.

Bhakat grasped the proffered arm, he wondered if the Shif could detect the feeling in some way. Perhaps sensors in the suit? "Welcome to the crew.

Chapter 18

Gianni opened his eyes and then immediately closed them as the light burned into his head, and he took a wincing breath. He had forgotten how bad a fernta headache could be. "Damn," he said as he sat up slowly. He needed to drink some water. He probably needed a bath as well.

He'd stayed up listening to Welemaan plot the Rajani attack on the Krahn home world and been plied with fernta the entire time. He hoped the headache would be worth gaining Welemaan's trust and confidence. As far as he could see, it was the only way to keep Yvette safe. Which shouldn't have been his job, but with James out of the picture, he felt a certain protectiveness towards her.

He sat, leaning back against his pillow in the bed that he'd been afforded by Welemaan. Much better sleeping arrangements than last time at least, he thought, remember the small room he'd stayed in when last on Rajan. Then his thoughts strayed to Kieren. If she had lived, would any of this be happening? She had been the diplomat of the group. Perhaps she would have been able to persuade Welemaan to give up this crazy plan to invade Krahn and focus on the future of the Rajani. Maybe she could have persuaded them to live out their lives, and the life of their species, in peace.

He remembered how tired and hurt and just plain burned out they all had been at the end of the fighting on Rajan, just before they left. If Kieren had lived, maybe they would have stayed longer and helped the Rajani and Sekani rebuild. It could have been enough to deter them from their plans for revenge on the Krahn. It could also have meant that Welemaan never seized power over the hearts and minds of most of the population.

But it didn't really matter. She had died. He had attended her funeral, the same as everyone else on Rajan, it seemed. She had been beloved by humans and aliens alike. Now it was up to him and Yvette to do something to stop Welemaan's plans from coming to fruition. When Yvette had refused to even contemplate it, he knew that he had to somehow work from the inside to try and stop events that would be catastrophic for peace for both planets.

He thought he had given Yvette enough hints as to his intentions but wasn't sure. She could be convinced that he had taken Welemaan's side in all of this. He wouldn't know until he talked to her again. If he ever talked to her again. He also had David to worry about. The man was a psychotic serial killer. Who knew what he would do to get his revenge on Yvette for hurting him.

◊

Yvette woke with a start, her head pounding while she fumbled for the cup of water next to her bed. She finally got ahold of it and gulped down the liquid in the cup. *And I didn't even drink any fernta,* she thought, rubbing her temples.

She assumed that the headache had something to do with the inhibitor being taken off her head. After Derreg had performed the procedure, she had suddenly felt tired and had asked if she could sleep somewhere. Mazal had been more than accommodating and had given her a large room on the second floor of his house.

She propped up her pillow and sat for a while until the pain in her head subsided to a dull roar. At least now she wasn't feeling nauseous from it. She slowly stood and her head didn't give her any more protest waves of pain, which she took for a good sign.

She walked over to a mirror that was set on the wall and looked at her reflection. She looked like hell. There were dark circles under her eyes and her skin looked pale. And of course, she had a hole in her head that couldn't be ignored. She looked closer at it and noticed that it looked better than it had even a few hours earlier. She hoped it meant that it would heal quickly.

Well, she thought, no use putting this off any longer.

She suited up and felt the familiar sensation of power around her. She looked at herself again in the mirror and didn't notice anything different. One of the first things she had done when they arrived home to Earth was suit up in front of a full-length mirror. She hadn't had a chance to do that on the trip to Rajan and certainly didn't have a chance while she was there, so she hadn't truly known what she looked like while powered up.

Now, she noticed that her head felt much better. Perhaps she needed to power up to tap back into the Stone's powers, including faster healing. Whatever the inhibitor did, it really screwed up her link to the Stone. She powered down and then looked at herself in the mirror again. The dark circles under her eyes were gone now, and she had regained color in her face. She shook her head, both happy that she had the Stone and still a little scared as well at the thought that she had an alien organism inside her body and would for a very long time.

◊

Gianni had eaten breakfast with a room full of Rajani whom he didn't know. When he'd been on Rajan last, he had spent most of his time with the Sekani. He thought about visiting Zanth and seeing what he could learn from him but wasn't sure if he could get away from Welemaan long enough. His initial conversation with Zanth gave Gianni the feeling that the Sekani were all in on the war with Krahn, but he wanted to find out why.

There was so much to stay and improve on Rajan, why would they agree to go along with Welemaan to fight the Krahn once again? Was it revenge? Bloodlust? A perverted sense of justice? If he could manage to drive a wedge between the Rajani and Sekani, maybe they would give up on their plans.

First, he had to ingratiate himself to Welemaan so that he could get the damn inhibitor device taken off his head. He felt naked without the ability to call up his powers, which by now were second nature to him. Plus, he wanted his powers back in case there was another attack from David.

He had thought about things while eating and now knew that there was only one thing to do: visit Tumaani.

◊

Yvette met again with Mazal and Derreg for a late breakfast—she hadn't realized how long she had slept until she was dressed and left her room in Mazal's house. She wasn't surprised at this, though, after having experienced so much in the days before.

"How was your rest?" Mazal asked.

"Good, though I probably slept too long."

"Understandable," he said.

"I've been thinking," she began. "I think it would be safer for you if I didn't stay here any longer than I have to. My presence here puts you and your people in danger."

"I agree," Derreg said. "The Rajani could come here looking for her at any time."

Mazal was silent for a moment, then nodded. "Yes, I suppose you are correct."

"Is there a more...private place where I can go?" Yvette asked.

"Maybe one of the farms?" Derreg said, looking at Mazal.

"Yes, that could work," Mazal said. "The Rajani hardly ever go out to them unless there is a problem." He thought for a moment more. "I think I know where you should go. I should warn you, though. Although my people have taken over the running of the farms, there are many who work there that have been there for a while, including Rajani and Sekani. At this house, I know my people are loyal and would never betray your location. On the farm is a different story altogether."

"I understand," Yvette said.

"I will have Derreg escort you..." Mazal began.

"No," Yvette said. "If the Rajani see me with any Jirina, especially one so close to you, they'd know that you were helping me. If you could just provide the directions, I can make my way there."

Mazal frowned, but then thought it over and relented. "I can see your logic on this, though I don't like it. James the Human would never forgive me if you came to harm, and I was responsible for it."

"Don't worry," she said, smiling. "I'm a big girl. I can take care of myself, especially now that you've removed the inhibitor. Thank you again for that."

"Our pleasure," Mazal said, standing. "If you'll excuse me, I have some other matters I must deal with."

"Of course," Yvette said, standing as well.

"We will speak again before you leave," Mazal said.

"I would suggest you leave when it's dark once more, to diminish the number of prying eyes."

"I agree," she said.

◊

Gianni walked out of the building where he was staying and felt the heat of the Rajani summer. It wasn't too dissimilar to a summer in Chicago, with a little less humidity so that he wasn't instantly drenched in sweat, which was nice.

His plan was to take a walk around the city to see what he could see, then figure out how he was going to go to the prison and see Tumaani. As he walked, he noticed the looks of suspicion he was getting from the Rajani he passed. He was surprised by the reactions. Wasn't he one of the saviors of Rajan? It felt a little ungrateful on their parts, but then, he figured they had all bought into the lies being given by Welemaan and his people, so he decided to ignore them as much as possible.

He also noticed that while many of the structures were rebuilt since the Krahn invasion, they didn't look nearly as grand as they had before. It was as if the Rajani had done just enough to rebuild them, but their hearts weren't in it to restore them to their former glory. There was no motivation to do so. It made him sad to think about it. He wondered what Rauph would say, seeing how things stood on Rajan. He would probably be disappointed, Gianni thought, seeing that there seemed to be no one laughing, nor even smiling as he passed them by. Of course, they were all males; no women or children, which could explain a great deal about their single-minded resolve to go to war.

He oriented himself as he saw a familiar-looking building and headed in what he thought was the direction of the old prison. He remembered heading towards the prison when they had first come to Rajan, after having ejected in escape pods while the Tukuli crashed with Rauph and Bhakat aboard. He and Kieren had been leading a group of Sekani when they had met up with James and his group of escaped Rajani prisoners. They hadn't known at the time that the women and children had already been slaughtered by the Krahn Horde.

Now that he thought about things, he never had gone to the prison while he was there the last time. He had no idea of where the entrance would be, or how he would be able to convince the guards to let him in to see Tumaani. He would just have to do his best to act like he knew where he was going and had the authority to see the prisoner. It wouldn't be the first time he'd had to fake his way through a situation.

He walked slowly, not wanting to draw too much attention to himself among the crowd of Rajani. He nodded and smiled to anyone who made eye contact. No need to set off any alarms within the community. He was just taking a stroll, seeing the sights.

He noticed that the closer he got to where he thought the prison was located, the more the crowd thinned. Probably no one wanted to work within sight of the large facility. Too many bad memories. He finally caught sight of it and casually made his way towards it. He stopped once to offer his help to a Rajani who was carrying a large load of what looked like electronic parts. The Rajani just shook his head and moved on. Gianni stood there for a moment and watched the Rajani as he struggled to not drop any of his load.

Things had definitely changed in the time that he was gone. He turned and headed back in the direction of the prison. He was aware that he was out in the open. Back on Earth, he would have been aware that more than likely, everywhere he went would be on some type of camera or another, whether CCTV, or something like the personnel cameras on people's houses or employment. He wasn't sure if the Rajani had that capability on Rajan, but he wasn't going to take any chances, so he kept his face passive and didn't make any sudden movements.

He finally made his way to the facility and looked up at the top of it, not seeing any guards atop it. He wondered how many prisoners were being kept in it, and how many of them were captured Krahn. He wondered if the leader of the Krahn Horde was inside. He'd killed the mate after she had killed Kieren, but he wouldn't say no to a chance of being alone in a room with Ronak for an hour.

Gianni moved around the prison facility, trying not to look like he was too interested in it. He saw a few Rajani walking past, and he smiled and nodded to them. Finally, he saw what looked like a large doorway. There were a couple of Rajani standing guard in front, both dressed in black fatigues and holding rifles. This must be the place, he thought. He put on his best smile and approached them.

Both of the Rajani guards noticed him approaching at the same time. They stood a little taller and one of them adjusted his grip on the rifle he was carrying. Gianni kept his smile in place. "How are you two?" he asked in his best Talondarian Standard. Neither of the guards spoke, but the one who had adjusted his weapon nodded in acknowledgement. That was all Gianni needed to bring his focus on that guard.

"I'm Gianni," he began. "Don't know if you remember the last time us Humans were here."

"We remember," the guard answered. "We thank you for your help in liberating our world."

"What do you want?" the other guard cut in before Gianni could say anything.

"I was wondering if I could see a certain prisoner," Gianni responded. He stepped closer to them, though out of arm's reach. "Just a quick visit, really."

Both of the guards frowned, and Gianni tried to think of something else to say. A thought popped into his head. "They say you may have Ronak locked up in here," he said conspiratorially.

The guards looked at one another. Gianni pressed on. "You might know that my...my mate was killed by Ronak." It wasn't entirely the truth, but he didn't want to go into too many details. "I would love to see that monster locked up."

The guards looked at him, but at least they were no longer frowning. "Just a few minutes?" he added.

"Fine," the one guard said to him, sighing. "But only because of your past service."

"But..." the other guard began.

"I said it's fine," the first guard said. He turned to the door and brought out a large key. He inserted the key into the lock and pulled on the door, opening it just enough to allow room for himself and Gianni to enter. He closed the door behind them. "My name is Kendle. I was in the final battle, as was my fellow guard there. I saw you and your fellow Humans fighting. Fighting for us."

"We all fought together, Humans, Rajani, Sekani, and Jirina," Gianni said. "And we lost so many..."

"Yes. Yes, we did," Kendle said, frowning once more.

"I've never been inside this prison," Gianni said, changing the subject. "Could you explain its layout? Are you holding only Krahn prisoners here?" He hoped he hadn't gone too far with the question, but the guard shook his head.

"No, we have some other prisoners here. Those who have broken the laws since the end of the war. Some that shouldn't be in prison."

Gianni tried to show little emotion at this last remark. Was the guard a sympathizer to Tumaani? "Our prisons on

Earth are full of Humans who claim to be innocent of the crimes for which they were convicted."

"It is the same here, I'm sure," Kendle said. "I am not privy to the trials of those we have here. I only guard them, from both escaping and from anyone who may come in with the thought of revenge upon them." He looked closely at Gianni when he said this.

"I assure you," Gianni said, "I only want to see Ronak behind bars."

The guard looked at him for a moment before turning and heading along a hallway. Gianni followed.

"We keep Ronak in the solitary confinement portion of the prison," Kendle said. "It's only for very sensitive prisoners, as you can understand."

"Yes," Gianni said. "Are there any other 'sensitive' prisoners there? I heard that Tumaani was here as well."

The guard stopped and looked at him again.

"Or was it just a rumor?" Gianni asked.

"Tumaani is there," Kendle said. "I...don't understand why he was sent here, to be honest."

Gianni nodded. "Maybe I could ask him?"

Kendle looked at him a moment more as if weighing his decision. He began walking again. "They say you are a guest of Welemaan."

"Oh, yes, though not exactly willingly. My friend Yvette and I were brought here against our wills by a bounty hunter that Welemaan employed."

Kendle nodded. "How do you feel about that? And about the reason you were brought here?"

"I'm not sure I'm in agreement with it," Gianni said. There was no going back now, he thought. If this guard was sympathetic to Welemaan and his cause, he would find himself locked up in the prison as well.

"Nor am I," Kendle said, turning to look at him. "As I said, I was there at the final battle, when we were triumphant and Ronak and his ilk were captured. I thought it meant peace for us, and a return to our normal lives. I was wrong."

"I'm sorry," Gianni said.

Kendle nodded. "I became a guard so that maybe I could be left behind when the invasion ships are launched. I am tired of fighting. Was tired of fighting before we were finished the last time. I lost so many friends. So many whom I loved, as did you."

"Yes," Gianni said. "I still miss her every single day."

Kendle nodded. He straightened up when another guard approached them. "Taking Gianni the Human to see the Ravager." The other guard nodded, though his eyes stayed on Gianni for a while as he passed.

"The Ravager?" Gianni asked.

"Yes, that's what we've come to call Ronak."

"It fits."

"Yes. Tumaani is this way." He led Gianni around a corner and down a flight of stairs. They passed a few more guards, but none of them challenged their passing. Kendle must be well-respected, Gianni thought.

◊

Starspanner mission journal. Captain Atalik Nar recording.

I made a show of getting in my ship and taking off from Rajan. The Rajani are too busy to worry about whether I left or not, but to be sure, I went back around the planet and re-entered the atmosphere in an uninhabited area before returning near the city, keeping low to evade any sensors the Rajani may have.

I am not happy with my dealings with Welemaan. The Rajani leader had promised me a Stone, and then had reneged on that promise when it came time to pay.

My plan now is to steal a Stone.

Which brings me to a choice: I've thought about which Human to capture (or recapture) to obtain their Stone. My protocols for capturing the two on Earth may not work as well here, and I don't have one set up for the Human who was already on Rajan.

But then I remembered something. Welemaan had mentioned that one of the Humans had been killed by the Krahn during their invasion and buried on Rajan, somewhere along the coast. Which means that there is a Stone lying unguarded and away from the city.

◊

Yvette left in the middle of the night. She'd made her goodbyes to Mazal and Derreg, and they had given her a bottle of water and some fruit for the trip, although they said it shouldn't take her too long to get where she was headed.

There was little light available as she moved in the direction they had pointed out to her. Now that she had her powers back, however, she could see as if it was broad daylight. Even so, she made her way slowly, careful not to make too much noise. She'd spent most of her time on the last trip to Rajan in the city, so she wasn't familiar with much of the areas outside of it. Kieren had told her about her trips to the farms with Rauph and the strange fruits and vegetables that they grew.

She kept in mind the name of her contact; a Rajani named Dreben who had been in charge of the farms for a long while, according to Mazal. The Rajani had been kept on after the Jirina had taken over farming so that he could train new personnel. His assistant farmhand was another Rajani named Terin.

Just then, she heard a noise to her left and she crouched down to listen. All was quiet for a moment, then she heard the sound of a footfall near her. There was someone, or something, close to her position.

She heard another sound and finally pinpointed where it was coming from, when she saw movement and instantly suited up, ready to attack. Then she saw the Jirina girl, Henme, walking towards her. She powered down again in an instant, not sure if the girl had even seen her yet.

"What are you doing out here?" she whispered to the girl.

"I...I thought you might need some help with directions to wherever you're going."

Yvette sighed. "It's dangerous out here."

The girl kept her face impassive as she looked up at her.

"Okay," Yvette said after looking at her for a moment. I'm going to a farm. The one where Dreben lives."

"Oh, I know that one, follow me."

"No, you can't come with me."

"Why not?"

"Like I said, it's dangerous."

"Not for me. I'm out all the time on my own. My mom goes to bed early. She works a lot, so she's tired early."

"What about your dad?"

"He got killed during the fighting when I was small."

"Oh, I'm sorry."

The Jirina girl looked up at her again, not saying anything.

"Fine, but we need to be careful. And quiet."

Henme smiled at her. "This way."

◊

Gianni followed Kendle down another hallway before they came to a cell door where Kendle stopped and looked through a small hole in the door. He nodded, then turned to Gianni. "He is here."

Gianni nodded to him. Kendle turned back to the door and pulled out a set of keys, placing one into the lock and turning it. The door opened outward, and Kendle stepped back to allow Gianni to walk through.

The first thing he noticed was the smell. He'd always thought that the Rajani smelled like animals, but the stench of the cell was even stronger than the monkey house at the zoo. He held his hand to his nose for a moment while he looked around. It was a small cell, perhaps six by four feet. There was a hole in the floor in one corner that he assumed was the toilet. On a small cot lay Tumaani, covered by a light blanket. He was shivering.

"Tumaani!" Gianni said, kneeling down next to the bed. He looked back at Kendle. "What the hell is this?"

"Welemaan has been very specific on how he wants Tumaani treated, unfortunately."

"I bet," Gianni said, looking back to Tumaani. He could see now that the Elder's eyes were open. "This is unacceptable."

"Gianni?" Tumaani said thickly. His lips looked parched, and Gianni wondered how long it had been since the Rajani had been given a drink of water.

"Bring water," he said.

"But," Kendle began.

"I said bring some water. And another blanket."

"Fine," Kendle said.

Tumaani tried to sit up, but the effort proved too much for him. "Gianni," he said again. He and Gianni had not interacted much the last time Gianni had been on Rajan, so he was surprised that the Elder remembered his name.

"Yes," he said. "It's Gianni. I've sent for water."

"Thank...thank you."

"Why are you being treated this way? Why is Welemaan doing this?"

"He is...changed. Ever since his family...and Kedar."

Gianni nodded. "I understand. Maybe Kedar could have kept him in line."

Just then, Kendle returned with a small bottle and another thin blanket. Gianni stood and took the items. He covered Tumaani with the blanked and then knelt again, offering the Elder a drink from the bottle. Tumaani eagerly drank, and Gianni pulled back so that he wouldn't drink too much too fast. When Tumaani nodded, he gave him another drink before placing the bottle on the floor.

"That's better," Tumaani said. "Thank you."

"So, basically, Welemaan went off the deep end after we left, and imprisoned you for speaking against him?"

"Yes, that's...that's about it."

"Damn it," Gianni said. He stood and faced Kendle again. "I don't care what orders Welemaan has given. Do you understand that if this treatment keeps up, that Tumaani will probably die?"

"It's outside of my control."

"Bullshit. I'm now giving you orders. Tumaani is to be kept warm and fed from now on. And a shower wouldn't hurt, either."

"But..."

"Enough arguing. You can tell Welemaan to speak to me if you want, but this will not continue." He turned back to Welemaan. "I promise, I'll do what I can to see you freed."

Tumaani nodded, smiling. His shivering had stopped, at least, from what Gianni could see.

◊

Yvette and Henme stopped to rest at the ruins of a building that had not been rebuilt after the Krahn invasion. The sight of it brought back memories for Yvette, and she felt sad that the Rajani had left it, deserted, on the edge of the city. Yvette noticed that it was beginning to get lighter. It was still many hours until dawn, but it was now early in the morning, rather than late at night.

"Are you hungry?" Henme asked her.

"Yeah, I could eat," she replied, smiling at the young Jirina. She took out her container of water and took a long drink. "How old are you?" she asked as Henme handed her a piece of dried fruit. It was dark purple to her enhanced sight but tasted similar to a dried mango.

"Fifteen Standard years," Henme replied.

"You're older than I thought."

"How old are you?" the girl asked.

Yvette sighed. "Thirty-one."

"You are older than I thought," the girl replied. She didn't smile at this, so Yvette wasn't sure if she was making a joke or not. She also wasn't sure if she wanted to go into the fact that she had an alien symbiote in her body that kept her at a prime physical health and appearance, so she laughed, and was grateful when the girl laughed as well.

When she'd returned home from Rajan the first time, she'd taken a good look at herself in the mirror and was surprised by the fact that she now looked to be in her early twenties. And she had glowed magnificently in all her pregnant glory, or so all of her father's friends had told her.

"Do you have any young ones?" Henme asked.

"Oh, oh yes," Yvette responded, caught off guard by the question. "I have a daughter named Kieren who is five years old."

"Do you miss her?"

"Yes, very much. And I miss my father and my...friend, James." She'd been about to say "husband," but that wasn't really the case. They had never officially been married. Definitely not something she wanted to go into detail about with the girl.

"I hope you can reunite with them soon."

"Me too," Yvette said. "How about you, do you have any siblings?"

"I have an older brother named Meden."

Just then, they both heard a noise and Yvette instinctively powered up. She stood up and saw that Henme was looking at her with wide, fearful eyes. She realized that the Jirina girl had not seen her in her power suit. "I'm sorry, I didn't mean to startle you."

The girl nodded, still looking as if she might run. Another noise, and Yvette switched her full attention back to being alert. "Stay here," she said. The girl nodded again, and Yvette carefully walked to the edge of a partial wall that provided most of their cover. She looked around, hoping she could see any movement. After a moment with nothing alerting her senses, she turned back toward the Jirina girl just in time to see a large shadow move behind her.

Yvette jumped to the side before she heard a weapon fire. She got to her feat in a crouch. It occurred to her that the sound of the weapon and the shadow were familiar. She did her best to quell the feeling of rage when she made the mental connection.

The alien bounty hunter was standing over Henme, who was now cowering on the floor of the building. Yvette saw his gun and extended her right arm out in a spear shape and pierced the side of the weapon in a shower of sparks. She slowly stepped out into the open.

"Step away from her or the next one goes right through you," she said.

The bounty hunter dropped the now inoperable weapon and raised his hands. He took a step back.

"Sit down," she said. "Henme, get behind me." The girl crawled over to where Yvette stood and then looked back to where the bounty hunter had sat before she stood up and moved around to put Yvette between her and him.

Yvette took three steps towards him. "Now, why are you trying to capture us? Did Welemaan hire you?"

"No," he said.

"Then why are you here?"

When he didn't answer right away, she took another step and extended her left arm out until the spear point was only inches from his face.

"I won't ask twice."

"It's a long story."

"Well, we don't have a lot of time, so you'd better summarize."

He sighed. "When I was hired initially by Welemaan, my price included a Johar Stone as payment."

"Welemaan didn't tell you that all of the Stones gone now?"

"No, he didn't."

She knew where the conversation was headed now. "So, you were going to kill me and take mine."

He was silent. She leaned forward until the point of her spear was now pushing on his forehead. "You wanted to kill me and take my Stone."

"Yes," he responded. "But that wasn't my first plan."

"What do you mean?"

"Welemaan had told me that one of your team had been killed during the fighting during the first Krahn-Rajani war."

"Is that what they're calling it?" She said out loud, not directing it towards him.

"Yes," he answered. "I've studied what little is known about the Stones to know that they don't die when the host body dies. They go into hibernation. I went to a place where I knew there was a Stone in hibernation."

Yvette pulled back her spear as she rushed forward and then grabbed the alien by the front of his clothes and lifted him over her head. "What did you do? What did you do to Kieren's gravesite? Tell me!"

"I...I dug it up," he finally answered. "But..."

"But what?"

"There was no Stone," he said. "It wasn't there."

Yvette dropped him. "You son of a bitch, I should kill you now."

"I understand," he said, painfully sitting up from where he'd fallen. "I do. She was your teammate."

"She was my friend," Yvette said.

He nodded, wearily. "I promise you; I placed her remains back where they were and recovered the grave site."

"Like I'm supposed to believe that."

"It is true," he said. "But you are missing the point here."

"What is that?"

"The Stone is gone, which means that someone else had already collected it. Had already disturbed the grave site."

Yvette paused when the realization struck. Someone had a Johar Stone. Someone had ransacked Kieren's grave to get it. There could only be a few who knew of the Stone and its location.

"Are you going to kill me now?" he asked.

She thought for a moment. "I should, for bringing Gianni and I here against our wills, taking me away from my family, my little girl." She was silent again as she thought. Finally, she extended a spear and stopped it at his throat, the point sinking in a moment. He winced but did not move back.

"I have a better idea," she said. "You really want a Stone? Well, I know where you can find one." She pulled back her spear. "The Human named David. He's with Welemaan right now, and you are free to take his. But if I ever see you again, or if I hear that you tried to take Gianni's, I will kill you."

"I understand," he said.

She bent down to him. "Do you?"

"Yes."

"Good," she said as she brought her arm down hard on his head, knocking him out.

She turned to the young Jirina. "Are you good?"

The girl stood up slowly and nodded. "Yes, I think so."

"Good, let's go. We have a lot of work to do."

Chapter 19

Dar had been unable to check to see if payment from the Krahn had been made in his account yet, but he had no reason to believe it wasn't. Nevertheless, he still felt uncomfortable just sitting around in the room that had been prepared for him. The others were in their own rooms as well, presumably bathing or sleeping.

He had thought about taking a nap—it had been a while since he'd had a decent night's sleep—but he also had a lot to think about. He had built his team's reputation on being impartial. They would take anyone's money for any type of job. He'd proved it by first being hired by the Rajani named Rauph and then again by the Krahn. He wasn't aware of many mercenaries who would have worked for both parties.

But in the end, they were still just mercenaries, not soldiers. He didn't know what Maliq hoped to achieve by having them there when the Rajani invaded. The three of them wouldn't make much difference in the fighting. He wondered what would happen if they turned down their offer to stay. He was still pondering this question when the chime rang that signaled that someone was at the door to his room.

He rose from where he sat on a surprisingly comfortable

couch and walked to the doorway. He pushed the button to open the door and was not surprised to see James standing there. The Earth man smiled, and he returned it. He really had become fond of the human.

"Can we talk?" James asked. "I don't want to bother you if you were taking a nap."

"Can't sleep. Come in."

"Took me a while to find your quarters," James said. "They have me in a different area of the building. Closer to the throne room. Probably so Maliq doesn't have to go far to find me."

"Ah, I see. Would you like a drink of water? Seems to be all they have available here." He motioned towards the couch and chair in the quarters near the bed and James sat in the chair. He sat on the end of the couch nearest the man.

"No thanks," James answered. "Just need to speak with you about our present situation."

Dar sat expectantly, waiting for James to speak further. The man sat a moment, thinking. It's one thing he appreciated about James—he didn't just blurt out what was on his mind. He was a measured speaker. Unlike Reilla and Jurl, who were constantly speaking, it seemed, without any type of filter between mind and mouth.

"I'm having a tough time weighing Maliq's offer. When I look at him, I keep getting flashes of my time on Rajan fighting Ronak and his warriors. I can't seem to separate them in my mind. Maliq seems too good to be true, even after speaking to him at length."

"I would not be surprised if this was true for every species," Dar said. "There are good and bad individuals in any society. Is it not the same on your planet? Some look to conquer and make war while others work for peace? I know that's what it was like on my planet."

"Yes, I suppose you're right," James said. "Meanwhile, there's the question of you and your crew. Have you made a decision yet on whether you are going to stay or leave?"

"It's not much of a decision," Dar said. "We can't leave unless you do."

"That," James said, then paused for a moment. "No one should feel like a prisoner here. I've thought about it, and if you all wish to leave, you can take the *Bright Journey*."

"Are you serious?" Dar asked, surprised. "You would entrust your ship to a crew of mercenaries?"

"It would keep the ship out of the thick of the fighting when the Rajani arrive," James said. "And it would take you back to your ship. I think Bob is smart enough now to be able to pilot it back to me when I need it."

"You are truly an extraordinary man," Dar said. "I don't think I would ever trust someone else to take my ship like that, with no real guarantee of its return."

"Then its settled," James said, standing. "Talk to your crew and let me know what you decide. I have to get some rest before I fall over."

Dar stood and held out his hand, which James grasped. He was reminded just how large the human was, as the man's hand engulfed his own. "Thank you, James."

◊

James had spent a few hours dozing and tossing and turning because his mind would not settle down. Finally, he had given up and sat up in the comfortable bed provided by the Krahn and just let his thoughts flow. Inevitably, they turned towards Yvette and Kieren, as they so often had since he'd left Earth.

He missed them both terribly and wondered what they were doing. Wondered if Yvette was on Rajan and preparing to attack the Krahn, or if she'd turned Welemaan down.

Wondered if Kieren missed her parents and was okay alone with Yvette's father, who while doting on her, was getting advanced enough in age that he may not make the best guardian of her. He wondered if Belani had been able to contact them.

There were so many unanswered questions in his mind. Was he really prepared to stay on Krahn and help them? It would be a daunting task, even with his powers. The Rajani were formidable fighters. Would the Sekani and Jirina join them in their invasion. He didn't think Mazal would allow it for his people.

One thing he did know was that he wasn't ready to lose Yvette or his daughter. If the Rajani were successful in their war against Rajan, would they stop there? Or would they go on to other worlds, continuing their conquering ways? Could Earth be one of those worlds?

He sighed and stood up and began to dress. He'd made up his mind.

◊

Jophen Dar woke suddenly in the dark. He'd had the nightmare again. He saw his house burning fiercely, knowing there was nothing he could do about it. No way to save his wife and young son. It was an old dream, but it still made him wake gasping for air.

He put his hands over his eyes for a moment and wiped away silent tears, feeling the wetness over the scars on his cheek. He'd been lucky to keep his eye from the injury. He'd been lucky to survive, if he was being honest. He'd stormed into the throne room on Talondaria in a rage, knowing who had given the order to kill him and his family.

He'd been the in the service of his cousin, the king of Talondaria, all of his life and had been loyal to him even after finding out that he'd been killed under suspicious circumstances. The king's brother did not and would not ever hold this same level of loyalty. Dar had never liked him, and knowing at a gut level that he was responsible for the death of the king and his family made Dar furious.

He'd spoken out against the new king both in private to his wife and then in the court. He'd been banished from the court under penalty of death, and had for a brief while, become the de-facto leader of the resistance on Talondaria. Their rebellion had been quashed forcefully, and ruthlessly, by the new king. And then the king had killed his family in an act of retribution.

He'd fought his way through the guards and physically attacked Millen Tordor. In the ensuing struggle, the king had raked his fingers down Dar's cheek, leaving deep wounds from under his eye to his jawline. Dar had broken the king's arm but had then been swarmed by guards before he could finish him off.

He'd been sentenced to death but had been broken out by other remaining members of the resistance and had fled off planet with little of his personal belongings. Only a ring with the royal seal of his cousin and a space suit.

It had been Reilla who had begun calling him the "man of tears" after they had met. He'd slowly put together a crew and had worked as everything from mercenaries to private security to smugglers, until they'd made enough to buy their own ship.

Deciding he'd had enough sleep for the night, he quietly got dressed and headed for the door to his quarters. Perhaps James would offer a little company and diversion from his own thoughts.

◊

James headed towards the throne room, remembering the way from his previous visit. He wasn't sure of the protocol to speak with the Vasin, but there were no guards at the stairs, so he began to walk up them.

"Wait up," said a voice behind him. He turned to see Dar hurrying to catch up. He waited for the Talondarian to get to the foot of the stone stairs.

"Did you get any rest?"

"A little, but it was not great," Dar said.

James nodded and began to walk up the stairs. "These stairs lead up to the throne room."

They walked up the stairs in silence until they reached the top. There was one guard outside the doors.

"I need to speak to the Vasin," James said. The guard looked him over and then the same with Dar before he turned and opened the door to allow them inside. James guessed that Maliq had left word to let the human enter when he arrived.

He turned to see the same expression on his face as he'd probably had when he first entered the throne area. "Close your mouth or you might swallow a wattoe," he joked.

Dar smiled. "I wasn't expecting this."

"Neither was I the first time," James said. "Although it wasn't raining like this yesterday." He saw the water pelting the outside of the windows but wasn't surprised. They were at the equator of the planet. It probably rained there every day.

He turned and saw Xenic walking hurriedly towards them. The guard must have informed him that they were coming. He stopped a few feet away and bowed. James nodded to him. "The High Vasin is currently partaking in breakfast. He bids you join him."

"Gladly," James said.

"Could you please have the other members of my crew woken and bring them as well?" Dar said.

"Yes, I will have a guard tend to them," Xenic said.

"Follow me." He turned and led them to Maliq's private lounge, when he had met with James the day before. They saw that Maliq was seated while looking over information on a small, handheld screen.

He finished and placed the screen next to him on the lounge chair before looking up at them. "Welcome. I've had breakfast, but you're welcome to help yourself." He pointed to an alcove that had a table set up with bottles of liquids and some platters with fruit.

"My Qadira, I must attend to the other members of their crew."

"Thank you, Xenic," Maliq responded. He turned back to James and Dar. "Please, sit."

James nodded and went to the table. One of the bottles held a liquid that looked like fruit juice. Another held a clear liquid that he hoped was water. He poured himself a glass of this and drank, happy that it was. He looked at the platters of fruit and saw that there was an empty platter that had some dark red liquid on it that was beginning to congeal.

"We are fortunate that the jungle outside provides many of the foods that we eat every day," Maliq said, coming closer to where James and Dar stood. Dar was eating a piece of the fruit, but had a look on his face that suggested that he wasn't sure if he liked it or not.

"Are Krahn omnivores?" James asked. "Do you eat both plants and animals, like my species?"

"Yes," Maliq answered. "I wasn't sure of your dietary needs, so I thought plants were best to serve. You probably don't want to know what this was," he said, pointing to the empty platter. "Just as you wouldn't enjoy watching us eat." He made the sound again that meant he was laughing. James smiled, though he suddenly remembered seeing Krahn eat on Rajan. His smile disappeared quickly.

"Um," he began, "I've thought about what you said yesterday, and I would like to stay and try to negotiate with the Rajani, if I can. Though I know that their current leader, Welemaan is not someone who thinks first, unfortunately."

"That is wonderful," Maliq said. "And you?" he asked, looking at Dar.

Dar looked first at James and then at Maliq before speaking. "I...we spoke last night, my crew and I, that is. We've decided that we need to get back to our ship and make sure that our other crew member is safe. From there, we will decide on what we're going to do."

"I understand," Maliq said. "It's not easy knowing that a comrade may be in need of your help, though I wish you would stay." He turned to James. "And they have permission to take your ship? I cannot spare any."

"Yes, they will take my ship. It should be able to return on its own."

Maliq nodded. He looked at Dar. "I do wonder if I can employ your services for one last task."

Dar set down his drink, possibly expecting something that would force him to stay after all.

Maliq stood and walked quickly to a single door at the side of the lounge. He knocked once on it and it opened. A small Krahn walked through the door holding a baby Krahn in her left arm and the hand of a young Krahn with her right hand.

"This is my mate, Qarela, and my children," Maliq said, placing a hand on his mate's shoulder. "I ask that you take them with you—away from the fighting. They are the future of my clan."

◊

Dar sat in shocked silence for a moment. Maliq's request had come as a surprise. He also knew that the ship they were returning to may not even be operational. He wasn't sure if he wanted to take civilians into that situation. He stood slowly, using the extra time to think. He thought about it for a moment more and decided that they would be safer with him than they would be if they stayed on Krahn.

"I would be honored to watch over your family," he said. He bowed to the Krahn ruler, his ambassadorial instincts kicking in as he did so.

Maliq returned the bow. "Thank you, Dar," he said. "And thank you, James, for agreeing to stay here and help us."

James stood and bowed as well, though he wasn't as practiced in the act, Dar noted.

Dar walked over to where Qarela stood with her children. He bowed to her as well. "We will work with your mate's people to ensure that you journey aboard the ship is safe and comfortable."

She nodded. "I thank you. This is Tareq," she said, motioning to the young male Krahn at her side. "And this little one is Sirala."

"You are welcome aboard my ship," James said from where he stood next to the breakfast table.

Just then, Xenic arrived back with Reilla and Jurl following him. They all turned to look at the new arrivals.

"What?" Jurl asked, noticing their scrutiny.

Dar laughed. "Sit and eat. We'll fill you in on our plans for the future."

◊

James had been surprised by Maliq's request at first as well. Then his thoughts strayed to Yvette and Kieren. He knew he would do anything possible to keep them safe. He felt that Maliq's family would be relatively safe with the Outsiders, as long as they stayed away from conflicts. He assumed that the bounty hunter they had confronted above

Earth was now on Rajan.

He was walking down the air-conditioned tunnel towards his ship as he contemplated how best to help the Krahn. He hoped that the Rajani wouldn't just begin firing on the planet below when they arrived in their ships. If he could open a channel of communication with Welemaan, he could possibly avert any bloodshed. It was a long shot, but one he had to take.

He saw Dar and his crew carrying boxes onto the ship, and waved when he saw Dar turn to look at him. He walked closer before speaking. "Where's Maliq's family?"

"Already safely stowed aboard in their own rooms," Dar replied, walking towards him. Xenic is quite the taskmaster when it comes to the Qadira's family. He was barking orders and directing Krahn for about a Standard hour. You should have seen it."

James laughed. "I can imagine. He seems like a serious pain in the ass."

"Well, the best thing is that they loaded up your ship with all kinds of supplies. At least we'll be eating well on our trip back to our ship."

"If it's still there," James said.

Dar grew serious. "Yes, there is that. If it's not, we'll have to head back to Mandaka and get everyone settled there."

"Just as long as you promise to send my ship back," James said.

"Of course," Dar said, mock seriously. "I promise. Not a scratch."

"Good, because Bob would not be happy if you did anything to his body."

"Oh, don't worry, he's already told me in no uncertain terms that he'll be watching my every move."

"Good, good," James said, smiling once again. "Seriously

though, don't take any chances, especially with the Krahn royal family on the ship. If you get to your ship and the bounty hunter is there, or it's too damaged to move, get everyone to a safe harbor. That's your first priority."

"Thank you again, James," Dar said, holding out his hand. James grasped his hand for a moment and then let go. He waved to Reilla and Jurl, who had stopped and stood watching them from the hatch of the ship. Then he turned back up the stone tunnel, hoping he would one day see his ship again.

Chapter 20

Welemaan felt tired as he rose for his early morning meeting with Zanth and the Sekani. Tired not only in his mind but in his body as well. It had all sounded so simple at the beginning—rouse his fellow Rajani to gain consensus on the plan to invade the Krahn home world. Yet once that happened, and it happened much quicker than even he thought it would, then came the planning. The logistics. The meetings. Endless meetings.

He walked slowly to the designated meeting place and waved his hello to the Sekani waiting there, including Zanth and his assistant, Jinda. Throughout the meeting he found it difficult to stay focused on the topic at hand, which happened to be food supplies for the joint Rajani-Sekani forces. At least Zanth seemed prepared, which was helpful. This would be the last time they met before taking off in separate ships towards Krahn. Zanth had made several salient points, not one of which Welemaan could remember. He hoped that the Jinda was taking copious notes.

Jinda. That was another problem that needed to be dealt with sooner rather than later. As the meeting wound down to a closing point, Welemaan stood and smiled at Zanth and said the expected pleasantries and goodbyes to both Zanth's people and his own. He looked down at Jinda and knew it was time.

"Zanth, can I borrow Jinda for a little while?" I want to go over his notes from the meeting and make sure I can impart them to my team later today."

"Yes, yes, that's fine," Zanth replied, smiling. He turned to Jinda. "Come see me when you're finished here, if you would."

"Of course," Jinda said, bowing slightly to Zanth.

Welemaan sat and watched his team and the Sekani leave. Jinda had stayed standing, giving off an air of nonchalance. Once the others were gone, he turned to look at Welemaan and his face became somehow sharper and more focused. "Is there a problem?"

Welemaan sat and contemplated his words. "Are we doing the right thing? Is this the right path forward?"

"Don't get sappy on me," Jinda said. He walked over to where Welemaan sat. "I thought we had settled this. Do you not remember what they did? Who they killed?" He stopped for a moment, thinking. "Is it the Humans? Did they say something?"

"No," Welemaan said, quietly, though that was part of it. "Of course I remember who they killed. If we go to war, though, there will be more Rajani to mourn. More faces haunting me every night."

"There will be justice," Jinda said with a sneer. "Or at least...vengeance. And you will have closure. Peace. For you and all of the Rajani."

"Oderey..." Welemaan began.

"I am Jinda!" the Sekani yelled, his face full of rage. He stood for a moment, silently calming himself. "I am Jinda here," he continued. "Don't say the other name again, Welemaan. Zanth would be...confused."

"Apologies," Welemaan said. He stood and wiped his eyes with both hands. "I'm just tired."

"Then go home and get some sleep, but we don't need you backing out of this. Not after all we've done. All of the preparations and planning."

"We?" Welemaan asked.

"You know who I work for, Welemaan."

"Yes, I know. You tell him that I need assurances that he'll hold up his end of the deal."

"Of course," Jinda said, now that his composure was restored. "I am his voice here. His forces are even now preparing to launch in support of your war. But it is your war, Welemaan. It has to look like your war to the Galactic Alliance. Only then can he send his peacekeeping forces to Krahn. Then you will have your military support."

Welemaan nodded. "I understand."

"Do you?"

"Yes."

"Then we won't speak like this again. There's too much at stake for the Rajani-Sekani alliance to fall apart over any... misunderstandings. It will fall apart if Zanth finds out who is backing you in this war. Goodnight, Welemaan."

The Sekani didn't wait for an answer, only walked from the room without a backward glance.

"Goodnight, T'van," Welemaan said, feeling better and also getting in a final dig at the Sekani. He walked slowly to the doorway and touched the button on the wall that turned off the lights.

◊

Ronak's cell door rattled as the key was placed into the lock and turned. He sat up, the sleep instantly leaving him as he wondered what new beating he was about to receive from his accursed captors. He looked and saw that it was

Welemaan himself standing in the open doorway. If he didn't feel so weak, he would have jumped at the Rajani and done his best to kill him. Instead, he sat and waited.

"Good morning. Almost time to go," Welemaan said.

"To Krahn?"

"To Krahn."

"And what if I refuse to help?"

"I don't think that would be a good idea," Welemaan said. "I told you, help us, and we may leave enough of Krahn standing for you to become its new leader. But only if you help us."

Ronak sat for a moment. "And all I have to do is explain my brother's defenses?"

"That's all," Welemaan said. "Or, you can stay here and starve to death in your cell. Your bones will lay here for a long time. Which will it be?"

Ronak sat for another moment before speaking again. "I...will help you."

"Good choice. You just saved your own life." He stepped back from the open door and slammed it shut, turning the lock once more and leaving without another word.

Ronak sat and plotted his escape. Whether it would be before or after they launched would have to be seen.

◊

David walked into the war room that had been set up by Welemaan and his followers. It was a situation room where Rajani and Sekani took part in the planning for the attack on the Krahn home world. Personnel from both species were hurrying about on various errands. David paused for a moment while he looked for Welemaan. He finally saw him in a corner of the room speaking with Seliban and a Sekani while pointing out something on a screen that he held.

David walked over to where they stood and waited

patiently for Welemaan to end his conversation—something that he'd been working on recently as well. He was so fast now that he had to concentrate on bringing himself back to normal living speed at times. The stone gave him precognitive abilities so that he could react to things happening around him while running, and he had to work on not reacting to what people were telling him before they said it.

Finally, Welemaan dismissed the other two and turned to look at him. "David, did you find her?"

"No," he answered, frowning and folding his arms before him. "But I will."

"You don't have time," Welemaan said. "Our ship is loaded and ready to embark."

"I'm not going with you," David said. "Not without finding her first."

"You're joking," Welemaan said, stopping to look at him. "We don't have a ship to spare. We cannot leave one behind for you."

"I know."

"Leave her for now," Welemaan said. "She'll be here when we return from Krahn."

"Maybe. Maybe not."

"What's that supposed to mean?"

David didn't answer for a moment. He didn't want to tell Welemaan that he'd begun to see flashes of events further into the future than just seconds before they happened. He'd begun to see glimpses of the future. He'd seen a fleet of ships land on Rajan—and they weren't Rajani returning from Krahn. If he didn't get Yvette now, he may never have the chance. "It means I'm staying here."

"Look, David," Welemaan said, placing a hand on his shoulder. "I don't have time to debate this right now. Why don't you come to my house for dinner later and we'll speak together."

"Fine, but you're not changing my mind about this," David said as Welemaan led him over to the door.

"You keep looking for Yvette the Human, and then we'll speak later," Welemaan said, tapping his shoulder and smiling.

David nodded and then walked out of the room. He then ran, and within seconds was at his sanctuary place. He knew he'd end there—knew that her presence was somehow still there.

Then he saw fresh, disturbed dirt on her grave. Someone had disturbed the grave site. Kieren's grave. He felt rage welling up within him and he thought about digging up the grave before coming to his senses again. Desecrating her grave once more would serve no purpose. He needed to find Yvette and enact his revenge. But for the time being, anyone in his path would pay the price for his anger.

◊

Zanth was enjoying a late breakfast when his assistant and counselor, Jinda, approached him. "Ah, Jinda," Zanth said, smiling. He had to admit that the Sekani—who was only few years younger than himself—had been a revelation ever since he'd appeared after the Krahn invasion. He had escaped his Krahn captors further to the north of Melange just as the fighting was wrapping up. Zanth had still been recovering from his injuries, and Jinda had proven his worth in organizing the Sekani for rebuilding efforts and coordination with the Rajani.

"Do you have a report of the final numbers?" he asked the Sekani.

"Yes," Jinda answered, pouring himself some fruit juice and taking a gulp. He put the glass of liquid down and then leaned forward. "We have full troop levels in our squadrons," he said. "A contingent will stay behind and protect the remaining Sekani—mostly older Sekani, women, and children."

"How many?"

"Two hundred," Jinda answered.

"So little a number to protect our people?"

Jinda shrugged. "Most of our troops want to go where the fighting happens."

"I don't like the idea of keeping so little a number back to protect our most vulnerable," Zanth said. "Double the number."

"I'm not sure if that's possible and this late date," Jinda said. "The fleet will leave tomorrow. At this short notice..."

"I don't care, Jinda. Make it happen." He put down the glass he was about to drink from. "Do you realize that this invasion force of ours means that our planet will be almost defenseless while we are away? Anyone could walk in here on a whim and take over."

"I understand. It will be done," Jinda said. He stood up and finished his glass of juice. "I had better go see to it now."

"See that you do, and thank you, Jinda," Zanth said.

Jinda nodded and turned to walk away.

"One more thing, Jinda," Zanth said, standing up.

Jinda turned and looked at him. "Yes?"

"I want you to stay here and lead our remaining troops."

"But Zanth," Jinda began.

"I will brook no argument," Zanth said, brushing away the other Sekani's protest. "There is no one I trust more than you to see to the safety of our women and children."

Jinda hesitated a moment before speaking. "You honor me, Zanth. Though I do wish I could be by your side in the fighting."

"I know you do. And I will miss your valued counsel.

Thank you for taking on this important responsibility," Zanth said.

Jinda nodded and turned away. Zanth didn't see the Sekani's scowl turn to a gleeful grin as he walked away.

◊

Gianni sat in his room aboard Welemaan's ship, wondering how he had got himself into such a mess. He was happy that they had finally removed the restraining device from his head, but he had agreed in return to not try and leave the ship. He had refused to board the ship with the restraining device still on, telling Welemaan that was the deal. He told the Rajani leader that if he was going, then there was no reason to have it on anymore. The real reason he'd wanted it removed was to protect himself. He knew that David would be aboard somewhere as well, and the only way he would be able to fight back if attacked was if he had his powers.

He'd asked around, hoping for any news about Yvette, but no one seemed to know anything about her or her whereabouts. He supposed that was good, but he still worried about her. He wondered if James was coming to her rescue but had no hope for it. They were on their own, and he had to do the best he could to stop this war from happening. He didn't feel up to the task.

◊

David rang the bell at the front door of Welemaan's house and waited. He wasn't feeling hungry, but the Rajani leader had invited him to dinner, and it would be prudent to show up, even if he wasn't about to change his mind on staying behind. He had made up his mind.

The door opened and Seliban stood there. He saw that it was David and nodded to him, then moved to the side so that he could come in. David nodded back and entered the house.

He saw that Welemaan was dining alone at a large table set with food. Seliban limped ahead of him and sat down at the table, wincing as he did so.

"David," Welemaan said. "Sit down, please. Eat."

David sat and prepared a heaping plate of food. He might be angry with Welemaan and the revelation at Kieren's grave today, but he needed to recharge. He was about to eat a piece of meat into his mouth when he suddenly felt a sense of great danger. "Welemaan, get..."

An explosion rocked the building as the wall to the right of where he was sitting exploded inward. David had suited up instinctively, which saved him as the table turned over and landed on top of him. It was heavy—made from a local stone that was cut from a quarry in the cliffs near the ocean. He looked up as the dust and debris from the explosion was beginning to clear. He could feel the pressure from the heavy table on his back and legs. For now, he was trapped.

A large figure came through the spot where the wall used to stand. David recognized the bounty hunter, Atalik. He stopped to look down at the body of Seliban, who David could see was dead. His open eyes stared straight ahead from his broken skull. He looked over to where Welemaan had been sitting but couldn't see him.

Atalik walked forward to stand above David. "This worked out better than I could have imagined," he said. "Your fellow human, Yvette, broke my immobilizing weapon, so I wasn't sure how I was going to catch you."

"I'm going to kill you," David said. He began to lift himself off the ground in hopes of freeing himself.

"I doubt that," Atalik said. "And I don't think you can maintain your power suit forever. I've been observing you. I know that the suit takes quite a lot out of you in particular when you use your powers. It's only a matter of time before it either falters or you fall asleep from lack of food. I have the time. I've always been patient."

"Why are you doing this?" David asked him. He could feel one of his legs loosen, but the other one was still solidly pinned down.

"I would think that was obvious," Atalik said, squatting down near him. "I want your Stone. Welemaan promised me one when he hired me, and then reneged on the deal. I aim to get what I'm owed."

Suddenly a large hand, surrounded by a power suit, grabbed Atalik by the scruff of the neck and threw him against the opposite wall. The force of the impact sent cracks spiraling outward. Atalik slumped to the floor, stunned.

David looked up to see Welemaan, fully suited up, standing over him. "Welemaan? What...?"

"Be quiet, David," Welemaan said. He bent down and punched David in the head. The impact of the two power suits coming together sent a shockwave outward through the house, and objects that had not already been knocked over from the explosion fell over and off shelves. David felt groggy and then another punch landed, and he felt the full weight of the table as his suit disappeared. He screamed from the pain.

"You're coming with me whether you like it or not," the Rajani said. Welemaan reached down and placed an inhibitor on his head. David felt it click into place and the exquisite pain as it locked into his skull. He screamed louder this time. His body was going into shock, and he felt close to passing out. He looked up enough to see Welemaan stride over to the slumped form of Atalik and pick up the large bounty hunter like one would a rag doll. He shook him and smashed him back against the wall, which groaned as if it might cave in.

"You attack my house? My house?" He shook him again.

Atalik stirred as if he was waking up. Welemaan held him up easily with his left hand. "I was merciful. I was allowing you to leave with payment for services rendered." He shook him again, and Atalik opened his eyes slowly. "No one takes what is mine!" He screamed in the bounty hunter's face. "Do you understand? No one!"

David could feel the last of his energy seeping away. There was nothing he could do. He laid his head down on the ground, feeling his vision clouding. The last thing he saw before it went to black was Welemaan's right hand rearing back and then punching through the chest of the bounty hunter named Atalik. He pulled it back and David could see the ick dripping from it. Then it was all gone as he passed into unconsciousness.

◊

Gianni sat in his chair aboard the Rajani starship that they called Coldana Naa, which meant basically, Swift Vengeance. The chair was on the bridge of the ship, and Welemaan was sitting in the captain's chair to his right. There were four pilot chairs spread out before the captain's chair, and all of them were occupied by Sekani pilots and technicians, all of them busy pressing buttons and calibrating systems for liftoff.

He'd been woken up early and told that the fleet would be taking off from the planet's surface in a few Standard hours. He'd spent at least one of those hours contemplating whether he should go forward with his initial plan of accompanying Welemaan or try to stay on Rajan and find Yvette to make sure she was safe. In the end, he had to force himself to trust that she could take care of herself.

"Status report," Welemaan said loudly. "Engines."

"Up and ready," said one of the Sekani techs.

"Gravity."

"Up."

"Life support."

"Up and functioning."

"Communications."

"Verified."

"All systems are a go," Welemaan said. "Pilot, prepare for liftoff."

"Acknowledged," said the Sekani pilot.

Welemaan turned and smiled at Gianni, and Gianni returned the expression, though his mind was racing, thinking about how he could talk sense into the Rajani and Sekani leadership before they arrived at the Krahn home world. Zanth was on a different command ship, and Gianni didn't think he would have a chance to speak to him again in person before the fighting began. He wished James was there. He always seemed to have a plan for these situations, and Gianni missed his leadership. He hoped he was safe somewhere, since the bounty hunter had seemingly failed to capture him.

There was a tremor as the ship's engines were engaged, and he closed his eyes, trying to calm his nerves as the ship lifted off the planet's surface.

The war against the Krahn had begun.

The End, Outsiders

Look for

Rajani War II: Invasion
by Brian S. Converse

Coming soon!

Updates on

www.BrianSConverse.com

www.ingramcontent.com/pod-product-compliance
Lightning Source LLC
Chambersburg PA
CBHW061528210726
48287CB00006B/1878